RELUCTANT PSYCHIC

SASHA URBAN SERIES: BOOK 3

DIMA ZALES

♠ MOZAIKA PUBLICATIONS ♠

Copyright © 2018 Dima Zales and Anna Zaires
www.dimazales.com

Published by Mozaika Publications, an imprint of Mozaika LLC.
www.mozaikallc.com

Cover by Orina Kafe
www.orinakafe-art.com

e-ISBN: 978-1-63142-358-1
Print ISBN: 978-1-63142-359-8

CHAPTER ONE

A HELLISH CLAMOR rips me from the welcome arms of slumber.

Heart hammering, I jolt up to a sitting position.

It takes me a moment to pinpoint the source of the offending noise.

It's my phone.

Grabbing the evil device roughly, I stare at the caller ID.

Instead of a number, it says, "Private."

"Nope," I say to the unknown telemarketer—or whoever the nuisance is. "I don't pick up when I don't know who's calling."

The phone keeps ringing insistently, so I tap the screen to reject the call and wait to see if they leave a voicemail.

They don't.

Then I see the time of day, and it makes me so angry I nearly throw the phone at the wall. It's my usual get-up-for-work time, but I don't need to go to work today—one of the few pros of quitting a high-paying job.

Making matters worse is my extreme grogginess. I clearly still owe myself sleep from that all-nighter for Nero.

The manipulative bastard.

My stomach rumbles.

If I'm up, I might as well grab a quick bite to eat.

Getting to my feet, I put on some sweatpants and a comfy T-shirt to celebrate my unemployment, and tromp into the bathroom to take care of business.

The orc bruise on my shoulder looks purplish yellow in the bathroom mirror, but it doesn't hurt much—courtesy of the frozen pea compresses, no doubt.

Yummy smells waft from the kitchen, and my nose drags me there to investigate.

"It's not just stuff," Felix says to Fluffster, whose tiny tea saucer with oats is sitting next to Felix's pancakes. "I nearly got killed."

"Morning." I beeline for the counter, grab myself a plate, and put some pancakes on it. "How are things going?"

"Felix is moping," Fluffster mentally replies, and the expression on the face of my chinchilla/domovoi is as close as a rodent could ever come to a smirk. "First, he complained about sleeping on the living room couch, then he said that he'll never get a female, and now he's upset that—"

"That was a private conversation." Felix threateningly points his fork at Fluffster's furry body.

I look at the fork incredulously. Did Felix forget last night, when Fluffster turned a hopped-up-on-sex succubus into a bloody smoothie?

"Sasha knows what happened," Fluffster replies as though no fork is near him. "So how is this private?"

"And I think you *are* going to get a female, Felix," I say, sitting down with my pancakes. "At some point," I add with a wink, spearing the carb-laden goodness with my fork. "Especially if we define the words 'get' and 'female' loosely."

The front door bangs open, cutting off Felix's rebuttal. He looks at his phone, likely checking the security footage, and informs us, "It's Ariel."

"Finally," Fluffster says in my head, and I experience a pang of jealousy that he can be so eloquent with his mouth full of oats. "She never came home last night."

"We're in the kitchen," I yell out to make sure Ariel doesn't think she can slink into her bedroom and pretend all is well. "There are pancakes."

I finally put a piece of pancake into my mouth, and the explosion of flavor makes me moan in appreciation.

"Made of potatoes," Felix explains gruffly, his mopey expression easing. "It's a traditional Russian dish." More somberly, he adds, "After nearly getting killed, I felt like eating something my mom would make for me when I was little."

"Hi, all," Ariel says with the enthusiasm of a

hyperactive kid hopped up on chocolate and amphetamines. "Good to see Fluffster is doing so well. How are the rest of you doing?"

She's wearing last night's clothes, but she must've done something with her makeup, because she seems to be glowing from the inside.

"It's a long story," Felix says and exchanges a confused glance with me.

If he's thinking what I'm thinking, he has the right to be confused. This is the strangest "walk of shame" behavior we've ever seen.

Could Ariel and Gaius be in love? After all, movies say that when you're in that state of being, you act kind of crazy.

Alternatively, maybe she's doing something new to self-medicate for her PTSD?

As though to highlight my musings, Ariel whirls through the kitchen like a tornado—no doubt using her Cognizant powers to move so fast. Before I can spell motion sickness, she's already sitting at the table with a plate full of pancakes, a fork, a knife, and an eager expression on her perfect face.

"Tell me what happened," she says excitedly and stuffs a potato pancake into her mouth. Even her chewing seems to be on fast forward.

I clear my throat. "So, remember Harper—the thing that used sex to nearly kill me at Earth Club? Well, he—or as it turned out, *she*—was here last night."

Ariel gapes at me and audibly swallows her third

pancake. "I knew she was a *she*. But what was she doing here?"

"You knew she was a *she*, and you didn't tell me?" I forcefully halve a potato pancake with my fork.

"I didn't know that you didn't know." Ariel shrugs. "It was obvious to me what she was."

"It doesn't matter." Felix readjusts his plate. "The important bit is that she tried to kill us last night. Nearly succeeded, too, but Fluffster saved the day."

Fluffster proudly puffs up his tail and sits up straighter—which makes him look like a fluffy meerkat instead of giving him the gravitas he was probably after.

Ariel drops her fork and stares at me and Felix with varying levels of accusation. "You guys left the house after I dropped you off? But then how did Fluffster—"

"No," I say. "She was *here*, at the apartment, right after you dropped me off."

Ariel pales. "How could a succubus get invited—" She looks at Felix and smacks her forehead. "That was your date?" Her voice rises. "You invited a succubus into our home?"

"I didn't even know she was a Cognizant of any kind," Felix says. "There was no aura. How was I supposed to know?"

"The smell," Ariel and I say in unison.

"What smell?" Felix sniffs the air as though Harper's scent might still linger. "Are you talking about her perfume? It was exceptionally nice-smelling, but—"

"Forget it," Ariel says, her shoulders sagging so

much I expect them to drop to her ankles. "You don't go to clubs, so you've never met one of their kind. This is all my fault. I should've been here." She covers her face with her hands. "I'm so sorry."

"Look," I say consolingly, uneasy with her sudden mood shift. "We're fine. With Fluffster around, nothing bad can happen to us. Not inside this apartment."

Fluffster's tail puffs up so much it's now bigger than the rest of his body.

"Tell me exactly what happened." Ariel lowers her hands, but her face is still uncharacteristically pale. "Every little detail."

Felix and I take turns explaining. He starts with how he met Harper, became smitten, and invited her over for Netflix and chill, "as per Ariel's own suggestion." I then tell her how I entered the apartment, smelled the enemy, and tried to fight her—and how Fluffster sealed the deal.

"I'm so sorry," Ariel says again when we're done. "I should've been here. It's not excusable. If this had gone any other way, I—"

She stops talking, and an actual tear streaks down her cheek.

Felix and I exchange extremely concerned glances. Felix, like me, had probably thought Ariel's tear ducts went out of business long ago.

"Could she be bipolar or something?" Fluffster asks —presumably only in my head. The little guy is clearly on the same wavelength. "I saw something about that condition on YouTube."

I give the chinchilla a shrug.

"I'm sorry," Ariel mutters again, then stuffs her mouth with a pancake.

"I actually have a question," I say to make sure she doesn't start apologizing again. "Can we get in trouble with the Council because of Harper's demise?"

Ariel swallows her food. "You were acting in self-defense. More importantly, she didn't have an aura, so she wasn't under the protection of the Mandate." Her voice steadies a bit. "In fact, if human authorities were to come snooping around, we could call upon the Council to make the cops look the other way."

"Oh?" I raise my eyebrow.

"Imagine if a long-lived Cognizant gets a life sentence," Felix chimes in gleefully. "Their slow aging might get noticed after a while—not to mention what happens when the prison sentence runs an unnatural number of years."

"But don't let that be an excuse to break human laws." Ariel's brows furrow. "For example, if you hack the database of an important bank"—she looks pointedly at Felix—"the Council could well decide to let you rot in prison for a while, especially if you don't have flashy powers that—"

"What is it with everyone breaking confidences today?" Felix grumbles. "I share with you that one time—"

"You always brag about your hacking," I say in Ariel's defense. "You told me you got into the DMV just the other day."

Felix gives me an annoyed look and also stuffs his mouth with a pancake.

"Why wasn't Harper under the Mandate?" I ask. "She didn't seem too young for it. Is her kind also persona non grata—like the necromancers?"

"No," Ariel says. "Very few types of Cognizant are that."

Felix clears his throat. "It's likely they both came here from the Otherlands. When you told me about the vision conversation between Chester and Beatrice, he said something about 'here' and 'liberal attitudes'—which makes me wonder if our villains hail from a pre-Mandate world. Those places sometimes have negative attitudes about pairings between different types of Cognizant—and sometimes, like in more conservative societies here, about same-sex relationships."

I feel a pang of pity for Beatrice and Harper. If Felix is right, all they wanted was to live together in peace, but Chester took advantage of that, setting Beatrice on her deadly path.

Then again, being a victim of prejudice on some distant world is no reason to agree to kill *me*. That choice, whatever her reasons, is why Beatrice is dead. Ditto for Harper—though I have to admit, her actions are even easier to relate to.

If someone had killed a person I love, wouldn't I want vengeance?

Felix also looks somber as he continues. "Alternatively, if they were from here, then Harper might not have gone through with the Mandate because her girlfriend, being a necro, wasn't allowed under it."

Ariel looks thoughtful. "That makes sense."

"It does?" I ask.

"Imagine having a lover, but being unable to speak to them about what's most important in your life," Felix says.

I nod, recalling Ariel bleeding from her nose, eyes, and ears when I asked her pointed questions about the Cognizant world prior to me being under the Mandate.

Ariel's phone chirps, breaking the momentary silence.

She glances at it, then looks up with a guilty look. "I have to run."

"Is it work?" I ask as casually as possible. "Or—"

"See you guys later," she says as though she didn't hear. She then repeats her Tasmanian Devil impersonation, cleaning up after herself and vacating the kitchen fast enough to break some highway speed limits.

Felix and I eat in silence until we hear the door in Ariel's room slam—which hopefully means she just changed her clothing. Then the front door bangs shut, followed by the sound of keys locking the door.

I look at Felix. "Is it just me, or are Ariel's comings and goings a bit odd? She didn't even shower."

"She does usually go to the hospital at this time, so it might be that," he says unconvincingly.

"I'm concerned," Fluffster mentally says, summing

up my feelings perfectly.

"Let's keep an eye on her." Felix finishes the last of his food and says, "I also have to run now. In my case, definitely to work."

"I'll clean up then." My appetite ruined, I mindlessly spear my last pancake. "Thank you for making breakfast."

"Fluffster told me about Nero," Felix says, getting up. "I'm sure you can get another Mentor—and a job."

I nod, but when Felix leaves the room, I say, "I didn't realize you were such a gossip, Fluffster."

"I was just concerned about the finances," the chinchilla replies, nonplussed. "You told me and Ariel, so I figured Felix can know too."

"I'm just messing with you." I scratch him behind the ear. "I was obviously going to tell Felix."

I then finish my food and begin tidying.

Just as I'm almost done in the kitchen, I feel a strange sinking feeling in the pit of my stomach, and a wave of fear rolls over my body. It reminds me of how I felt when Nero's orcs staged those accidents for me the other day—except I know that I should be safe here, in Fluffster's presence.

The phone rings in my room.

Could that be the source of my malaise?

Getting up carefully to avoid tripping over something and creating a self-fulfilling prophecy, I hurry to my room and take a look at the caller ID.

It's a private number.

Just like this morning.

CHAPTER TWO

GRABBING THE PHONE, I contemplate answering the call.

The anxiety symptoms worsen.

Is this a nightmare? Am I in *The Ring?*

I did watch a video tape recently…

I let the call go to voicemail again, and the fear abates.

Clearly, my intuition doesn't want me to talk to whoever is calling.

I do want to know what's going on, though, so I need to figure out who the caller is.

I run for the door and intercept Felix just as he's about to leave.

"Is there a way to figure out who's calling on a private number?" I ask, waving my phone around.

"Sure. There are a bunch of apps for that. Some block private calls, and a few try to unmask the number for you. Why?"

"Someone woke me up with a private call today, then called again just now," I explain. "I got a weird feeling about it both times."

"Probably a telemarketer," Felix says. "Try a few apps, and if that doesn't work, let me know."

He leaves, and I spend a few minutes playing with my phone, installing a bunch of apps that promise to unmask private numbers, as well as block them if I wish.

Having set the technological trap, I wait for another mystery call.

After two minutes of staring at my phone, I realize my mistake. If I watch it like this, it will never ring; Murphy's/Chester's Law will make sure of it.

So I do what I would've done if I were waiting for a tea kettle to boil: pretend I'm not interested in the phone at all.

I start my charade by cleaning up the kitchen some more, and then I move on to the bathroom.

I begin with the tub's drain—which has a giant hairball in it, a mixture of Felix's and my hair.

Felix sheds like a Beagle and will probably be bald by the time he's forty. I lose a ladylike amount, all things considered. The interesting case is Ariel, who never seems to lose a single hair from her head (or elsewhere as far as I know).

Is this part of her super strength?

I throw the disgusting hairball into the garbage, wash my hands, and examine Ariel's hairbrush.

Zero hair, as usual.

I used to think she had OCD about picking up her hair after every brushing session and shower, but that was before I knew about the Cognizant and her powers. Now I wonder.

On a whim, I go into Ariel's room and check for hair on her pillow and other likely places.

Zilch.

Is this why her hair always looks like she's stepped out of a shampoo commercial?

For a moment, I fantasize about swapping powers with Ariel. How awesome would it be to be super strong?

Resuming my tidying efforts, I take the garbage bags from the kitchen and the bathroom and walk out of the apartment to put them in the garbage disposal.

Great minds clearly think alike, because Rose is walking to the same destination. As usual, she's dressed to the nines.

"Sasha." She beams a warm smile at me. "How are you this morning?"

"Okay," I say cautiously. "But I now have more crazy adventures I can share with you."

"You still owe me the story of how you joined our ranks." She stuffs her garbage bags into the chute, her nose crinkling in displeasure. "We should have lunch now that you're not so busy with work."

"Sure." I send my own bags after hers. "Do you have a place in mind?"

"How about something at Le District? Lots of

options there." She holds her hands away from her body.

"Deal." I close the garbage disposal. "When?"

"How about today at one?" she says and starts walking toward her apartment.

I fall into step next to her. "That works. Want to walk there together?"

"No." She clasps her door handle clumsily with her left hand—probably because that hand didn't touch the garbage disposal. "I'll go for a stroll before that."

She goes in and closes the door behind herself, so I don't get the chance to offer to stroll together—which is probably for the best, as I need to do a bunch of things before lunch.

I get back to the apartment, wipe away some more dust in the most obvious places, and walk back into my room, yawning.

"Are you going to start your job search?" Fluffster, who's sitting next to my laptop, taps it with his furry paw. "Rent and utility bills don't pay themselves."

My blood pressure instantly rises. "I guess I *am* starting a job search." Opening the laptop, I mutter under my breath, "Furry slave driver."

As I update my resume, I consider the direness of my finances. I have ninety thousand left from Nero's unexpected bonus, plus some savings that preceded it. Anywhere but Manhattan, this kind of cash would last a while, but in this city, I have to worry—especially given the inevitable calls from Mom, pricey massacre cleanups courtesy of Pada, illegal gun purchases, and who knows what else.

Of course, if things get really dire, I could always pawn the expensive-looking necklace Nero gifted me for the Jubilee. Then again, the diamonds in it might not be real, and I don't know what the centerpiece stone—the one Nero had magically turned into a polygraph during my Council encounter—would be worth. I also have a couple of very rare magic books that had cost my dad an arm and a leg, but if I were forced to sell them, I'd probably cry.

So, with a heavy heart, I tailor my resume for a position in the financial industry—the lesser evil.

I'd always pictured my next job being that of a full-time TV illusionist, but that dream is over. Instead, I get to find out if other places on Wall Street are going to be as bad as Nero's fund—or worse.

My knowledge of the finance industry—or my psychic powers—tells me they might indeed be worse.

When I get to the job site, dozens of postings sound like a good fit with my education and experience. In fact, there are so many of them I soon tire of applying to them all.

"I'll apply to more later," I say out loud, in case my chinchilla is looking over my shoulder, ready to assume his monster form to make sure I have a better job search ethic.

Fluffster is nowhere in sight, however, so I reward myself for my job-search diligence by planning a good illusion to show Rose at lunch. It takes me a few minutes to come up with something rather devious, and I prepare what I'll need, including an outfit. My spoiled-by-job-search mood noticeably lifts as I put the decks of cards into the pockets of the pants I'll wear to lunch.

Picturing Rose's expression, I inwardly smile.

Since I have time before lunch, I decide to re-watch the meditation part of the tape Darian sent me. If I could take conscious control of my powers, I might be more in control of my life in general.

I turn on the TV and un-pause the tape.

"In a nutshell, you need to learn a special type of meditation," Darian says from the screen again. "Part of it is to teach you to clear your mind; another part is to have you believe in your powers without a shadow of doubt. This isn't something I'd expect you to master anytime soon, and I wouldn't even try it in your current sleep-deprived state. To start, you have to learn to breathe in and out to a count of five."

I realize that I'm still not fully caught up on sleep, but curiosity overrides my fatigue and I try following the rest of the instructions.

"Sit in any position where your back is straight." Darian contemplatively brushes his goatee. "It can be the stereotypical lotus pose or simply a chair"—he eerily looks from the screen at my chair—"or even the edge of your bed." He looks from the screen at my bed. "The key is to sit with a good posture."

I pause and experiment with different ways to sit. Settling on the lotus pose, I cross my legs, placing each foot on the opposite thigh, and make my spine as straight as possible.

My breathing grows slower as I un-pause again.

"Close your eyes and follow your breathing," Darian says. "Pause the recording now and try."

I do as he says, focusing on the air coming in and out of my lungs.

When a stray thought—like, say, an image of Nero's piercing gaze—enters my mind, I just let it go and focus on my breath again.

Thanks to a few yoga classes and the breathing exercises Lucretia taught me, this part of the training isn't as hard for me as it might be for some other New Yorker. Very soon, I feel as calm as a Hindu cow on Valium.

I un-pause the recording and close my eyes again, ready to attempt the next step of the training.

"This step is not needed every time," Darian says. "Only in the beginning." I peek through my eyelashes, and he actually winks at me on the screen—as though he knew I'd do that in that very moment. "I need you to firmly believe in your powers. Become that belief. Be a seer. Breathe it. Live it."

"Easier said than done," I mutter and pause the tape again.

Closing my eyes, I focus on the reality of being special.

I assault my natural skepticism with the best weapon—evidence. The truth is, I've had numerous visions that came true—too many to discount. I've also had countless intuitions that turned out to be valid, and, thanks to Nero's evil machinations, I've even predicted the unpredictable forces of the market.

With each breath, I make myself dwell on this new reality, and if any doubt arises, I tackle it with more irrefutable evidence.

It takes a while, but a moment comes when I have no doubt about my abilities. I can now define myself as a seer first and as an illusionist at a distant second.

Feeling ready, I un-pause the video once again.

"Now you have to empty your mind completely. Turn it into a calm lake," Darian says and gives some tips as to how. "Eventually, you will enter Headspace," he continues, "which is the key to conscious prophecy."

"How will I know if I succeeded?" I mutter under my breath.

"You'll know when you've accomplished your goal, believe me," Darian says from the screen. "I wish I could also give you detailed instructions for Headspace itself, but I can't. When you're actually in Headspace, you'll understand why. All I can tell you is, don't give up. While most seers take decades or longer to get to that level, you should be able to do it much sooner. With your natural ability and the boost you've gotten from the TV performance, you are more powerful than you can imagine."

"Great," I grumble, realizing I'm losing my hard-earned calmness. "Let me give this a try."

I pause the tape again and follow my breathing, as per Darian's instructions. Next, I perform what he called "the body scan"—where I have my awareness move from my feet to the middle of my forehead.

"Pretend you have a new eye there," I recall him saying, so I do exactly that, picturing my face looking like one of the seer masks at the Rite—the ones with an eye on the forehead.

Nothing happens.

Not unless Headspace is the same as feeling extremely sleepy—because that's the only result I get.

I sit in lotus pose for what feels like another hour, and my back starts to hurt.

I try to incorporate the back pain into my meditation somehow, but then my legs cramp up.

Soon, I tire of controlling my breathing and start dozing off, nearly falling onto my side.

"Maybe I need to try this again when I've had enough sleep," I say to the paused screen. "Or maybe Headspace happens when you go to sleep?"

Darian has no answers for this, so I yawn and get out of the meditation pose.

"Maybe just a quick nap," I say, stretching out on my bed.

I expect to have difficulty falling asleep with the light streaming from the window, but as soon as my eyes close, a wave of pleasant drowsiness drags me into unconsciousness.

———

MY STOMACH MAKES A LOUD GROWL. So loud, in fact, that I wake up.

Lying in a lazy haze, I contemplate going back to sleep. It doesn't seem likely to happen, though, so I open my eyes.

I'm in my room, and it's midday.

That was a nice nap. I could get used to this perk of unemployment.

Getting up, I realize I didn't get any dream visions as I slept. So I guess Headspace isn't dream space, which in turn means I didn't complete my meditation properly.

Oh, well.

I check the phone.

It's 12:35 p.m., which means I'm late for my lunch with Rose.

Springing into action, I get ready and head out.

———

AS I WALK through the shops of Le District, I uncover a flaw in our plan. We didn't agree on a specific restaurant, and there are many here.

To make matters worse, Rose doesn't believe in cell phones, so I can't just text her to find out where she is.

Figuring this is as good a time as any to rely on my intuition, I let my legs carry me where they want.

My seer powers are alive and kicking. It takes me but a minute to locate Rose. She's standing in line at a place with the most heavenly smells, and I realize I could've just let my nose do the searching instead of my psychic mojo.

I examine the line she's standing in and do a double take.

Rose isn't alone.

Standing here, in the middle of all these people, is Vlad, Rose's broody, much younger-looking vampire lover.

And, he's the least broody I've ever seen him. The corners of his eyes are crinkled in a hint of a smile as he listens to something Rose is saying.

I approach Rose and give her a greeting hug.

When I pull back, Rose worriedly darts her gaze from me to Vlad. I extend my hand for Vlad to shake, and she visibly relaxes.

Note to self: don't get too touchy with Rose's significant other.

"I take it you can be out during the day?" I ask Vlad, letting go of his icy hand.

It then clicks that I'm referring to his nature in public. However, the Mandate doesn't make me hurt, so perhaps the statement is too ambiguous to cause trouble.

"Don't believe every rumor you hear," Vlad says noncommittally. The earlier hint of a smile is gone, but he still sounds courteous.

"Clearly," I say and look at Rose. "How was your stroll?"

"Most delightful." She reaches over to clasp Vlad's hand. "We'll probably resume it after lunch."

"Where do you guys want to sit?" I ask, looking at the people around us. "I was going to tell you something rather private."

"We can get a table over there." Rose points at the empty row of tables with inferior views but superior privacy. "Besides"—she squeezes Vlad's hand—"I just heard some of the story."

Of course.

Vlad was there when the Council interrogated me, so he knows quite a bit of what took place.

We make small talk for the rest of our wait in the line. Then Rose orders some savory crepes, I get myself a Croque Madame sandwich, and Vlad gets a coffee.

"Do vampires follow an exclusively liquid diet?" I whisper as soon as we get to the most distant table—out of earshot of non-supernatural ears.

"I'm not actually going to drink this." Vlad places the coffee in front of Rose. "I just wanted to purchase something."

"That's very nice of you." I hungrily cut up my sandwich, letting the soft egg yolk run all over my plate.

"You're dilly-dallying," Rose says. "Tell me your story." She salts her crepe, earning a chiding look from Vlad. Is he worried about her blood pressure?

I'm salivating for my food, so I rattle out a short version of the events, from the TV performance with the first-ever vision to the zombie attacks that followed to the showdown with Beatrice and the two variations of my encounter with the Council—vision and real.

When I mention that Gaius threatened Ariel's life to get me to stay quiet about his and Darian's involvement in the TV performance, Vlad's expression darkens.

Crap.

Vlad is Gaius's boss—the head of the Enforcers—and Gaius admitted he wasn't acting in official capacity when he helped Darian. He was doing it to get a vision.

Did I just mess up?

"You don't think he'll still do something to Ariel, do you?" I say uncertainly, looking at Rose for support.

"Vlad isn't going to confront him. Right, dear?" Rose lays a calming hand on Vlad's forearm.

Vlad's mouth tightens. "Gaius is too ambitious for his own good."

"If he tries something, you'll put him in his place again," Rose says soothingly. "If I give you a—"

"Let Sasha continue with her tale," Vlad interrupts. "I won't confront Gaius about this. Not yet, at least."

I want to know what Rose was about to say when he interrupted her, but I can tell it would be rude to ask. So I finally bite into my sandwich. The combination of ham, melty cheese, and crunchy bread complements the sauce and the egg so perfectly that I vow to write the place a glowing review.

And maybe marry the chef, sight unseen.

"You wouldn't have let the Council actually kill Sasha if the vote had gone according to her dream vision, would you?" Rose gives Vlad a stern look as I continue to stuff my face.

"I'm sure Nero would've stopped the execution long before I would've had to interfere," Vlad says, and the crease in his forehead returns to its natural gloomy position.

Is he right?

In my vision, Nero did step forward to say something, right after that vote. Maybe he was about to say, "Councilors, that is my cash cow you just voted to kill. That's a no-go. She's mine to torment, and anyone objecting will be ripped to shreds—"

"You take your Enforcer responsibilities far too seriously," Rose tells Vlad before taking a large bite of her crepe.

I study Vlad curiously. "Why do you think Nero would've protected me?"

"He offered to be your Mentor." Vlad's dark eyes seem to suck in the light of the halogen lamps around us. "That was the first time he'd ever done that."

"And probably the last," I say, stabbing what's left of my sandwich. "As I said, I quit his stupid Mentorship."

Vlad gives Rose an unreadable look.

I use this opportunity to place another heavenly morsel into my mouth.

No one says anything as I chew. Is Nero's Mentorship a taboo subject?

To break the awkward silence, I proceed with my story, filling in any gaps they might've had when it comes to what happened with the orcs. Then I finish by telling them about the late Harper.

Vlad's face now resembles a tropical sky before a hurricane. "Gaius should've reported the club incident to me." His voice is biting.

Rose is frowning too, but she lays a hand on his arm again, massaging the tense muscle gently. "It wasn't Earth, dear. If he was going to report it to anyone, it would've been the Gomorrah authorities."

His nostrils flare. "Fine. But we're still going to have a talk one of these days."

I swallow the last bits of my sandwich and attempt to diffuse the grim atmosphere. "So," I say with forced brightness. "Vlad, you're out during daytime. You couldn't explain before. Can you do so now?"

Rose and Vlad exchange a quick glance, and she says, "His kind can be out during the day without any ill effects." She smiles at him shyly. "They do, or did, hunt at night like many other predators, so that's probably where the human legends stem from."

"We're usually too busy during the day to be prancing around," Vlad clarifies. "Since we don't need to sleep, we do our work during the day and enjoy leisure activities"—he looks meaningfully at Rose—"at night."

"Except you're here during the day," I observe.

"I'm with Rose whenever possible," he says, that hint of a smile returning.

Oh no.

Are they about to make out again?

As happy as I am for them, it was really awkward to witness the last time.

"Did you know Rasputin?" I ask Vlad, in part to prevent the public display of affection and in part because I really want to know. "Or were you in France during his time?"

"I knew him when I lived in Russia." Vlad's black eyes take on a distant look. "But I was in France when he got into all that trouble with the St. Petersburg Council—"

"Wait," I say. "What trouble?"

"You don't gain fame in the human world without consequences," Vlad says. "As you found out yourself."

That's right. Rasputin became an almost mythical figure—which goes against the spirit of the Mandate and probably pissed off the Cognizant around him.

"So what happened?" I ask, meeting Vlad's unblinking gaze.

"From what I've heard, Grigori faked his death and went into exile somewhere." Vlad shrugs. "Obviously, a seer—especially one that powerful—wouldn't let himself be poisoned by mere humans, let alone get shot by them, then beaten and drowned, as the history books say."

"But how do you fake something so intricate?" I ask. "All the online articles say—"

"How did the people in that TV studio forget the zombie attack?" Rose winks at Vlad before looking back at me. "How did the people at that Vegas hotel explain the shootings when you and Ariel battled Beatrice?"

"Of course." I pat my lips with a napkin. "If Rasputin had help from a vampire, glamour could've been used to make humans believe any story."

"It sure explains why the legend of Rasputin's murder sounds so farfetched," Rose says. "Don't trust anything you read in human records. Those are highly unreliable."

Vlad doesn't look comfortable speaking about his kind's powers so openly, but he does nod in agreement.

"So is everything known about Rasputin fake, then?" I ask, looking at Vlad. "Or just his death?"

"Anything can be faked," he says. "But some information is not worth covering up, so I doubt it was."

"What about children?" I ask. "Human history says he had some."

"I wouldn't trust that," Rose says. "If he had children, he would've taken steps to conceal their identities before he went into exile."

"He might've also taken them with him," Vlad says.

"Do you have any idea where he went?" I ask him.

"No." Vlad hands a wad of napkins to Rose. "If such information were known, Grigori would be dead. He really made a mess of things in St. Petersburg."

I look hopefully at Rose.

She shrugs, wiping her hands. "If Vlad doesn't know, I wouldn't either," she says. "I only knew of Rasputin by his reputation."

I sigh in disappointment—which is when the sense of danger returns, stronger than ever.

Rose frowns at me, and Vlad raises a questioning eyebrow.

I must look as pale as I feel.

"Someone just walked over my grave," I say quietly, and as though in reply, my phone rings again.

CHAPTER THREE

I LOOK AT THE "PRIVATE" label, take a calming breath, and unlock the phone.

One of the apps I installed reveals a number that doesn't look familiar, but does have a local 718 area code.

"Give me a sec," I tell Vlad and Rose and Google the number.

No luck.

I forward the number to Felix along with a text message.

App revealed the private caller, but I still don't know who it is. Can you help?

Felix replies almost instantly.

Have a ton of work to do now but will tackle this as soon as I can.

I thank him and turn my attention back to Vlad and Rose. "Someone has been calling me for some reason," I explain. "It's probably nothing, but Felix is on it."

"You let us know if it's trouble." Rose curves her hands around the cup of coffee Vlad purchased. "You've been through enough already. I refuse to let someone hurt you again."

"Oh, thank you. You're so sweet." I shake my head in the hopes of clearing away the adrenaline overload, then recall that I have the world's best stress relief with me today.

"Do you want to see something cool?" I ask my companions.

"A magic trick?" Rose's face lights up, giving me a glimpse into her long-ago childhood.

Vlad raises both eyebrows.

"I know the Council forbade me from performing for humans," I say to Vlad. "But if I show an effect to the two of you, it should be fine."

Rose gives Vlad a beseeching look.

"If it's something only we can see," he says, "there's no problem."

"It's a close-up effect," I promise. "Now, Rose, do you want to be my helper, or should it be Vlad?"

"Me," Rose shouts in the voice of a ten-year-old. "Pick me!"

I look at Vlad, and he nods, the tiny smile back in the corners of his eyes.

"Rose," I say, my hands going into my pockets, "please name any playing card out loud."

"Seven of clubs," Rose says without a second thought.

Inwardly, I'm dancing a jig, but outwardly, I just

nod approvingly and take my right hand out of my pocket.

"Please shuffle these," I tell Vlad and pantomime a riffle shuffle for him.

Vlad takes the cards out of the box and expertly gives them a table riffle.

"Thanks. Now put them back into the box and give them to Rose to hold between her hands."

I pantomime how Rose is to hold the cards, and Vlad places them gently into her outstretched hands. I can't help but notice how he uses this chance to brush his fingers caressingly against her palm.

"Sorry for stating the obvious," I say. "But just to point out, now that the cards are held this way, I can't change anything about them."

Rose nods.

"Now," I say, fighting to keep the excitement out of my voice—the hardest part about being an illusionist for me. "Name a number between one and fifty-two."

"Forty-two," Rose says without thinking again.

"Are you sure?" I ask. "You didn't say it because it is, say, the answer to Life, the Universe, and Everything in a famous book?"

"Can I change it to twenty-four?" Rose holds the cards tighter in her hands.

"Hmm." I scratch my chin, pretending to consider it. "I'll tell you what… I'll let you change your mind if that's what you want." She looks at me eagerly as I continue. "In fact, I'll even let you change your twenty-four for something else if you wish, but only if you do so in the next five seconds."

I start to count silently with my fingers.

"I like twenty-four," Rose says after some consideration. "I'm sticking with it."

"You sure?" I put on my best poker face.

"Positive," Rose says. "Twenty-four."

"Okay. So your free choices are the seven of clubs and twenty-four. Correct?"

"Yes." Like many people in this situation, Rose begins to look uneasy.

"And you could've changed your mind," I remind her.

She nods, her uneasiness growing visibly.

Channeling my best illusionist impersonation, I pointedly stare at her hands.

The hands that are clutching the deck of cards as though Rose's life depends on it.

"No," she says. "That would be impossible."

"Please take the cards from the box and count to the twenty-fourth one," I say imperiously. "Let's see if we can see the impossible become possible."

Rose takes the cards out and begins to count.

On ten, her hands begin to shake with either fear or excitement—it's hard to differentiate.

On twenty-four, I can tell she doesn't want to turn over the card, so I prod her, saying, "Please turn over the card. I don't want to touch it and be accused of some kind of sleight of hand."

Rose turns over the twenty-fourth card.

It's the seven of clubs.

Rose's eyes turn into tea saucers, but Vlad looks annoyingly calm, all things considered.

"How?" Rose mutters. "Did you master your powers already?"

"Vlad shuffled those cards," I remind her, but the high I was feeling from Rose's initial reaction is ruined. I don't need to be a seer to know that her theory is how everyone will explain a huge chunk of everything I've been doing. "You would have to have been the seer, not me, to guess the card's location so easily."

She nods, but uncertainly.

"I wasn't done anyway," I say, and it's the truth. "This next part can't be explained by seer powers at all." I take the seven of clubs into my right hand and make a stylish gesture.

The card disappears from my hand.

Rose gasps.

"It didn't actually evaporate." I show my hand on both sides and wink conspiratorially. "The card teleported."

I stare at Rose's pocket, and when she sees where I'm looking, she puts her hand to her chest, as though she's about to faint.

"Please put your hand into the pocket." I point.

Rose gingerly obeys—and when she touches the card inside, she jumps as though it's a rabid tarantula.

"Take it out," I order. "Let's see what card it is."

As if working under water, Rose takes out the card and turns it over.

The card is the seven of clubs.

Rose audibly gasps. "I don't think I *want* to know how you did that. And I'm a witch."

I smile, the earlier dopamine high returning.

"Aren't you impressed?" Rose asks Vlad after she regains her composure.

I can't blame her for asking. Vlad's face was completely expressionless throughout the proceedings, as though I'd just read the menu instead of performing some of the best effects from my repertoire.

Maybe he's one of those people who feels the sense of awe on the inside, like my dad, instead of showing it on his face, like Ariel and Rose?

"I know how you did that," Vlad says, his face as passive as before. If he were Felix, he'd look triumphant right about now. "However, since Rose said she doesn't want to know how it's done, I'll keep quiet."

"I just had a change of heart," Rose says. Turning toward Vlad, she makes puppy eyes at him, and in an exaggeratingly pleading (and somewhat disturbing) voice, she adds, "Please. Please tell me."

"How can I refuse?" Vlad gives me an apologetic look. "May I?"

"It's a free country," I say as calmly as I can. Gathering the cards into their box, I pocket them and mutter, "Besides, what are the chances you actually know what I did?"

"The card in Rose's pocket." Vlad gently pats Rose's side. "You planted it there when you hugged her."

"She did?" Rose looks at me admiringly. "I thought you were just really happy to see me."

"One would have to be very skilled to put that card in there so fast and without Rose feeling anything," I say to Vlad noncommittally. "Are you sure about that theory?"

He crosses his arms and nods.

Damn vampires.

They must have supernatural attention to detail because I did exactly what he said. It's called put-pocketing and is the closest to pickpocketing I get with my close friends. Both pick and put-pocketing are among the core skills I've developed over the years of fantasizing about my own show, and despite Vlad catching me, I'm still glad to have had a chance to practice it.

"Now let me explain how your card was at your chosen number," Vlad says and pointedly looks at Rose instead of me. "The deck of cards used was made up of fifty-two identical sevens of clubs—so every number you named would've yielded the same result."

"Again, are you sure about that?" I smile cockily and take out the deck from my left pocket.

As cool as an Antarctic cucumber, I take the cards out of the box and make a stylish fan—displaying the different indices for them both to see.

"That's not the deck I shuffled," Vlad says with unshakable confidence. "That one is in your right pocket."

If I ever create a show for the Cognizant, I will have

a new rule—no vampires in the audience. Or perhaps no Vlad. I'll need to check if other vampires are as annoyingly attentive as he is.

I'm tempted to deny having a deck in my right pocket, but that would open me to the possibility of Vlad checking my pants.

Rose wouldn't like him checking my pants. Not even a little bit.

I decide to sidestep the issue. "To have a whole deck of seven of clubs in my pocket implies I knew Rose would name that exact card, and so does put-pocketing a seven of clubs into Rose's pocket during a hug. But how could I know she'd name the seven of clubs? Did I make her say it?" Deciding to throw in a little lie, I add, "She had the chance to change her mind."

"That's true," Vlad says thoughtfully—and I inwardly smile.

I didn't actually give Rose the chance to change the *card* after she named it; I was too happy she said what I wanted her to say to risk such a thing. Instead, I made a big deal about letting her change the number she'd named.

"So," I say to Vlad. "Your whole chain of logic crumbles."

"You used your seer powers," Vlad says, but without earlier conviction. "You foresaw what card she would settle on."

"Wrong." I grin. "I told you earlier; I didn't use my power for this effect."

"But wouldn't you say that regardless?" Rose rubs her temples.

"I didn't use my powers," I repeat. "I can swear any oath you'd like. For that matter, I'd let you use your powers to see if I'm telling the truth."

This isn't a bluff. The way I knew Rose would name that card is so much simpler that I can't believe she doesn't realize it. A year ago, I was performing for Rose and asked her to name any card. She named the seven of clubs. Then, a few months later, I was doing another, similar effect, and she named the same card. So I decided to take a gamble today. Had she named any other card, I would've taken the normal all-cards-different deck and performed another one of the countless card tricks in my repertoire.

Then I realize something. Vlad didn't comment on how I made the seven of clubs disappear from my hand. Does that mean I was so good that even a vampire can't catch me? I was using a combination of backward palm and a few moves that I invented myself, and it's great to know it works so well.

"I think she's telling the truth," Vlad says after a long pause. Was that a tinge of frustration in his voice?

"So, are we back to not knowing how she did what she did?" Rose looks at Vlad, and I could kiss her for her logical fallacy. She thinks that if he was wrong about one element of the effect, he was wrong about all of them.

"Can you do the whole thing again?" Vlad says, now definitely frustrated.

"That would be so anticlimactic." I wink at him. Then, realizing Rose might get jealous, I also wink at her. "Besides, as they say in my business, 'once is magic, twice is education.'"

"It's probably for the best," Rose says, getting up. "I wanted to take another stroll." She loops her hand through Vlad's elbow. "To help digestion."

"I better go too," I say, and make my escape before the two love birds get it into their heads to start making out again.

———

INSTEAD OF GOING HOME, I walk around and do a little food shopping for later.

When nature calls, I make my way to the ladies room, place my shopping bag on the sink under the mirror, and try the door on the nearby stall.

The door is locked, as is the one next to it.

I feel a slight wave of uneasiness.

Is my phone about to ring again?

Instead, there's a clicking sound of someone else's phone behind the door, followed by some giggles.

Are teenagers texting on the toilets now?

No wonder manufacturers are so intent on making electronics waterproof.

The last stall is free, so I push away the uneasy feeling and use it quickly—not tempted in the slightest to pull out my own phone as I take care of business.

I'm washing my hands and looking at myself in the mirror when the two stalls swing open.

Staring at the girls who step out, I instantly understand the source of my unease.

I know these girls, though I can only recall the name of one of them.

Roxy.

The second one is either Maddie or Ashley, but the name doesn't matter. The key is that she, along with Roxy, is part of the clique of bullies from my Orientation class.

They're literal bitches—as in, female werewolves.

Roxy sees my face in the mirror, and her smile transforms into a lupine scowl.

Clearly, she's still upset about the other day, when I saved Maya by playing Russian roulette with Roxy and her b-hive.

Unfortunately, I don't currently have a gun, and we're the only ones in the bathroom.

They can turn into their wolf shapes and attack me at their leisure.

Something in their eyes tells me an attack is exactly what's about to happen.

Without a second thought, I bolt for the door.

CHAPTER FOUR

MY SHOES SLIDE on the tiles as I rush past the sinks.

I grab the germ-infested doorknob, yank the door open, and dart through, then slam it shut behind me—right into Ashley/Maddie's smug face.

Not looking back, I sprint for the nearby escalator.

In the reflective surface of a column I pass, I confirm that they're chasing me in their human form.

Was running a miscalculation? Are they like dogs who chase whatever runs because the mere act of running marks one as their prey?

Well, I always have the option of pulling a cat on them—standing my ground in a scary enough way where they start wondering why they chased me at all.

If only I had a gun.

No matter.

I'll save the cat strategy for the same situation as the felines do—in case I'm cornered.

A half-baked plan forms in my head, and I run

down the escalator, dodging people on the way as I exit toward Battery Park.

The b-hive follows me, and is actually catching up, despite both girls running in high heels.

I get onto a jogging path and run toward my destination—a secluded gazebo that is Rose's favorite spot.

The hope is that she and Vlad are there and can help me out.

A bicyclist nearly rams into me but swerves just in time.

I speed up and almost knock over a little girl on a skateboard.

I glance back. The b-hive have tossed their high heels aside and are gaining on me faster.

Making a sharp turn through the perfectly manicured shrubs, I sprint down the grassy patch that leads to my destination.

For a second, I wonder if they didn't see me get off the road, but then a rustle of the shrubs behind me bursts that bubble.

At no point do I see any hint of Rose and Vlad— which is bad. But they may be inside. Or, since the gazebo has two entrances, they might've just come out of the side opposite me.

As I approach the gazebo, I push my muscles to the max.

My heart is hammering in my chest.

I dive for the entrance.

Rose and Vlad are not here.

Crap. Hopefully, I can catch them on the other side.

I sprint there, but hear panting right behind me.

I turn and see Ashley/Maddie about to catch me.

She sneers and looks behind me.

I follow her gaze.

Roxy is entering the gazebo on the other side—sandwiching me between the two of them.

Sounds like it's time for that cat strategy now.

"What do you think you're doing?" I give Roxy a scathing glare. "Did you not learn your lesson the last time?"

I reach into the back of my pants—as though for a gun.

They follow the movement of my hands with their eyes but don't back away.

When I don't produce an actual gun, Roxy's mouth curves in a predatory smile, and she starts to strip at an impressive speed.

I pivot toward Ashley/Maddie and find her already naked.

This is my chance.

Is tackling a naked teen easier than a dressed one?

If I were in their shoes, I'd feel vulnerable—but they look anything but that.

A flash of energy tells me it's too late.

They've both turned into wolves.

With a sinking feeling, I back away.

Both beasts show me their teeth, and Roxy leaps at me.

CHAPTER FIVE

I JUMP TO THE SIDE, and Roxy's crushing teeth clank right next to my ankle.

There's some kind of movement behind the wolves, but I focus on dodging Ashley/Maddie's attempt to chomp on my knee.

Roxy momentarily puts her weight on her haunches, then leaps.

A pale hand snaps Roxy from the air by her neck, like a kitten, and at the exact same time, a booted foot pins down the second werewolf's tail.

"Is this how ladies behave?" Vlad growls, his perfect features transforming from brooding to furious.

Rose shows up behind Vlad, pointing each of her index fingers at her lover's captives.

Blinding streams of energy smack into them, and with another flash, the wolves turn back into naked teens.

Vlad removes his foot from Ashley/Maddie's butt,

but keeps holding on to Roxy's neck, seemingly oblivious to her state of undress. "Did your father put you up to this?" he asks her sternly.

Suddenly finding herself in Vlad's hold must be too overwhelming for Roxy's tiny brain, because she just stands there, gaping at him, then at Rose, then at me.

Finally twisting out of Vlad's grasp, she crosses her arms to cover herself. "What does my father have to do with anything?" she petulantly asks.

"He and Sasha have a history." Vlad's voice is hard. "You're not a good enough actress to pretend you know nothing about that."

"But I don't." Roxy's arrogance appears shattered so badly I almost feel sorry for her. "He never tells me any—"

"Who is her father?" I ask, though I can guess based on the context.

"Chester," Vlad says, confirming my suspicion. "The former Councilor who—"

"Oh, I know who that is," I say and look at Roxy.

Yes.

Now that Vlad has pointed it out to me, I can see that Roxy has Chester's exact cheekbones and chin.

Except he's not a werewolf.

Then I recall our last Orientation lecture.

Roxy raised her hand when Dr. Hekima asked whose parents are different types of Cognizant. I jokingly thought then that her non-werewolf parent had to be a harpy or the unleashed kraken—and it seems I was close, as Chester is worse than both of those combined.

Does she have double powers?

Can she manipulate probabilities like Chester?

Dr. Hekima said that was rare, but he also said probability manipulators have an edge in that regard.

Her having Chester's powers could explain how I had such bad luck bumping into her and Ashley/Maddie.

Then I recall something else—something Gaius told me before my Rite.

Chester's beef with Darian was over a dead wife. A dead *werewolf* wife who'd committed suicide in response to a prophecy in which she was to be the cause of her daughter's death. Was Roxy that daughter? Does she know? I hope not. That would mess with any child's psyche. Maybe I should've been nicer to—

"I have no idea what you're talking about," Roxy says, getting her spunk back. "We met at Orientation last week, and when we saw her again, we decided to have some fun."

Rose's smooth forehead folds into a full-blown scowl. "I have the power to prevent you from changing for days, young lady—maybe even weeks if I wish." She extends her hands toward Roxy, and energy starts to crackle around her fingers.

Roxy pales, but for whatever reason, gives *me* a death stare.

Like Rose's threat is my fault.

"Sasha," Vlad says to me. "You better head home while Rose discusses ladylike behavior with these girls."

He doesn't need to ask me twice.

Keeping my posture as straight and proud as I can, I walk out of the gazebo and hightail it home.

———

BY THE TIME I get home, I'm relatively calm. Despite their deadly wolf form, it's hard to view Roxy and her gang as anything but bratty teens. Plus, I can't help but feel sorry for Roxy. With her mom's suicide and Chester as her father, the poor girl is entitled to be a little prickly.

Fluffster greets me at the door, so I grab him and get some pet therapy as I tell him about what happened.

When I'm sufficiently relaxed, I decide to give Darian's teachings another go.

In order to avoid pausing and re-starting the tape, I re-watch it until I have every step of the meditation committed to memory.

Recalling my earlier back and leg discomfort, I sit in a chair instead of a lotus pose and close my eyes.

I do the recommended breathing and slide my awareness around my body until it settles on my "third eye."

My mind is now as serene as a Zen monk's.

Even if I don't reach Headspace, this is bound to be good for my stress levels.

"Back on track," I remind myself and focus on the third eye again.

I'm so in the moment that the passage of time becomes hard to track. Floating on a cloud of relaxation, I feel my palms grow warm.

So warm they're almost hot.

According to what I've read, warm palms and feet are classic signs of the "relaxation response"—just as cold appendages are the body's reaction to stress.

I keep breathing and empty my mind again.

My palms are so warm now they feel like they're on fire.

Some intuition makes me open my eyes, and I see lightning forming on my palms.

I gasp.

Instantly, my autonomic nervous system turns my deep relaxation response into its complete opposite.

I'm breathing at a hundred miles an hour, my heart pounding against my rib cage.

All warmth leaves my palms—and the lightning fizzles out.

My fight-or-flight response doesn't go away, though. Instead, it goes into overdrive as I realize what the next step of the meditation would've been.

The lightning was going to go into my eyes.

CHAPTER SIX

I TAKE IN A CALMING BREATH, but it doesn't work.

The idea of lightning hitting my eyes bothers some primal part of my brain—the place responsible for fear of spiders, falling, and snakes.

This fear is obviously irrational, and likely made worse by the adrenaline that's been swimming in my system after the encounter with the b-hive. When I had my first-ever awake vision yesterday, lightning streamed from my palms into my eyes. Felix showed me a video that proves it.

Unfortunately, merely knowing that the lightning is harmless doesn't help. I've always been sensitive about things going into my eyes. I've even refused glaucoma tests after the first, horrific one, choosing to take my chances with the disease.

Why didn't Darian say anything about the lightning?

He sure talked a lot about everything else.

For that matter, what does he really want? Why is he teaching me?

I don't buy the Jubilee gift explanation. I bet it's all part of some plan of his—a plan that somehow culminates in the two of us together... assuming he didn't lie about having that vision.

Either way, that vision is not going to come true—not based on my current levels of annoyance and frustration with him.

Then an idea comes to me—one that should've occurred to me yesterday.

Worried that I'm too late, I rush to the door to see if the box Darian used to ship me the VCR is still there.

I exhale in relief.

The ripped-up box is where I dropped it last night. It's a good thing my earlier cleanup wasn't that thorough—or that my roommates aren't bothered by junk lying in the hallway.

On the shipping label, right below Darian's name, is an address.

Unlike on the tape package—which Darian pretended to mail from the TV studio where he may or may not have worked—this address is on the Upper East Side, a mere forty-minute subway ride away.

I enter the address into my phone, quickly get dressed, and head out.

It's time I asked Darian some very pointed questions.

———

SURPRISE, surprise. Darian's posh building has a doorman with a long-tailed coat, white gloves, and a hat.

"Take the elevator to the fourteenth floor," he tells me when I explain whom I'm here to see. "Let me get that for you."

As I follow the man, I nearly jump up and down in excitement. Until this moment, there was a real chance that Darian just put a random address on the package. In that case, the doorman wouldn't have known who Darian is—but he does.

Now I have to wonder if Darian put his real address there because he wanted me to come.

The building has four elevators but one button. The doorman presses the button for me, and the leftmost doors slowly open.

I get in, press the button for my destination, and the doors close just as slowly.

Then—just like the other day when I was standing outside Felix's room—lightning bolts explode in my vision.

———

I'M bodiless in a corridor of a posh building.

Right in front of me is Nero. He's holding Darian by his throat, easily lifting him off the ground with one hand.

Nero's free hand blurs into that morbidly familiar claw I saw yesterday, during the orc massacre.

In a voice that would be comically deep and guttural under other circumstances, but is chilling in this context, Nero growls, "You knew the orc would bruise her. And what I would do to them as a result. And that she'd walk in on me while I was slaughtering them. And how she'd react."

"You wanted to know if she would live if you hired the orcs, and I told you she'd be fine. And she is," Darian chokes out, his face turning an unhealthy shade of purple.

Nero's claw flies for Darian's chest.

Darian squeals, and I fully expect bits and pieces of him to fly in every direction.

But he's intact.

Nero's talons stopped right next to Darian's shirt.

"You screamed," Nero says, and if I had a body, I'd shudder from the cruelty in that deep voice. "Does that mean you didn't foresee if you'd live or die?"

"Stop this now," Darian chokes out, his eyes bulging out of their sockets. "She's about to step out of that elevator." His gaze darts to the leftmost doors. "If you kill me now, she'll see it—and her reaction will be worse this time."

Nero can tell if people are telling him the truth, so I have to assume Darian was honest because Nero lets Darian fall, looks at the door in question, and growls, "If you come near her again, you'll die. If you send her another package, be it another tape, or a vinyl record, or an email, or a DVD, or a fucking carrier pigeon —you'll die."

Darian looks like he's about to say something, but then there's a bright flash near his face and he stays silent. Does that mean the seer lightning just hit his eyes, and Darian foresaw what would happen if he talked back?

Whatever Darian glimpsed in his vision—assuming I didn't imagine that flicker of lightning—must've really impressed him, because he nods his agreement so vigorously there's a real chance of whiplash.

"Scram," Nero snarls.

Darian turns his back to Nero and stabs the elevator button as if his life depended on the speed of its arrival—which I guess it does.

The doors of the rightmost elevator open, and Darian jumps in.

———

I COME BACK to my senses and look around the elevator car in confusion.

It must've been another awake vision.

That means Nero and Darian are about to have that conversation.

I press the fourteenth-floor button forcefully, but that doesn't seem to improve the crawling speed of the elevator.

Something occurs to me.

Just like the last time, the beginning of the vision felt like I had lightning streaming from my hands directly into my eyeballs—and it wasn't so bad. Next time I do the meditation, I need to remember how unpainful the unsolicited vision was.

Then again, perhaps it feels different under conscious control.

After what seems like an hour, the elevator stops.

Jumping from foot to foot, I press the open-door button, over and over, but the uncaring doors crawl apart at the pace of a drunk snail.

I leap out of the elevator—and come face to face with Nero.

"Sasha." He tilts his head to the side. "What are the chances?"

"Don't," I hiss and jump back into the elevator.

Pressing the first-floor button as fast as I can, I toggle the close-door button in the hope that the doors slide shut quickly enough to allow me to catch Darian downstairs.

The doors barely move.

Nero stares at me, his piercing blue-gray eyes bringing to mind the myths about snakes being able to hypnotize their prey.

I lift my chin in a wordless challenge.

His limbal rings seem to visibly thicken, creating the illusion that the dark circles are eating away the whites of his eyes and the irises.

"You won't make it," his eyes appear to say. "And even if you do, I'll kill him if he talks to you."

"You wouldn't dare," my own eyes reply. "If you kill him, I—"

The doors finally close, stalemating our staring contest.

The ride down feels even longer than the ride up.

Can't the people in this uber-expensive building spring for a better elevator? It might be more useful than a doorman.

The elevator stops.

The doors begin to crawl open again.

In the distance, I see Darian's back. He's running out of the building so fast his soles are flashing.

As soon as I can fit through the crack between the opening doors, I do so—and launch into a sprint.

The doorman watches me in puzzled fascination.

Darian is outside, hailing a cab by the time I reach the door.

I rush out of the building.

He gets inside the cab.

I run to catch him, or better yet, to get into the same cab.

With a screech of tires, the cab jolts forward just as I grab for the door handle.

Darian stares ahead, refusing to look at me.

I try to hail a cab, desperate to follow him, but Murphy's/Chester's Law is at it again—the next three cabs already have passengers.

By the time one stops, I lose track of Darian completely.

"Let's go home," I tell the cabby in frustration.

"And where would home be?" the guy says with a gap-toothed smile.

I give him my address and sit there sullenly, processing what just happened.

Nero doesn't want Darian to train me, or even speak with me. It might be because Nero has plans for me, or because he still sees himself as my Mentor, and Cognizant rules state that it's a big sign of disrespect to teach someone else's Mentee.

Or maybe it has something to do with me telling Nero about the future Darian allegedly foresaw—the one where Darian and I become lovers. But that would imply that Nero is jealous, which would in turn imply that he has human feelings—something that seems farfetched.

Whatever his reason, Nero has just made sure I can't ask Darian for any help.

As confusing as Nero's motives are, there are other questions just as big.

How did Darian get caught by Nero in the first place?

He's a seer, a powerful one, yet he let himself get into a situation where he was dangling in the air by his throat.

Was that part of some scheme, or did his seer abilities fail him in this, just as they did when he kissed Kit (a.k.a. fake me) at the club the other day?

Maybe he knew he'd get off with a warning due to my timely arrival—which wouldn't have happened if he hadn't written his address on the package.

Perhaps this encounter was actually the best-case scenario for Darian. After all, only his pride was hurt in the end. For all I know, Darian might've glimpsed a multitude of futures and chosen the one where Nero's assault becomes a catalyst for something bigger. Hell, that something bigger might simply be my attitude toward Nero.

Perhaps Darian wanted me to see Nero at his most ruthless to eliminate what he perceives as romantic competition.

No wonder people hate seers so much. All these plots within plots are exhausting.

Then, the most important question of all hits me like a sledgehammer.

How did Nero know about the VCR and the tape Darian sent me? I got both of those items in the mail and watched them in my room yesterday, all by myself.

With a sinking feeling, I recall the theories about Nero having cameras around the fund—theories that explain how Nero knew about the bruise the orc gave to me.

Is it possible that Nero has similar surveillance in my apartment?

In my bedroom?

Blood leaves my face as I recall all the times I've gotten naked in that room, or worse, my encounters with Copperfield—my Hitachi magic wand massager.

No. Even Nero wouldn't be so—

I stop myself. Who am I kidding? If the last few days have proven anything, it's that Nero is capable of all sorts of horrible things.

Was *this* what Darian intended? To expose Nero as a peeping perv?

Getting out my phone, I text Felix.

When are you getting home?

His reply arrives a few moments later.

Finished my workload, just about to figure out this phone number thing for you.

I debate if I should tell him to drop everything and come home, but the phone number issue is important, so I reply with:

Thanks! Please let me know what you find out.

Felix texts back with an affirmative, and for the rest of the cab ride, I practice breathing for seer meditation —which has a nice bonus of calming me down as well.

I definitely need that.

I'm walking into our building when Felix's text arrives.

I figured out who that number belongs to. Or more accurately, which business. It's Izbushka Na Kurih Nojkah. It's not their main number, but it's theirs nevertheless. I wouldn't answer it if I were you. I'm going home now. Talk soon.

In a haze, I enter the elevator.

When translated from Russian, *Izbushka Na Kurih Nojkah* means "a hut on hen's legs." It's the name of the restaurant that belongs to Baba Yaga—the witch who helped Fluffster remember his last owner, Rasputin, in exchange for, and I quote both the witch and the Godfather, "...someday, and that day may never come, I will call upon you to do a service..."

Looks like that "someday" is today, the day after our meeting.

Great.

Now that I've had more sleep and no near-death encounters for a few hours, I'm certain that agreeing to grant Baba Yaga a favor was a bad idea. Not that I had much choice last night, but still. I stipulated that she not ask me to do something illegal, but with my mind now clearer, I can easily think of a number of unpleasant things that wouldn't be strictly illegal, like, say, eating tapeworm larvae.

On that cheerful thought, I enter my apartment.

Fluffster prances over and mentally says hello.

"Hey, bud." I bend down and rub under his chin. "You hungry?"

"I could eat," he says, so I give him some organic hay in my room.

Despite the earlier thoughts of tapeworms, my stomach rumbles as Fluffster dives into his dish. I make my way to the kitchen, toast a couple of bagels, and garnish them with cream cheese and lox.

As I'm doing that, an idea forms in my mind.

Taking out my phone, I text Felix again.

Let's have a little picnic in Battery Park.

The reply from Felix is a single character—the question mark—so I text back, *It's time for me to feed you for a change.*

Once we settle on a particularly picturesque location, I pack the bagels and a couple of water bottles into a big brown bag and put on my shoes.

Just as I open the front door, the now-familiar, but no less unpleasant, dread overcomes me, and I get the phone out.

As expected, the infernal device rings a few heartbeats later.

It's Baba Yaga.

Again.

CHAPTER SEVEN

I DON'T PICK UP.

Instead, I put the phone on top of the shoe rack and head out the door, all the while wondering whether my powers will still give me panic attacks if Baba Yaga calls when the phone is far away from me.

Planning my conversation with Felix in my head, I make my way to our meeting spot. It's near a scenic grill-oriented restaurant that Ariel always drags us to.

Felix isn't there yet, so I grab a seat on the bench and do my best to calm down.

"You're alone?" Felix says a few minutes later—startling the bejesus out of me. Seeing my hand on my chest, he lifts his unibrow. "Jumpy much?"

"You can't just creep up on people like that," I tell him as he sits next to me on the bench. "And yes, it's you and me. Ariel wasn't home."

"Hmm." Felix takes off his backpack and places it on

the bench, then reaches into the brown bag and gets a bagel. "Ariel should be home by now."

"I've never been home on a Tuesday at this time, so I didn't know that."

"Fair enough." Felix takes a bite of his bagel and looks around, as though to make sure Ariel isn't hiding behind him. "There's no pattern to her new, Gaius-contaminated schedule."

I get my own bagel out. "That thing parents always tell you about bad influences—there's something to it, I guess."

Felix shakes his head and chews contemplatively as he stares at the soothing New York Harbor view.

I follow his gaze to the Statue of Liberty. "Thanks for figuring out that phone number."

He looks back at me, his face unusually serious. "Whatever Baba Yaga wants, it's bad news. Here." He hands me a phone. "This is brand new. It should take her a while to figure out your new number—assuming she ever does. Meanwhile, you have plausible deniability. After all, you can't break your promise to do a service if she can't ask it of you."

"That's a great idea. Come to think of it, my current phone is my old work phone. I should've given it back to Nero when I quit. Now I will do just that, and it will deepen the plausible deniability you speak of."

"I knew you'd be good at this deviousness game," Felix says proudly. "So, what's up with this picnic?"

I tell him about my encounter with the b-hive and

with Nero, and how the latter led me to the conclusion that I have a camera in my room.

Felix looks thoughtful as he absentmindedly breaks his bagel in half. "Why do you think it's video surveillance? In contrast to an audio-only bug, I mean."

"I guess I was thinking about your surveillance in our hallway and assumed Nero's would do the same thing." I take out one of the water bottles and take a big gulp. "Plus, he knew about Darian's tape, so I figured—"

"If Nero had an audio bug, he could've recognized Darian's voice when you played the tape." Felix takes a bite of the bagel half in his right hand. "In any case, I find the whole idea of a bug—video or audio—improbable."

"But you yourself—"

"I don't know if you know this about me, but I'm very paranoid when it comes to Wi-Fi devices." Though the bagel portion in his right hand is unfinished, Felix bites the half in his left hand. "I know what every wireless device in the building does, and to whom it belongs. That makes me fairly sure there isn't a bug, or at least, not one that uses Wi-Fi." He bites his right bagel half. "That makes Nero's job that much harder," he says through a mouthful. "Just think about it, when would he have planted such a thing?"

"When we were at—" I don't finish the thought when I realize that Fluffster makes planting anything in our absence impossible. "Maybe it was there before we moved in?" I suggest instead. "Nero does own the building."

"How did he know which room was destined to be yours?" Felix looks at both bitten halves in his hands, shrugs, and stuffs what's left of the right half into his mouth.

"All our rooms might be bugged," I say. "That's what I'd do if I were Nero."

Felix shakes his head as he finishes chewing. "There was never such a thing in my room," he says with unshakable confidence. "And I, in general, find it hard to believe he could've had hardware in our apartment all this time, recording and passing along info without me noticing. As you know, I'm quite familiar with surveillance equipment."

"Familiar" is an understatement. Felix could stand in for Q in a *James Bond* movie when it comes to tech. Like hacking, it has to do with his "technomancer" powers.

"I'm glad you brought that up," I say. "Because it's actually your skills that I wanted to talk to you about outside of Nero's possible earshot." I inadvertently squeeze my bagel, and some cream cheese drips on the pavement at our feet. An aggressive pigeon eats it up as I continue. "I think it's time we turn the tables on Nero and hack his ass. Not just to find out if he's been spying on us, but to learn his secrets, in case some of them are useful."

Staring at me as though I've grown horns, Felix tries to bite into a bagel in his right hand and gets his empty palm instead. "You want me to penetrate Nero's security."

Trying to radiate calm, I bite my bagel, take a sip of water, and casually nod. "Yes." With a fake smile, I add, "I want you to penetrate Nero."

Felix chuckles humorlessly. "In other words, you want me dead."

"Why would you be dead?"

"Because Nero would catch me 'hacking his ass,' as you put it, and he'd kill me." Felix scoots away from me on the bench.

"Why don't we place all the blame on me? Can't you set up the hack or whatever so that it looks like I'm the only one responsible?"

"So he kills you instead of me? That is, until he figures out I was involved, and then kills me too."

"I don't think he would kill me." I take another bite, but the bagel no longer has any flavor. "And as I said, I'd bear *all* the blame."

Felix unscrews a water bottle. "I designed Nero's security in the first place. It's—"

"Awesome. Use some backdoor," I say. "You left one for yourself, didn't you?"

"I was working for a walking, talking polygraph exam who could squish me like a cockroach at any point." Felix puts his unfinished bagel back into the brown bag. "Of course, I *didn't* leave any backdoor. And I'm glad I didn't because he asked me if I left a backdoor after I was finished. I truthfully told him no, and look, I'm still alive."

"But you're always preaching that no system is uncrackable."

"I didn't say the setup I made for Nero is uncrackable." Felix gulps some water. "It's just the best security I've ever set up—without a backdoor."

"So you *can* do it?" Deciding to play dirty, I make puppy eyes. "Pretty please? I swear I'll take all the blame."

"It's too difficult," he says, displaying an amazing resilience to the puppy-eyed look.

"But not impossible." I upgrade the look to that of a hungry basset-hound puppy, one with big, droopy ears.

Felix's unibrow dances on his forehead as he thinks for a good half a minute. Then he looks around again, as though Nero might be lurking in the bushes. "You'd have to get a physical device near his workstation and keep it there until I'm done, which could take hours."

"What kind of device?"

Felix rummages through his backpack, takes out a circuit wafer of silicone the size of a playing card, and hands it to me.

"Did you get that out of a phone?" The card magician in me notes that the gizmo weighs as much as ten cards, is as thick as about four, but the dimensions are actually smaller, which would make palming it both harder in some respects and easier in others.

"I made that." Felix sits up straighter. "I call it Felix's Extranet Low Latency Access Trojan Input Output. Or F.E.L.L.A.T.I.O for short."

I look at him for any signs of humor and find

none. "Let me get this straight. This is called *fellatio*?" I make the gizmo vanish as I did the seven of clubs for Rose and Vlad, then make it come back with a flourish. "Don't you find there's enough sexual innuendo in hacking already? Penetration. Backdoor—"

"You're the one who said we should 'hack his ass.'" Felix snatches the gizmo from my hand. "It's just easier to remember this way, and besides"—he scratches the back of his head—"this FELLATIO is pronounced 'fella,' as in, young fella, 't,' like Mister T, and i.o., like in computer parlance."

"Sure it is," I drawl, and a possibly hysterical chuckle escapes my lips. "And you're sure that *fellatio*"—I use the more traditional pronunciation—"is required to penetrate Nero properly?"

"I'd need it near Nero for hours before I could *get in*," Felix says with a trace of a smile. "Hence, this is impossible."

"Let's say the gizmo magically got into Nero's pocket," I say, though a bunch of nervy butterflies divebomb my stomach as I vividly imagine implementing such a feat. "Would that help?"

Felix takes out what remains of his bagel, takes a small bite, and chases it with some water, looking thoughtful throughout. "Yes. If FELLA—I mean, this device—made its way into Nero's pocket, I think I could pene—I mean, get into—his system." He stares at the New Jersey skyline across the Harbor. "Maybe."

"Sounds doable," I say with a certainty I don't feel.

"Except, what happens if Nero finds the FELLATIO in his pocket?"

"I'll be as good as dead." Felix looks back at me. "But I *can* use my power to command the silicone in the device to turn into dust at any point I wish, so there's that."

"For that, you'd need to see him going for his pocket."

"I can get a visual of Nero fairly quickly through his own security cameras," Felix says, some color returning to his face. "Triggering a security alert is a bigger concern, though—"

"But you put the security in, so you wouldn't trigger any such thing," I say confidently.

"I guess not." There might be a glimmer of something like excitement in those black eyes.

"Great." I grin and outline the beginnings of my insane plan.

"You better hope you're right when you say that Nero wouldn't hurt you," Felix says when I finish. "Because you're going to put that to the test."

"I don't think he would," I lie.

"Okay," Felix says and goes into his backpack again.

He takes out his laptop and types on it so fast I'm half-certain he's just pressing random keys to make himself look impressive.

Then, the FELLATIO device makes a loud beep.

"Here." He hands me the gizmo. "Do not take it out or speak of it once we get home."

I nod solemnly, take out a deck of cards, throw

away the advertising cards and the jokers, and stash the FELLATIO in the freed-up space.

"It might be best if we don't even return home at the same time." I pocket the cards and get up.

"You go there," Felix says. "I'm going to go do a little shopping, fill up that empty room of mine."

"Sounds good." I start walking back, and over my shoulder say, "Thanks, Felix. I owe you one."

"A big one," he grumbles and leaves.

———

I MAKE my way home and catch Ariel just as she's leaving the apartment. She's wearing the dominatrix-meets-Catwoman outfit from our Earth Club outing and is clearly unhappy I caught her in it.

"So, you got a chance to finally change your clothes," I say caustically.

She hides her gaze. "I've got to run. We'll catch up soon."

"Sure," I say with a deep sigh and watch Ariel strut to the elevator.

My roommate isn't acting like herself. Soon, Felix and I will have no choice but to stage some kind of an intervention.

Making my way into my bedroom, I give Fluffster more hay.

"How is the job search going?" he asks mentally, oblivious to the reality of communicating with his mouth full. "The bills—"

"Let me check on that." As graciously as I can fake it, I add, "Thanks for the reminder."

I soon discover something odd happening with my job search. My inbox is chock-full of replies from the companies I applied to.

I open the first one, from a hedge fund that's Nero's minor competitor and the most promising job opportunity for me.

The email regrets to inform me that the position has already been filled.

That's strange. Usually, if you apply for a job and they don't want you for whatever reason, you never hear from them. Maybe they saw where I worked and wanted to be extra nice in case they want to recruit me later?

I open the next email.

"We regret to inform you the position has been filled," writes the Director of HR at a major investment bank.

That's weird.

Frantic, I open the next email, then another and another.

They are *all* informing me about filled positions.

I go online and look up some of these job postings at random.

All are still posted on the job search site.

Given that it costs good money to keep a posting listed, why are so many companies advertising jobs that they've already filled? And how did so many companies fill their positions at the same time?

More importantly, why are they so uncharacteristically responsive and vocal about it?

An impossible explanation occurs to me. Could Nero have blacklisted me somehow? Could he have ordered other firms to tell me that the job is already filled if I apply?

No.

That's very hard to believe.

He *is* powerful in the financial sector, sure, but can anyone have this much pull?

Gritting my teeth, I seek out some positions outside the financial industry. I find a gig as an entry-level quality assurance tester at a media company. It only requires the applicant to have a bachelor's degree, so I apply to it. Next, I locate similar easy-to-qualify-for listings in the health industry, as well as with a few software companies.

I don't share what just happened with Fluffster, who's happily munching on his hay. He already worries about our finances, and this could give him a heart attack.

Instead, I sit there, staring blankly at the laptop screen.

What would I do if my crazy hypothesis is true? What if Nero is really blacklisting me? Would I take one of those entry-level jobs I just applied to? Or, assuming I master my powers, could I use them to simply win the lottery instead?

Would that break the spirit of the Mandate?

Yes, I decide. Given my fifteen minutes of fame

among the humans, winning the lottery might indeed be perceived as a public exercise of my powers—so that's out.

Making money doing what I love is out too; the Council explicitly forbade me from performing as an illusionist.

I could try my hand at day trading. My powers should help there, for sure. However, on the off chance my intuition misleads me, I could lose whatever savings I do have. Not to mention, to successfully live off the daily stock fluctuations, you need quite a bit of capital to start with—something my measly savings don't qualify for. Also, if I'm too good, I might get on the radar of the SEC, which would be bad enough on its own, but infinitely worse if it leads to trouble with the Council.

I imagine an overly successful day trader might be a lot like a lottery winner in their eyes—a Cognizant who's risking exposure of her powers.

Oh, and on top of that, if I trade any of the stocks I researched for Nero—which is a lot of stocks—I might be breaking the no-personal-trading clause in the agreement I signed when I joined the fund.

I dig in my emails and pull up the agreement. Yep, no trading of those stocks for me for at least a year, unless I'm willing to risk getting sued by Nero—and if he's being enough of an asshole to blacklist me, he'd be more than glad to sue me too.

Suddenly, I'm way more eager to execute my earlier

plan. I'll have to do a lot less acting now that I'm genuinely furious with Nero.

The plan, however, is for tomorrow. Today, my best bet is to master my powers. If I could see the future with any predictability, there are bound to be ways I could capitalize on it—financially or otherwise.

I shower, change into comfy clothes, and get into the meditation pose.

To my annoyance, I find that clearing my mind when I'm mad at a smug, manipulative bastard is an exercise in futility.

After a couple of hours, I give up and surf the internet for more info about Rasputin. Given what Rose and Vlad told me, it's all probable BS, so when I come across the Disney movie *Anastasia*, I watch a few clips featuring Rasputin as the villain.

The cartoon is as likely to be true as what's on Wikipedia.

Frustrated, I decide to go to bed extra early.

The earlier I get up tomorrow, the earlier I can storm into Nero's fund.

CHAPTER EIGHT

ENTERING MY FORMER OFFICE BUILDING, I walk through the long, sleek lobby to the security guard, explain that I no longer work at the place, and request a guest pass to "see HR about turning in my old phone."

I figure if I tell him that my actual plan is to storm into the chief's office, he'd not-so-respectfully send me away.

"You don't need a pass," the guard tells me after he examines my driver's license as though to see if it's a forgery. "Your ID wasn't deactivated. You can just go right ahead."

I verify his words by getting through the ID-activated turnstiles without trouble.

That's odd.

Is Nero in denial about my resignation?

If so, I'm about to disabuse him of that notion.

"Sasha," a familiar female voice says as a gentle hand touches my shoulder.

I turn to see Lucretia, the fund psychologist and one of the few people I might actually miss when I burn all bridges to this place.

"Hello." I smile at her.

"Is something wrong?" Lucretia asks. Leaning in so that her lips nearly touch my ear, she whispers, "I sense a huge tumult of conflicting emotions in you. Is everything okay?"

That's right. I recently learned that besides being a pre-vamp, Lucretia is also an empath—a rare combination of different Cognizant powers.

"Come ride the elevator with me," I say, and she nods.

We let a group of people grab the next elevator, then jump into an empty one. As soon as the doors close, I say, "Nero left me no choice but to quit this place."

I then press the stop button and give her a brief version of events, one that assumes she'll break doctor/patient privilege and report everything I say to Nero (or that he has listening devices in the elevator).

She listens with a vaguely disbelieving frown. "There's more to Nero than this," she says when I finish. "I can't break his confidence, of course, but when he talks to me, I can sense his emotions, and I doubt he's as ruthless as you say. Especially toward you."

I cross my arms in front of my chest. "Are you actually defending him?"

"No. That wasn't my intent." Her large blue eyes

gaze at the floor. "I just sense your own emotions toward Nero and—"

"This conversation seems to be going nowhere quick," I say and stab the stop button to release it. "I better go."

"I'm sorry if I overstepped." Looking genuinely apologetic, Lucretia tucks a long strand of black hair behind her ear. "Just know that you can be my patient regardless of your employment status at this firm."

"Thanks," I say, feeling slightly bad that my anger at Nero made me snap at the woman. "I don't think I can afford you—but I'm happy to be your friend, if that's free."

She smiles. "Sure. Call me if you need anything." She hands me her card and exits the elevator on the next floor.

I program her number into my new phone, set it to vibrate, and spend the rest of the ride up calming my nerves—unsuccessfully.

By the time I stomp up to Venessa—my least favorite peon in Nero's army of assistants—my heart wants to jump out of my rib cage.

"Yes?" Venessa drawls, her beady eyes staring at me as though I could be here for any reason except to see Nero.

"I'm expected," I lie and ignore the woman's outraged protests as I stride by.

I hide the action of palming the FELLATIO device by my angry march into Nero's office. Entering, I try to slam the door behind me, only to find that the stupid thing is automated to close with barely a puff of air.

Nero's fancy desk is in the standing position, and for a second, I almost lose my nerve as I see him there.

He doesn't usually wear suits, but he has one on today. It must be an insanely expensive bespoke creation by the best Italian designers, because it hugs his muscled frame like spandex, making me gape at him in dumb fascination.

I better snap out it.

So what if he's wearing a suit? That's great for the plan. Suit jacket pockets are much better for my purposes than pant pockets.

Nero doesn't show any sign that he's aware of me. Either he's laser focused on what he's doing, or he's just messing with me.

I pointedly clear my throat.

He still doesn't look away from the screen.

"Nero. Don't pretend you can't see me."

He looks up from behind the screen and lifts one dark eyebrow. "That didn't take long." He comes around the desk and spreads his arms, as though offering me a hug. "Welcome back."

The smug expression on that symmetrical face infuriates me—and that too is actually good for the plan.

"Here comes the suicidal part," I think to myself and stride toward him.

CHAPTER NINE

IT TAKES me a couple of seconds to close the distance between us.

When he's within arm's length, I stop my advance and gulp in a calming breath, inhaling his clean, woodsy scent with just the faintest hint of lime. Being this close to him reminds me of the time I danced with Kit in Nero's disguise—and that kiss she tricked me into.

His blue-gray eyes stare down at me mockingly, making me recall the plan.

"How dare you?" I hiss, and without further ado, I slap his chest with my right hand—just as my left one surreptitiously delivers the device into his pocket.

For a moment, he looks confused, so I capitalize on that, slapping his chest with both hands this time. In part, it's because I'm genuinely angry, but mostly so that he has the illusion of both my palms being in view at all times.

With a movement too fast to register, Nero catches my wrists in a vise-like grip, pinning my palms against his chest. I attempt to pull away, but it's like trying to escape a cement wall.

Our eyes lock.

Is he about to kiss me?

Or is he about to bite my head off?

Both seem equally likely in the moment.

"You're hurting my wrists." I make another futile attempt to pull away. Even through the layers of his suit jacket and shirt, my palms can feel the powerful beating of his heart.

Or is that my own pulse echoing in my hands?

As I keep staring into those blue-gray depths, a quote from Nietzsche pops into my head: "...if you gaze long into an abyss, the abyss also gazes into you."

Nero's grip loosens.

Circulation returns to my fingers.

Now it feels more like he's caressing my wrists—his strong, calloused palms hot on my sensitized skin.

"Let go." I put all my frustration into my words.

In reply, he stares at me so intently that I have to look away, aimlessly gazing around the room.

His painting catches my eye again. It's the surreal landscape one, with the silver Grand Canyon-like mountain ridge under unfamiliar star formations, with seven differently shaded moons and an aurora borealis.

To my surprise, he releases my wrists.

I make the mistake of looking back at him—and it feels as though he captures my gaze in his.

Why do I always feel like a rabbit hypnotized by a snake when we lock eyes like this?

I take a step back and gather my scattered wits.

"How dare you," I repeat with renewed fury. "Who are you to tell me who I can or can't speak with?"

He tilts his head. "You can speak with whomever you want," he murmurs, and steps toward me.

"So long as it's not Darian." I take two steps back this time.

"*You* can speak with whomever you want," he says, enunciating every word. "I wouldn't dream to 'dare' say otherwise."

"But Darian can't talk to *me*."

"That's that coward's choice." Nero takes another step in my direction.

My phone vibrates in my pocket at the same time as I say, "You didn't leave him a choice."

Our eyes do battle once more, making it very easy for me to pretend that I don't know what to do with my hands, so I stick them both in my pockets.

"You know," he says thoughtfully, "I'm beginning to think Darian let me catch him just so that we could have this pleasant conversation."

I had a variation of that same thought before, but I don't share that with Nero. Instead, I use the moment to palm the new phone and take it out in such a way that Nero won't be able to see me glance at it.

There's a text from Felix.

I now have access to the cameras. Get out of there.

"I don't care what Darian's motivations were," I say,

glaring at Nero as I slip the phone back into my pocket. "It's yours that are a problem."

Nero's eyebrows pull together. "I didn't tell Darian anything that wasn't my prerogative as your Mentor."

"Did you forget the part where I quit being your Mentee?"

Nero looks me up and down, and I take another step back as he says, "That isn't your choice to make."

I fight the urge to slap him for real as he asks with mock courtesy, "Was there anything else?"

My jaw tightens. "Did you blacklist me?" The plan doesn't require us to be talking anymore, but I'll be damned if I don't give Nero a piece of my mind.

"Did I what?" He takes another step in my direction.

I step backward again—and my back meets the glass wall. "Did you sabotage my job search?" I push away from the wall, my hands balling at my sides. "Did you tell everyone in the financial industry not to hire me?"

"You already have a job." Nero waves his hand, as though to encompass his building. "There's not a better job in the financial industry."

My desire to slap him intensifies. "Bullshit." Remembering my other reason for this visit, I pull my old phone out of the other pocket and shove it at him. "I quit. Remember?"

"You're taking a break," he says dismissively, showing no sign of taking the phone from me. "Thus far, you took a comp day to make up for your work on Sunday, but if you continue this, you'll be using up your vacation days." He pauses as though to make a quick mental calculation. "You have twelve days left."

Before I understand what I'm doing, I throw the old phone at his head.

With another supernatural display of speed, he catches the phone and smiles.

"I got myself a new phone," I say, seething.

"Give me your new number," he replies with infuriating calmness.

"I *really* hate you." I pivot on my heel, heading for the door.

"You forget," Nero says to my back, and I hear a smirk in his voice. "I can tell when you're lying—and it doesn't matter if you momentarily believe your lie yourself."

I jerk open the door, and it takes a monumental effort of will not to stomp out like an angry toddler.

Forgetting the lesson from my entry, I try to slam the door shut behind me, but the evil device just makes that impotent puff of air instead.

Venessa is standing in my way. In her bitchiest tone, she says, "You're—"

Something in my gaze must activate the woman's sense of self-preservation, because she stops speaking and moves out of the way.

I'm still fuming by the time I've walked a few blocks.

Taking out my phone, I dial Felix.

"You better tell me you're in that asshole's system," I say instead of a hello.

"Sadly, no. Nero set strong passwords just as I'd instructed him to do. I was hoping he wouldn't have done it, like many other users."

"Don't tell me I went into that office for nothing." I squeeze the new phone so tightly the plastic creaks.

"That's not what I'm saying," Felix says defensively. "I'm just going to need more time."

"Fine." I loosen my death grip on the poor device. "Let me know as soon as you have it figured out."

"I will," Felix says. "Oh, your mother just called me —so I gave her your new number."

I fight the strong desire to smack my phone against the asphalt. "I wish you'd have checked with me before doing that."

"She said she was worried," Felix says, confused. "I didn't realize—"

"Forget it." I take a deep breath. "Focus all your attention on penetrating Nero."

"Deal," Felix says and hangs up the phone.

I get myself a cab and try to calm down.

My phone rings.

This number I recognize.

"Hi, Mom." I do my best to keep any residual irritation out of my voice. "How are things going?"

"Sasha." Mom sounds like she's hyperventilating. "I was about to call you so we can talk about extending my stay in Paris"—I mentally translate this from Mom-speak to mean she was going to ask me for more money—"when Beverly called me."

She stops, and I can hear her inhale enough air to speak for a couple of minutes nonstop.

Beverly is the gossipy friend of hers who saw me have lunch with Dad the other day. If she called Mom, I can easily guess what this conversation is to be about. Mom wants to complain that I'm "cooperating with the enemy behind her back"—which is total self-centered BS that I'm going to put a stop to.

"I just saw Beverly the other day," I say before she can continue her tirade, deciding that this calls for the best defense—offense. "When I was having lunch with Dad. Remember I told you about that the other day?"

In reality, I called her and tricked her into thinking the call was cutting out, but unlike Nero, she's not a lie detection machine.

"You did call me." Mom audibly blows out the big breath. "Said something about sushi. But you didn't tell me—"

"I did," I say confidently. "Why do you never listen to me?"

There's a very long pause on the other line. I'm about to check if she's still on when she says, "You're trying to muddy the waters. What matters is that you took that cheating scoundrel's side, and we don't have much to talk about."

If she'd called me on any other day, I might've cringed, but today isn't that day.

"Talking to my father isn't the same as taking anyone's side," I say sternly. "And so that we're clear, 'nothing to talk about' obviously includes conversations about extending your stay in Paris."

A silence follows.

"I'm just trying to look out for you," Mom finally says, her voice quivering. "He'll break your heart, the way he broke mine."

"Thanks, Mom," I say with fake sincerity. "I'm a big girl and can look after my own heart."

Another silence follows. "About extending my stay," she says after a moment. "It would be great if—"

"Actually, I was about to call you about that," I say, deciding to go in for the kill. "I just lost my job. I could use some help myself, but if—"

"Oh. So you went to your father for money?" She sounds relieved.

"That's not what I was saying." I roll my eyes so hard I get dizzy. "Not even a little bit."

"Say no more," Mom says conspiratorially. "I totally understand."

"You do?"

"Obviously, you'll need to get yourself another job, sooner rather than later. Your father isn't reliable—"

"I was actually applying to some jobs right before you called," I lie. "Probably should get back to it."

"That's a good idea," she says. "I'm sorry if I distracted you."

"You didn't distract me. I'm always happy to hear from you."

"Still, I better let you get back to it," Mom says. "*Au revoir.*"

"Bye, Mom." I hang up and stare at the phone.

When I got out of Nero's office, I didn't think I could be more rattled, but I was wrong.

Maybe I should somehow unleash Mom on Nero?

The bastard definitely deserves it.

But no. I can't. He'd probably shred her like an orc, plus such below-the-belt tactics might be against the Geneva Convention.

Shaking my head, I text Felix, *How goes Nero penetration?*

He replies instantly.

Both my day job and my roommate are distracting me. Makes it hard to concentrate.

He's got a decent point, so I don't reply.

Instead, I do my best to practice meditative breathing—and by the time the cab drops me off by my building, I confirm what should be obvious: talking to Nero and Mom isn't meditation conducive.

When I get home, the first thing I do is pet Fluffster.

Touching his fur is so soothing that a whole branch of pet therapy should be created with chinchillas in mind.

Slightly calmer, I rethink my earlier encounter. So what if Nero refuses to accept that I quit? That's his problem, not mine. He'll come to terms with the new reality when I take another job. In fact, maybe I'll take one of those entry-level gigs, just to spite him.

Thus determined, I grab my laptop and schlep to the nearest Starbucks in order to have privacy from any possible Nero snooping.

The Starbucks is nice and empty at this time of day, so I get a venti cup of coffee and park my butt in the cushiest couch with a window view.

Carefully sipping the scorching brew, I open my laptop, get on their Wi-Fi, and check if I got any responses to my job applications.

My breathing speeds up.

I did get replies. *From every place I applied to.*

They all apologize and inform me the position has been filled.

My pet therapy effect instantly goes down the drain, and I barely restrain myself from smashing the laptop against the tile floor.

How is Nero doing this?

Did he get a vampire to scan all the job sites and glamour all the HR people at these companies to reject my applications? Or is he this influential in *all* these industries?

My phone rings and I jump to my feet, then sit back down again before looking at the screen.

To my relief, it's just Felix calling.

"Hey," he says. "Is it safe to talk?"

"I'm at Starbucks. Does that qualify?"

"Yeah, should be safe enough. I have good news and bad news."

"Give me the good news first." I warm my hands by grabbing the coffee cup.

"All right," he says. "I'm in Nero's system, and I've figured out how he knew about Darian's tape—and lots of your other conversations."

"That's amazing news." I nearly tip over the cup in excitement. "What's the bad news?"

He's silent for a moment. "Unfortunately, I did my job too thoroughly when I originally set up his security, and I can't use any of my usual methods to get more information. What's worse is that I see a really juicy shared drive with lots of files, but it's password protected and I'm having trouble getting into it. In fact, that's why I'm calling. I was hoping you could help me."

"Me help you?" I say as I try to process Felix's bad news. "How?"

"Wait," he exclaims in a worried tone. "Did you give Nero your old phone?"

"Yes. Why?"

"Whew." Felix loudly exhales. "Let's jump on a video conference and I'll explain."

"Wait, how did—"

Felix hangs up.

Both my phone and laptop notify me of a video call, so I eagerly pick up on the laptop.

I see a view of Felix's workstation from the side. His black chair and split keyboard are identical to the ones he has at home, which in turn look just like the setups in *The Matrix* ships.

Felix has an intense expression on his face as he stares at all the screens. There are little windows with command prompts all over his monitors, with the exception of one. On that screen is a big window that's showing the feed from the security camera in Nero's office.

Unlike during our earlier encounter, Nero has his desk adjusted to the sitting position. He's peering at the screen even more intently than before while his long fingers dance on his keyboard with the grace of a piano prodigy.

"This PuTTY window is where I'm trying to get the password." Felix points at a greenish box with black font.

"Hold off," I say. "You never explained how he did his spying."

"Oh." He looks away from the screen and into the camera of his phone, so that he's looking right at me. "That's easy. It was that phone you gave back to him."

"That bastard." I slowly shake my head. "This kind of makes sense. He gave me that thing himself."

"Exactly." Felix readjusts his keyboard. "It was your work phone. Corporations don't even pretend to give you privacy on your work equipment. When you joined the fund, you probably signed some paper that allowed Nero to spy on any phone he gave you—"

"Oh, I doubt a lack of legal pretext would've stopped him." I glare at the screen where Nero is obliviously typing away. "This explains everything, though. The phone *was* in my room when I watched the VCR. It's like a secret to a magic effect; now that I know how Nero did it, I wonder why I didn't think of it in the first place."

"Why didn't I?" Felix looks genuinely contrite. "The important thing is that you gave him the phone back and didn't take a replacement."

I inhale a quick breath as a new realization hits me. "My powers must've activated before we had that picnic," I whisper. "Thanks in part to Baba Yaga's incessant calls, before I came to see you, I left the phone at home, on the shoe rack. If I hadn't…"

Felix jams his hands into his armpits as though giving himself a hug. He must've just realized that if I didn't leave the phone where I did, Nero would've overheard our picnic scheming and known all about this penetration attempt.

"Back to the bad news," I say, eager to distract Felix from morbid thoughts. "Why can't you use your technomancer powers to get into this file or drive or whatever? Don't you have hacker tools or something else techy to help you out?"

"I already used my powers to secure this system to start with." Felix rubs his reddening eyes. "Nero forced me to make it 'Felix proof,' for lack of a better term, so I'm kind of battling my own self. A better self in a way —a self who had months to design the security. So I'm reduced to the most basic method of all—trying to simply guess the password. But, what makes it harder is that if I guess it wrong more than three times per ten minutes, it's game over."

"So guess it less often?" I say, unsure how I can help the mighty Felix in this, of all things.

"Right." He scratches the top of his head. "The problem is, doing it that way will take an eternity."

"Hmm." I drum my fingers on the table in front of

me, momentarily oblivious to its dubious cleanliness. "I still don't see how I can help."

"You know Nero better than I do." Felix glances at the screen with my typing ex-boss. "Maybe we can start with *your* best guesses?"

"I don't know him *that* well," I say bitterly. "No, wait. Scratch that. Try 'asshole' as his password. Or maybe 'heartless,' or 'evil,' or—"

Felix types something in the green screen and presses enter.

Nothing happens.

"Dude, I was kidding. Did you just actually try those out?"

"I don't have better ideas to try." Felix looks at me earnestly. "Could you somehow use your power to get at the password?"

"I have no idea how to do that," I say.

Suddenly, something makes my aforementioned powers tingle in alarm.

"Shit," I tell Felix. "Something's about to happen."

My voice must scare him because I see hairs lift on the back of his neck.

Venessa comes into Nero's office and puts a piece of paper in front of him.

He stops typing, looks at the paper, and says something harsh to Venessa.

Though no sound is available, I can guess what he says. Something like, "You imbecile. Why the hell are you bringing me a piece of a dead tree?"

Nero is obsessed with a paperless office to such a

ridiculous level that he exiled printers from his whole building.

The paper Venessa brought him must've come in the mail—and I bet part of his chastisement is about why she didn't just scan and email it to him.

They go back and forth, and to my shock, Venessa manages not to get shredded into chunks of meat.

My guess is that she tells Nero the paper is urgent, or something to that effect.

Finally, Nero looks pacified and searches for something around his impeccably empty desk—probably a pen to sign whatever the paper is.

Not finding what he needs, he looks expectantly at Venessa—who seems to shrink into herself. She clearly didn't anticipate that a signing might require a pen; in her defense, our office has no pens anywhere, either.

After Nero says something curt to Venessa, he begins to pat his pockets.

A wave of anxiety hits me then—one that makes Baba Yaga's phone calls seem like a minor inconvenience.

I understand what's about to happen.

Nero is going to reach into his pocket and find the device.

And when he does, we're dead.

CHAPTER TEN

"FELIX!" I shout so loudly that the Starbucks employees gape at me. "Destroy FELLATIO."

Chin trembling, Felix jumps to his feet and points a hand at the screens in front of him.

A ray of magenta energy flows from Felix's fingers into the screens just as Nero reaches into his right jacket pocket—the one with the gizmo.

I squint at the screen unblinkingly.

Nero's hand comes back out, holding something.

A pen.

"He must've gotten that pen as swag from some vendor," I tell Felix in a faint voice. "I didn't know he had it in that pocket."

"It's okay. I made the FELLATIO disintegrate in time," Felix says, plopping back into his ultra-ergonomic chair. "That was a close call." He sounds as relieved as I feel.

"We'll have to try again," I say, my frantic heartbeat slowing. "You'll need to give me a new device."

"Okay." Felix moistens his lips. "But we'll still have the password problem. Besides, how are you going to get close to him again?"

At the thought of getting close to Nero, a warm, strangely tingly sensation flutters through my body. It intensifies when I realize that we might have better luck if I place the device in his *pants* pocket.

Must be due to my stupid nerves.

"Let me worry about FELLATIO delivery," I say firmly, to cover up said nerves. "You figure out that password. Maybe you could see him typing it after he logs out and logs back in?"

"I'd have to wait until he wants to access those specific files," Felix says, studying Nero's screen with a worried expression. "Plus, the camera is too far away for me to know exactly what keys he's pressing."

"I'm sure you'll figure out a way," I say and beam my most confident smile at him. "Please think about it. Meanwhile, I'll stop distracting you. Let's talk later."

Before Felix can object, I hang up and gulp down my now-cooled coffee.

———

SINCE I'M out of the apartment already, I head to the gym to burn off some of my nervous energy.

Fancier than most spas, my gym advertises itself as "an executive's gym," and not having to pay the exorbitant membership fees is a perk of working for Nero. Given his earlier rejection of my resignation, I'm not surprised when my membership turns out to still be active.

I make my way into the locker room and change into the brand-name workout clothes the gym supplies.

I lift some weights and ride a stationary bike, but overall, my workout is rather perfunctory without Ariel's metaphorical whip. She's the one who dragged me into the gym to start with, and whatever muscle tone and stamina I now have is all thanks to her. Which reminds me: she hasn't dragged me to this place ever since she met Gaius.

I guess whatever "friendly" activities they do together is exercise enough for her.

I'm walking to the locker room, wiping sweat from my forehead, when I spot the yoga class gathering behind the glass.

I've only done yoga a few times in my life, but I recall it being referred to as "moving meditation" and the teacher saying how great it is to do yoga before an actual meditation.

Maybe this class could help me with what Darian has taught me?

I walk in, grab a mat in the back, and do my best to keep an open mind and follow everyone else.

As during the other times I've tried this, instead of a meditation, yoga reminds me of playing the game of Twister and Simon Says at the same time. Still, by the end, I'm pleasantly fatigued and eager to try meditation again.

After rewarding myself with a session in the steam room and the hot tub, I shower and go home.

———

FLUFFSTER IS NAPPING when I walk in, so I tiptoe into my room, change into comfortable clothes, get into lotus pose, and follow Darian's meditation instructions once more.

The yoga or the workout, or maybe the spa sessions, must really help with this. My palms get warm at record speed, and I do my best to focus on breathing instead of worrying about lightning about to hit my eyes.

I breathe in and out for what feels like another hour, and then, as expected, lightning bolts explode in my vision.

———

I EXPECT a vision but find myself somewhere indescribable.

Is this what Darian called Headspace?

No wonder he couldn't explain it.

My body is missing, like in some visions, but this time, my senses are gone too.

Or, as I soon realize, they are not gone.

They've been replaced by senses I have trouble comprehending.

Still, I introspect with all my willpower and soon decide that I'm floating.

I'm not really floating, of course, as that implies air that's lacking here. There isn't even a vacuum, or spacetime, or anything from a physics class.

Floating also implies that I have the senses of movement and balance, but I don't.

So I pseudo-float for a while, trying to make sense of where I am. Actually, "a while" is also an approximation, as is the concept of "where."

Wherever or whenever I am, I doubt it's part of the regular three (or is it four?) dimensional reality.

Though my sight is missing, I begin to experience something like it, though this has elements of taste and smell, along with heat and cold detection. For all I know, instead of sight, this is what the echolocation of a bat is like, or a shark's ability to sense electricity.

So I sort-of-see a warm cloud of multicolored shapes that have tastes and smells. These shapes defy geometry, and if I had a head, it would hurt trying to make sense of it all.

Some of the "shapes" look like contradictions of mathematical definitions—like a cube that's also a sphere at the same time—while others remind me of visual illusions made famous by artists like M.C. Escher.

Not a single one of the shapes is identical to any other, though the ones in proximity (for lack of a better term) to each other are more similar than ones "farther away."

Another sense, one closest to hearing, makes me realize that each of these shapes also emits something like music, but instead of vibrating the air, these pseudo-sounds create waves of foreboding and calm.

Eventually, I become aware of something like a sense of touch—though touch implies having appendages, which I lack.

Instantly, I yearn to "touch" the lukewarm, brown, pineapple-tasting, snowflake-looking shape next to me, but the foreboding music emanating from it stops me.

Some new sense tells me I wouldn't like it if I touched this snowflake—so I don't, opting to seek another, safer shape to touch.

But all the shapes near me play the same scary tune.

After a while longer, I figure out how to change my perspective in this place. What I do is a hybrid between moving around and zooming in and out with binoculars—all without arms, legs, or eyes.

If I zoom in on a shape, I find that it's made of other similar but not identical shapes. If I zoom in on any of these inner shapes, I find them made out of their own smaller shapes.

Zooming back out, I find the same recursive pattern replicated on a bigger scale. Groups of similar-looking shapes turn out to be like bricks (or perhaps molecules) making up a bigger shape, over and over.

Tired of examining the shapes in one spot, I try moving "forward," and as soon as I get farther away, I examine a burning-hot green strawberry-tasting round-pyramid shape that plays a calm melody.

This shape is also surrounded by ones like it, some more or less round, some with different temperatures, tastes, and smells. All, however, play similar lullaby-like music.

Overwhelmed with curiosity, I choose one specific shape and touch it.

I don't feel anything at the touch.

Instead, the shape sucks me into itself like a black hole.

I swirl in a whirlwind of sensory data until my consciousness short-circuits and my awareness ceases.

CHAPTER ELEVEN

I'M WALKING toward the kitchen.

There's a jingle of keys, and then the front door opens and Felix steps in.

"Hey," I say. "What are you doing home so early?"

"I always try to eat lunch at home when I can." He changes his sneakers for his home flip-flops. "I'm only here for an hour."

At the mention of lunch, my stomach growls like a grouchy dwarf.

Felix grins. "Yes, I'll make something for you too."

———

I'M BACK in my room. Back to sitting in a lotus pose.

I finally got to experience Headspace.

Now that I'm out of there, I can really appreciate how trippy that place was.

It also seems like I just had my first conscious

vision. That, or I saw the most uneventful hallucination in the history of mental illness.

Untangling my legs, I get up. According to my phone, it's lunch time.

Time to go plunder the fridge.

I'm walking toward the kitchen when it hits me.

If what happened was a prophecy, keys are about to jingle.

Keys indeed jingle, and the front door opens just as it's supposed to.

Felix steps in.

"Hello there," I say, deciding not to follow the script in the vision. "Home for lunch?"

"I always try to eat lunch at home when I can," Felix says, just like he did in the vision.

This is interesting.

Even though my script changed, his did not. Probably because I saw the future and know how to fight it, but he doesn't.

I wonder what this says about Felix's free will.

He changes his sneakers for his home flip-flops just as before.

"I'm only here for an hour," I say in my best imitation of Felix's voice. "That's what you were about to say, wasn't it?"

"Good guess," Felix says, but he looks a little spooked.

"Not a guess." My stomach growls just as loudly as it did in my vision.

Felix grins. "Why don't you explain it while I make us some lunch?"

"Explain what?" says Fluffster's voice in my head.

"You woke up?" I look at the furry domovoi.

He sleepily bobs his little head.

I bend down and pick him up. "Come, I'll explain what happened."

I make my way into the kitchen and place Fluffster on the table.

As Felix makes a large omelet, I tell them all about my meditation efforts and today's Headspace experience.

"Are you sure you didn't take any LSD today?" Felix drops three slices of cheese into the skillet. "Or Mescaline or DMT—"

"I'm sure." I scratch behind Fluffster's ears. "No drugs today."

"I'm jealous." Felix folds the omelet in half so that the cheese ends up melty in the middle. "I'd love to see those shapes and have synesthesia or whatever it was you had."

"Hold on," I say and run into my room.

I grab my laptop, put it next to Fluffster on the kitchen table, and search the work of M.C. Escher.

"Here." I bring up a lithograph called *Belvedere*. "This might give you a feel for the shapes, at least." I point at the man holding an impossible cube.

"That hurts my brain." Fluffster rubs his whiskers with his little paws. "How could you even draw that, let alone make it?"

"You can't make it," I say. "At least, not in the real world. You can make something that would look like that from some angles, but that's about it."

"Oh, I love Escher's work," Felix says over his shoulder.

I nod sagely. As a magician, I love visual illusions of any kind, and Escher was one of the true masters of deception. I don't mention any of this, though, because that might make them realize I use some of these visual illusion principles in my effects.

Felix brings the skillet over to the table, placing it in the middle. "Have you seen his *Ascending and Descending*?" he asks. "It has those endless stairs that also show up in *Inception*. His *Relativity* painting was featured in one of the *Night at the Museum* sequels, and in *Labyrinth*."

Instead of answering, I pull up the paintings in question for Fluffster. His beady eyes boggle at the strange gravity in *Relativity* and then follow the figures who trudge stairs in the never-ending square stairwell in *Ascending and Descending* until he looks away and mentally says, "That made me dizzy."

"I didn't see something this cool in Headspace." I get Felix and myself big plates, and a tea saucer with oats for Fluffster.

"Yeah." Felix plops a big chunk of omelet on his plate. "Speaking of Christopher Nolan's films, did Headspace remind you of what happened at the end of *Interstellar*?"

"Going through a wormhole?" I grab myself some

food. "Maybe when I touched the shape and swirled into the vision."

"No, I mean the part where Matthew McConaughey was inside the black hole," Felix says. "He was supposed to be outside of four-dimensional space and was able to see into and influence the past." He looks at Fluffster and adds, "Spoiler alert."

"Perhaps it was similar in spirit," I say thoughtfully. "I, too, felt like I was outside reality. The difference is that I had no body in Headspace. But now that you mention it, I guess each of those shapes was a bit like the black hole structure he was in."

Felix chews excitedly, swallows, and says, "Yeah. Maybe each of the shapes you saw corresponds to a vision of a place and time. Maybe similar shapes are similar locations at different times. Maybe the smaller shapes are shorter time intervals—which is why they're made up of bigger shapes and vice versa. Milliseconds make up seconds, and seconds make up minutes and so on—"

"Maybe." I mindlessly poke at my food, my hunger gone. "Also, maybe the foreboding music wasn't something I should've avoided. I chose a calm shape, and I saw a boring vision of you arriving home. Maybe the scary ones are of danger to my life—and that's what I would want to see in a vision, so I could prevent it in the real world."

"Your Headspace reminds me of some kind of user interface," Felix says. "The shapes are like icons you need to click; the visions are a sort of virtual reality. I bet being a seer is about how many icons you have access to and how good you get at operating the strange UI." He grins in excitement. "This is further proof for my simulation theory. Maybe Headspace is outside our simulated world—which is why you couldn't comprehend it with your normal senses. I bet that's how seers are able to—"

Fluffster yawns in my head—and judging by Felix's expression, the domovoi did so in his, too.

"Can we talk about something more important?" Fluffster pushes his half-finished saucer to the side. "Ariel didn't sleep at home again."

Felix and I exchange guilty looks.

"She was even more hyper the last time I saw her," Felix says. "But I'm not sure what we can do."

"Maybe I could talk to Vlad and Rose," I say contemplatively. "Learn more about vampire relationships?"

"That's a great idea." Felix stuffs the remainder of his omelet into his mouth.

"I'll stop by Rose's apartment right after this," I say.

"And I have to run back to work." Felix pushes his plate away.

"You go, and I'll clean up," I say. "Just leave me another FELLATIO gizmo before you go."

Felix looks extremely uncomfortable. "We still don't know his password."

"You're supposed to be working on that." I grab his plate and stick it in the dishwasher.

"Well." He gets up. "I'm no closer to it than I was before."

"I won't go face Nero again any time soon," I say, suppressing the rabid butterflies that accompany the thought of getting within put-pocketing distance of Nero. "You have time to figure it out."

"You should try using your powers to determine the password," Felix tells me. "Try getting a vision of what would happen if I tried 'apple' as a password, then try 'app1e,' then 'app13,' and so on, a bit like what I do when I guess the password by brute force. Only you'd be doing this in Headspace, with no danger of discovery."

"I have no idea how to bring about a vision so specific." I put away my own plate. "Also, even if I could, it takes a long meditation to bring about a vision. Guessing the password like that would take forever."

Felix sighs. "Can you at least look into the future and make sure I'm alive after we try this hack again?"

"That might be easier." I put the skillet into the dishwasher next. "I'll give that a try."

"Great," he says and walks out of the kitchen.

I continue tidying until Felix comes back, holding another FELLATIO gizmo. "I activated it already." He hands the device to me.

I take it to my room and hide it inside a deck of cards like the last time.

"See you later," Felix yells from the hallway, and I hear the door slam shut.

I return to the kitchen and keep cleaning.

When the counter is spotless, I decide to go talk to Rose about vamp relationships.

———

SHE GREETS ME EXCITEDLY. Before I get a chance to utter a single word, I'm forced to park my butt on her living room couch and accept a cup of tea.

Lucifur uses this as a chance to honor me with a rub against my legs.

"This is about Ariel," I say when Rose takes her seat in a stuffed chair across from me.

I explain about my roommate's "friendship" with Gaius. As I speak, Rose's expression darkens. Whatever she knows about this, I have a feeling I won't like it.

When I finish, Rose says, "I can't talk about this without Vlad being here." She bites her lip. "I swore I wouldn't, you see, and I don't want to break an oath to—"

"That's fine." I smile at her. "I can come back and talk to Vlad when he's here."

"He's rarely here during the day. And I don't think you should come here at night." Rose reddens.

"Say no more." My face must be as red as hers. "Just tell me when he'll be here during the day, and I'll swing by." I pull up the calendar app in my phone.

Rose gives me a couple of days and times when Vlad should be there, and I record them all.

Next, I share my Headspace adventures with her. By

the end of my explanation, Rose looks as proud as my parents did when I finished college.

"That's excellent progress," she says. "You should go practice your powers some more. I know I would if I were in your shoes."

She's right, so I gulp down my tea, step over her cat, and make my way back to my apartment.

———

"CAN I WATCH?" Fluffster asks after I get into my meditation pose once more.

"Sure," I say, closing my eyes.

I sit there, breathing for a while, but nothing happens.

Ariel's situation keeps popping into my head, as does my joblessness and the Baba Yaga phone calls.

Do I need to go to the gym and do yoga every time I want to get into Headspace? That would be great for my body, but not very practical in terms of actually using my powers.

"My mind wanders too much," I explain to Fluffster in another few minutes, after I officially give up and stand up to stretch my legs.

"Why don't you watch some YouTube?" Fluffster suggests. "That's what I do when I need to unwind."

I picture him watching cat videos and grin.

Making my way to the living room couch, I turn on the TV and put on Pen and Teller's *Fool Us*. On this program, two famous magicians provide up-and-coming illusionists with a chance to trick them, for a shot at a Vegas performance.

After a couple of episodes, I realize I'm as good as the hosts at figuring out how the effects are done.

Several more episodes later, I have a hypothetical plan for how I'd fool them if I had the chance. Of course, the pleasure of doing so is not worth getting killed by the Council.

Eventually, Felix comes home and we have dinner, after which he hides in his room, leaving me in possession of the living room TV.

I watch some more, then realize I never got back to meditation. Now it's too late. Yawning, I head to bed, painfully aware that Ariel is still not home.

Taking out my phone, I text her, *I miss you.*

Then, remembering that I got a new phone, I add, *This is Sasha. I got a new number.*

I wait for a reply until my eyelids grow heavy, then give up and go to sleep.

———

THE NEXT DAY, Felix feeds me breakfast again, then leaves for work.

When I check my phone afterward, I notice that Ariel texted me back at three in the morning.

Hey, Sasha. Sorry I've been so busy lately. We'll have to do something soon.

I consider a few replies and settle on:

Sure. I'm now free whenever.

She doesn't respond right away, so I get on my computer.

It's time to figure out how far Nero's influence extends.

I navigate to the Federal Reserve home page and look at their job listings. A few positions vaguely match my skills and experience, so I apply to them. If Nero is able to manipulate these people, I'd be very impressed.

Next, I apply to a bunch of government jobs, and a few listings outside New York state—not that I'd take them, but just to see if Nero's reach goes that far.

Then I apply to some completely silly postings. The Cirque du Soleil needs a contortionist, so why not? An upstate laboratory needs a snake milker—sure thing, I apply to that too. Having worked in the finance industry, I feel like I'm qualified to extract venom from poisonous snakes.

Tired of job searching, I decide to practice meditation and tell Fluffster he can watch me if he still wants—and he does.

I sit in the lotus pose, close my eyes, and breathe mindfully.

My palms start to get warm.

I focus harder, less worried about lightning hitting my eyes this time.

My phone rings.

The wave of anxiety isn't as strong as before, but I'm definitely startled out of my meditative state.

The number isn't private, but it isn't familiar either, so I don't pick up.

"Could this be Baba Yaga again?" Fluffster asks—clearly disappointed he didn't see the lightning forming on my hands. "If so, how did she get your new number?"

"I have no idea." I take my phone, navigate to the app store, and install the number-revealing app again—in case I somehow get a private call later. "One thing's for sure: further meditation would be an exercise in futility."

"You should relax, then try it again," Fluffster says and snuggles up to me.

"Petting you will not cut it, I'm afraid." I scratch under his chin, then get up and start changing my clothes. "I'm going to go to the gym and swing by a yoga class, and then try meditating after that."

Fluffster approves my plan, so I make my way to the gym.

———

AFTER I WORK out with weights, I stumble onto a kickboxing class and take it. Self-defense can come in handy with my unfortunate new lifestyle.

Muscles aching, I take the nearly empty yoga class next. It feels great to stretch after the earlier workout. Afterward, I reward myself with a visit to the steam room and a dip in the hot tub, and then have a nice healthy lunch in the gym's cafeteria.

There's a bounce in my step on the way home, and

I'm certain I'll be able to get into Headspace without a hitch.

Opening the door, I hear some noises in the kitchen.

Given what Fluffster can do to an intruder, I know this has to be one of my roommates, so I call out a hello.

"Sasha," Ariel shouts excitedly from the kitchen. "Is that you?"

"Yeah." I hurry into the kitchen.

"There you are." She lowers her sandwich and beams at me. "I'm glad we have a couple of minutes to talk before I have to run."

I examine her perfect features.

She looks great. Even better than usual. She could easily be on a cover of a fashion magazine.

Is this some kind of love-glow?

Are we worrying over nothing?

Munching on her sandwich, Ariel peppers me with questions about my latest and greatest. I bring her up to speed on everything as she finishes her lunch.

"I'm so jealous," she says, brushing the crumbs off her palms. "I want to go to the gym too. If you'd taken my call earlier, we could've gone together."

"You called me?" I take out my phone and look through missed calls.

All I see is that unknown number.

"I called from someone else's cell phone," Ariel explains, taking out her phone. "Mine ran out of juice."

"Is that someone else Gaius?"

"Maybe." She smiles mischievously. "Hey, can you do me a favor and delete his number from your phone? He'd be upset if he knew I just gave it to you without asking him first."

"Sure," I say and delete the missed call.

"Thanks." She walks to her room, and I follow.

Once inside, she puts her phone on the charger and opens her closet. Pulling out a pair of jeans and a T-shirt, she begins to undress.

"We can go to the gym tomorrow," I say, surreptitiously examining her body for any signs of bites.

To my relief, I find none.

"That's a great idea." She shimmies into her jeans with the grace of a ballerina. "And maybe we can stop by the gun range and get you a new gun on the way."

"Sure, that works."

"Well, I've got to run," she says apologetically, finishing changing. "But we have plans for tomorrow. Yay."

She then turns into a whirlwind, reapplying makeup and grabbing her bag, and rushes out of the apartment before I can properly question her about her relationship with Gaius.

Fluffster is taking his dust bath when I reenter my room.

"Ariel was here," I tell him.

"I know," he says. "I can always feel it when people enter and leave the apartment."

"I guess I'll try meditating again. Do you want to watch?"

"That would be great." He lies down on the floor in front of me. "Go for it."

This time around, I sit in a chair, but otherwise follow Darian's instructions as before.

Soon, my palms get warmer, so I redouble my efforts.

Lightning bolts explode in my vision, and I find myself in Headspace once more.

CHAPTER TWELVE

I ORIENT myself much faster this time, and float there, pseudo-staring at the impossible shapes all around me.

In my immediate proximity, most of the shapes are similar and look like a cloud of green, chilly, oatmeal-tasting cubes with more than six faces and more than twelve edges. They all emit music so foreboding it could be used as a horror movie score.

Ignoring the music, I try to touch one of these cubes.

I find that I can't.

Whatever serves as my appendage here simply twitches in fear—metaphorically speaking. I guess I'm not ready to see a future that frightening.

I move forward and locate a swarm of warm, chick-yellow, marshmallow-tasting hybrids between a hexagon and a cylinder. They play a milder tune, though also frightening.

Picking one at random, I try to touch it—but I can't budge again.

Deciding to be stubborn, I just float there, trying to touch the shape, over and over.

Each time, I'm on the cusp of succeeding. It's like trying to remember something that's just on the tip of your tongue.

Pulling my immaterial self together, I focus all my attention on overcoming the remaining reluctance.

Something seems to tear, and the touch finally connects with my target.

Just like the last time, I spiral into the vision.

———

I'M IN MY ROOM, sitting in a chair and overwhelmed with familiar dread.

The phone rings.

The call would be private, but thanks to the app I installed, I recognize the number.

It's Baba Yaga's restaurant bothering me again.

How did they get the number to my new phone?

I let the call go to voicemail and note the time of day—3:21 p.m.

When the voicemail dings, I bring it up and listen.

"Sasha," says Koschei in his corpse-like voice. "As part of the bargain you made, you are to appear in front of Baba Yaga tonight, at ten."

I pull the phone away from my ear, the dread intensifying into panic.

There's no way I'm going to Brighton Beach today—

———

SNAPPING OUT OF THE VISON, I look at Fluffster.

"That was amazing," he says in my mind. "I saw lightning go from your hands into your eyes. It was extremely brief and easy to miss, but I caught it—"

I ignore the rest of his excited babbling and do my best to orient myself in reality.

My ragged breaths hurt my chest after all that slow breathing.

Diving for my phone, I check the time.

It's 3:12 p.m.

In nine minutes, the phone will ring, and Koschei will leave that voicemail.

My mind racing, I open a browser on my phone.

I find a recording of the famous "this number has been disconnected" message that comes on when you call a truly disconnected number. Hands shaking, I quickly make it my voicemail.

It's 3:20 p.m.

My finger ready, I count down the seconds until 3:21.

The phone rings, and I instantly swipe "No" to send it to voicemail.

Then I wait.

If Koschei sees through my illusion, he'll wait for the "disconnected number" message to finish, hear the regular voicemail beep, and leave a voicemail as per the vision. But if I fooled him, he should give up long before the voicemail beep.

As I wait, I again wonder how Baba Yaga and her minions got my new number. Only Felix and Ariel have it. Well, and Gaius because Ariel used his phone to call me, but that's still a very small number of people.

Does Baba Yaga have a technomancer like Felix on her payroll? Or is there some other kind of Cognizant who can divine this sort of thing? If it's the latter, they might be useful when it comes to Nero's password.

After a minute, I exhale a relieved breath.

There's no voicemail.

I'll have to keep my phone off as much as possible, so that if he tries again, it goes right into voicemail without me having to react like a ninja.

Fluffster is looking at me with a mixture of worry and confusion, so I explain to him what I saw in my vision.

"Whatever Baba Yaga wants, it better be a small favor," Fluffster says when I finish. "I still haven't recovered new memories—and not for lack of trying."

"I have a feeling it's not a small favor at all. But this reminds me." I grab my laptop. "I need to research Rasputin some more."

"You do?" Fluffster's reply sounds rather disapproving in my mind. "What about your job search?"

"You're worse than my mother," I mutter but nevertheless go to my inbox.

Heartbeat speeding up, I stare at my email. "This is getting ridiculous."

Fluffster scurries over and looks at the screen with me.

There's a "sorry, position was filled" reply from the Federal Reserve, as well as from the government jobs I applied to. The out-of-state companies have also sent me the canned reply.

Most ridiculous of all is that I have an email from both Cirque du Soleil and the upstate laboratory. Instead of saying, "Hey, you can't be a contortionist snake milker," they both just inform me that the positions have been filled, like everyone else.

I stand up, fists clenched. "Nero is just showing off at this point."

If he were near me, I'd punch him in the smug face that I can so vividly picture.

"What does this mean?" Fluffster asks.

I explain, pacing back and forth, and Fluffster looks as miffed as a chinchilla can. "If he keeps doing that, we'll end up living in a cardboard box in the park."

"You don't know the half of it," I growl. "The bastard owns this building, so even if I magically made money, he could opt to not renew our next lease and hello, box in the park."

"You should invite him over," Fluffster says menacingly. "I don't care how powerful he is outside. Here, I'd teach him some manners."

The idea of Nero in my bedroom sends my

thoughts in a completely inappropriate direction, and my face flames uncontrollably.

To cover for my misfiring hormones and neurons, I sit back in front of my computer and log into my bank account to see how desperate the situation really is.

In shock, I gape at the numbers.

Money has been added to my checking account.

It's a familiar amount, but I double check it, just in case.

"That bastard." I jump to my feet again. "He paid me. Just like nothing has changed."

Fluffster twitches his bunny-like ear. "What are you talking about?"

"Nero," I explain grimly. "He refuses to admit that I quit. And now I've received my usual paycheck for last week *and* this week. The week *after* I quit."

"Isn't that a good thing?" Fluffster stands up on his hind paws. "It's free money."

"No, it's not," I say with such viciousness that the domovoi moves away from me.

Teeth clenched, I yank on some clothes, put the deck of cards with Felix's gizmo in my pocket, and storm out of the apartment.

It's time Nero and I had some words.

Again.

CHAPTER THIRTEEN

"FELIX, WE'RE BACK ON," I hiss into my phone as I stride into my not-so-former work building.

"I still don't have the password," he says. "You said you'd try getting a vision about it, remember?"

"I remember promising to see if you're alive in the future. If you don't help me, you won't be." I use my old ID card, and it works. Of course it does. "We'll just have to expedite the whole thing."

"I don't think it's such a good idea," Felix says frantically. "Why don't we—"

"I'm entering the elevator," I lie. I'm actually only waiting for one. "Get ready. Everything's going to go down like the last time."

I hang up as Felix tries to say something else.

Just as on my cab ride here, the opposite of meditation is swirling in my head as I ride down in the elevator. I'm boiling with anger at Nero and rehearse insults I can throw in his face. I fantasize about slapping him—for real this time.

On some level, I know my reaction is disproportional to his crime—which, after all, is giving me money.

It's just that it's the last straw.

And the principle of the thing.

Who the hell does he think he is?

The elevator doors finally open.

I storm in and face Venessa, mentally daring her to give me crap this time around.

"He isn't there," she says, her face unreadable. "He's in Europe for a few days."

"Bullshit," I exclaim, then look.

Nero's office walls are made of glass, and he doesn't seem to be inside.

I dart in anyway, ignoring Venessa on my tail.

Nope.

He's really not here.

Storming back into the elevator, I try to calm my overworked nerves.

When I exit the elevator, I call Felix again.

"You got your wish. We're postponing the operation."

"What happened?" There are annoying undertones of relief in his voice.

As I explain, I use four-letter words that make some of my not-so-former colleagues give me worried looks as I stomp through the lobby.

"It's really for the best," Felix says soothingly. "I

think we need to get the password first, then try this madness again."

"Fine." I hail a cab. "Talk to you later."

———

I'M much calmer by the time I get home, but when I try meditation again, I fail miserably.

I take a seat on the couch in front of the TV, but instead of turning the TV on, I just sit there, trying to figure out a way I could make money if I ever succeed at quitting my job.

Fluffster must sense my bad mood because he jumps into my lap and lets me pet his therapeutic fur.

My breathing evens out, and ideas begin to pour in.

Gambling is an obvious option. If someone were to let me into an underground poker game, I could not only use my seer powers but also the various magician moves that originated with card cheats in the first place.

"How about you come up with ways to make money that will leave your bones, fingers, and toes intact?" Fluffster suggests when I share my idea with him. "You can play poker online, for example, or bid on horse races."

"You're right." I smile, getting into the spirit of this. "People make money predicting election results—something I'm good at. There are also things like fantasy football…"

"Sure." Fluffster snuggles into my hand. "But, and

please don't yell, why don't you just keep Nero's money? If you don't like him, isn't taking his money a punishment of a sort?"

"I don't think I can explain it," I tell him. "I don't know if I understand it myself."

To prevent Fluffster from pressing the issue, I turn on the TV and watch a few movies—only to find out that I've gotten even better at foreseeing every plot twist and ending. Afterward, I contribute some predictions for the Good Judgement Project, and then Felix gets home.

We eat dinner, and then I reread my favorite books on card magic until I go to bed.

———

"WAKE UP, YOU LAZY BUTT," someone shouts through a giant loudspeaker. "Gun fun awaits."

I peer through one eyelid.

Ariel is jumping from foot to foot next to my bed.

I really need to put a lock on my door.

"Finally," she says in an annoyingly cheerful tone. "Now get up and let's go."

She cruelly opens my curtains and runs away, slamming the door so hard that any remaining hope of getting back to sleep is shattered.

I crawl from under my warm blankie and check the time.

It's nine-thirty.

Last week, I'd think myself lucky to be able to sleep

in this late. How had I gotten into unemployment mode so easily?

I get ready, and Ariel greets me with a sandwich by the front door.

"Let's get a head start." She thrusts the food into my hands. "You can eat this on the way."

She's brimming with excitement.

Too much excitement.

As we make our way down, I carefully ask her, "How are you feeling? You seem to be in a good mood."

"I feel great." Her grin could power a small village. "But you have to tell me what's been happening to you. Fluffster mentioned some craziness."

I give her the latest update and try to turn the conversation back to her, but she skillfully dodges my questions until we get into the car, and once we do, she goes into her official "silent driving" mode.

———

WE DRIVE through a familiar sketchy part of New Jersey and park next to the house of horrors where Ariel got me the last illegal gun.

"I want something smaller this time around," I say as she unbuckles her seatbelt. "I don't have any orcs after me, so I figure the caliber doesn't matter as much."

"How about a Glock 19?" Ariel says and launches into a sales pitch so thorough I suspect the good folks at Glock might be paying her commission.

"I have one here," she says in conclusion and reaches over, opening her glove compartment to take out a beige-colored gun. "Check it out."

I gingerly hold the weapon in my hand. It has some plastic parts and feels almost like a toy gun—especially in that color.

"Can you get me a black one?" I ask after a moment of consideration. "So that it looks more like a real gun?"

"Don't insult Precious," Ariel says in her best imitation of Gollum's voice as she snatches the gun from my hands and holds it lovingly to her chest.

"I'm sorry, Precious," I deadpan to the gun. To Ariel, I say, "I kind of pictured myself with another revolver."

"This will be easier to conceal," Ariel says. "It's more—"

"I trust you," I say quickly, willing to forego the Russian Roulette effect if that saves me from another gun lecture.

Ariel puts her Precious back into the glove compartment and heads into the asbestos-infected rat palace she uses as a gun shop.

Just like the last time, I lock the car doors.

As I wait, I practice meditative breathing.

My hands are starting to feel warm when Ariel comes back.

Either she was gone for a while, or I'm getting better at this meditation stuff.

"Keep this in the glove compartment for now," she says and hands me a black version of her Precious.

"Once we get to the range, we'll rent you one just like it, and they'll teach you how to handle it."

AFTER THE GUN-RANGE guy finishes explaining how to use a Glock 19, I decide that I prefer it to my deceased revolver.

My warm fuzzies toward the Glock intensify once I fire a few rounds into my target. The recoil is much milder, it's lighter, and it just feels more at home in my hands.

Also, having more rounds is convenient; with the revolver, I had to reload a lot more often.

Half an hour later, I'm certain this is a better gun for me.

What's really great is that my marksmanship scores improve with each new target they put up. Though, of course, it will probably take me years to get close to Ariel's insane hit rate.

"This was so much fun," Ariel says as we walk back to our car. "Do you want to go to the gym?"

My muscles are slightly sore from my earlier workouts but refusing to go with her is like taking candy away from a gym-junkie baby, so I can't help but agree.

Besides, if I do some yoga, it will go a long way in facilitating the Headspace practice I'd like to do later today.

———

WE GET HOME, change, and jog to the gym.

As usual, a workout with Ariel is like a Special Forces boot camp. By the end, I'm completely out of breath, and sore in places where a proper lady shouldn't even have muscles.

Ariel then joins me for yoga, and despite it being her first time ever, she's ten times better at it—a feat I attribute to her superpowers rather than my sloth.

"Should we stop somewhere for lunch?" Ariel offers after we pamper ourselves with some post-workout spa treatments. "Or would you rather eat at home?"

"How about Cuban?" I suggest. "There's a great place on the way."

As we exit the gym and turn onto the secluded side street where the Cuban place is located, a familiar feeling grips me.

Dread.

Strong dread.

Given that my phone is at home, whatever my powers are alerting me to isn't a phone call.

"Something is about to go down," I whisper to Ariel, frantically scanning the garbage-filled street. "But I don't know what it is."

Ariel visibly tenses. "Shit. My gun is in the car."

"I left mine at home." My heart rate continues to spike.

Ariel looks around, as alert as a predatory bird.

I look back.

In a blur, a black van with tinted windows makes a sharp turn onto our little street, its tires leaving burn marks on the pavement.

With a roar of the huge engine, it screeches to a stop in front of us.

We jump back.

The van's doors open.

Like a pride of lions, huge, grim-faced men stream out of the car toward us.

CHAPTER FOURTEEN

THERE ARE FOUR OF THEM, and each one has the kind of features that look great on mugshots. No Mandate aura—could mean they're human.

All are wearing suits except for the one approaching us the fastest.

He's also the biggest—so huge he could pass for an orc. With that wifebeater shirt and jeans, he must've been the only one to get the memo about casual Friday. I also notice tattoos of military-style epaulettes on his shoulders.

What is he? An admiral?

He reaches into the back of his pants.

His suited allies reach into the insides of their jackets.

Ariel launches into motion, punching the admiral in the chest.

He flies into a suited guy behind him, taking him

along for the ride. They slam into the van with a hard thud and slide to the ground in a spooning position.

Damn.

Ariel has clearly been eating her spinach.

As she chops at the gun hand of the other suited guy, I suck in a breath and leap at the closest goon.

The guy already has his gun out when I slam my shoulder into his stomach with all my might—as though trying to impress an NFL scout.

The exploding pain reminds me to let my poor shoulder fully heal before I do that again.

The guy's gun clatters to the pavement, but he recovers quickly and grabs me by my hair, like we're in a cat fight.

I kick the gun away, and while he's distracted, my foot continues its arc toward his groin.

My sneaker connects with something soft, and my opponent grunts, jerking my hair so hard that stars dance in front of my eyes.

When my vision clears, I see Ariel grabbing my attacker's hair-pulling arm.

Something crunches and cracks.

The guy howls and lets me go.

Heart pounding, I spin around.

The admiral is a few feet from us, raising a gun.

"Kick," Ariel orders, grabbing me by my forearms.

"Wait," I want to say, but she starts swinging me—human lasso style.

I understand her insane plan. As soon as my

sneakers are near the target, I execute a move I learned in the kickboxing class.

My foot crashes into the admiral's wrist.

His gun clanks against the pavement.

Ariel slows down the swing, dropping me behind her, and leaps for the growling admiral.

He swings his massive fist at her head, but she expertly sidesteps it.

He punches with his other arm, but Ariel blocks his hit, then unleashes a devastating uppercut that lands square on the admiral's chin.

He flies up, then performs a sack-of-potatoes impersonation as his back slams into the sidewalk.

Not trusting him to remain unconscious, Ariel kicks him in the head. She then repeats the precautionary measure with every one of the four before rummaging in the last one's pockets.

"No ID," she says when she finishes, and walks up to the next guy.

Deciding to speed this up, I also check the unconscious admiral for his ID, but the only thing in his pockets is what looks like a black knife handle.

I examine the object. It's a very fancy toy—an out-the-front extending automatic knife with double action. I test it out by automatically extending the blade, then retracting it.

Without giving it much thought, I slide the handle into my pocket.

This isn't stealing.

I'm basically confiscating it.

"Nothing on any of them," Ariel says.

"Same here," I tell her.

She shakes her head, then walks up to the van and looks around the empty street as I stand there, trying to catch my breath.

Sliding her palms under the side of the car, she assumes a deadlift position and strains all her muscles.

No.

She's not doing what I think she's doing.

Even with her powers, she can't be strong enough. Right?

Wrong.

The van lifts off the ground and flips onto its side.

"So they can't follow us," Ariel explains—clearly misunderstanding the incredulous expression on my face.

She then picks up each of the guns, and I half expect her to beat her earlier feat of strength by bending the weapons into pretzels. But no, she takes the wussy route and removes the clips, pocketing the bullets.

"Let's get out of here," I say when my roommate examines the battlefield for more items to add to her to-do list.

"Are you okay?" She frowns, looking me over.

"Fine." I brush my damp palms over my T-shirt, like I take down guys twice my size all the time. "Let's scram before someone else tries to assault us."

Ariel hurries out of the alley, and I follow.

When we get to a busier street, we slow our half-jog

to a socially acceptable speed walk, mimicking New Yorkers who are late—an extremely common sight.

We get home in five minutes without another unwanted encounter.

I turn both locks on the door, and slide the security chain into place—a first for me.

"What was that about? Have you ever seen those men before?" I ask, collapsing onto the living room couch.

"No." Ariel doesn't have the courtesy to even pretend to be winded after all that exercise. "I hoped you might know who they are."

Fluffster scurries into the room and looks at each of us. "Is everything all right?"

Between calming breaths, I tell him what just happened.

"You should've brought one home." Fluffster's rodent eyes gleam menacingly—reminding me of the urban myths about giant rats and alligators in the New York subways. "I would've asked them some pointed questions."

"Given recent history, we can safely assume they were after *me*." I wipe the sweat from my forehead. "Maybe Chester sent them, or Baba Yaga. Or maybe this was another 'lesson' from Nero."

"You did get into two fights with Chester's daughter." Ariel paces to the TV and back. "Not that he liked you to begin with."

"She started it." Realizing I just quoted my

kindergarten self, I say in a calmer tone, "You might have a point, though."

Fluffster stands on his hind legs and looks at me piercingly. "Regardless of who's behind the attack, we need to take precautions."

"I agree." Ariel sits on the edge of the couch next to me. "We're lucky you're unemployed. You can stay home under Fluffster's protection and only leave with my supervision."

"As in, I'm under house arrest?" I exaggerate my grumpiness. I'm in no mood to go anywhere anyway, but I also know how quickly I get cooped up.

"You're obviously free to go get killed." Ariel rolls her eyes. "We just like having you around."

"Fine." I recline the couch and lean back. "I won't venture out needlessly. Or if I do, I'll take a gun."

"And me." Ariel sits back.

"And you," I agree. "Assuming you're around."

"I'll be around," she says. "Just tell me where you want to go and when."

"There's another Orientation lesson this Sunday. I'm going to that."

"No problem." Ariel gives me a determined look. "I'll take you."

"I'd also like to do yoga again tomorrow," I say.

"I'd love to—"

The doorbell rings.

We all exchange glances.

"I'm not expecting anyone," Fluffster says in my

mind, his tone so deadpan you'd think he entertains tons of visitors.

"I doubt it's your friend the guinea pig." I jackknife to my feet, go to my room, and get my new gun.

Ariel must've had the same idea because when I return, she also has a gun in her hand—a different one than in her car.

Taking the lead, she unlocks the door and opens it as far as the security chain allows.

"Hello," says a hypnotic voice through the small gap. "Paranoid much?"

Ariel breathes out an audible sigh of relief and removes the chain.

When she opens the door, I put a name to the voice.

Gaius, Ariel's vampire "friend," is standing on our doorstep.

His pretty, pale face twists into a smug smile as he takes us in.

If the guns bother him, he doesn't show it.

Fluffster steps in front of me, his tail waving aggressively from side to side.

Gaius's smile falters when he notices the rodent-shaped domovoi. His arctic-sky eyes stare into mine, then turn to Ariel. "The young of this age have no manners, do they?" He looks at Fluffster for a reaction, but finds none. "Is no one going to invite me in?"

Ariel looks at me apologetically and mouths, "I've got to go."

"Wait—"

Before I can finish my thought, she slinks out of the apartment and closes the door behind herself.

I look at Fluffster, and he shrugs his furry shoulders.

I walk over to the door and put my ear to the keyhole, but I can't hear anything.

Peeping though the grimy peephole, I see that neither Ariel nor Gaius is by the door anymore, so I push it open and catch a glimpse of the two of them entering the elevator.

"She left with him." I close the door. "Just like that."

"Maybe you *should've* invited him in," Fluffster replies with a definite undercurrent of malice. "We could've learned more about their relationship."

"Maybe I should've." I lock the door but skip the chain. "Gaius was helping Darian the first time we met, so maybe he knows where Darian is."

"Assuming you want to find the coward," Fluffster says. "Can't you ask Ariel to query Gaius about this when she gets back?"

"I doubt she'd like being a go-between, but I might try," I say and head to the bathroom.

To relax and wash off the sweat from the combination of running and stress, I draw myself a bath—which does wonders for my smarting shoulder.

My skin all pruney, I locate Fluffster, and we both eat a nice lunch.

Next, I attempt to access Headspace.

I know that the remnants of adrenaline will be an obstacle to meditation, but that's why I want to give this a shot right now. For my powers to be useful, I need to be able to apply them in stressful situations.

The breathing portion of Darian's instructions takes me four times as long as the last time, but eventually, lightning streams from my palms into my eyes, and I again find myself in Headspace.

―――――

I'M FLOATING among the shapes. The ones nearest me are room-temperature, magenta-colored, mango-tasting hybrids between a pentagonal prism and a cone. Each is playing a frightening symphony that would make good Halloween music.

I try to touch the closest one.

It doesn't work.

I will my metaphysical appendage to touch the shape with all my being, but I might as well wish myself to defy gravity and float to the sky in the real world.

If I had a lip, I'd bite it in frustration.

Why is this not working?

Could it be that some visions are not meant to be seen?

Or am I not powerful enough? Experienced enough?

Or could it be that these shapes have nothing to do with me, and my powers are protecting me from having a possibly scary but completely useless to me vision?

Maybe this vision was of a surgery of a little baby in Belarus—an event that would be nearly impossible for me to change from the United States.

What I need is to talk to Darian or some other seer about this, but that will have to wait until I'm outside Headspace. For now, I need to practice using my power by seeking out accessible visions.

That reminds me.

Felix requested some predictions earlier. He wanted me to figure out what Nero's password is, and/or whether Nero will kill him for the hack in some distant future.

I focus on these two concepts as much as I can and float forward, soon finding myself among a new set of shapes.

Liquid-hydrogen-cold, black, BBQ-tasting ellipsoids with impossible angles, these shapes play a music that's much calmer than the earlier shapes, but still with an undertone of danger.

My memory is clearly working better each time I enter Headspace because I recall one more point Felix made earlier.

He suggested that the size of the shape determines the time duration of the vision.

Deciding to kill a few extra birds with a single test, I zoom in a few times. If Felix's theory is right, my vision should be nice and short.

These molecule ellipsoids are slightly less cold, and sound even calmer, so when I reach to touch the one nearest me, the vision starts instantly.

I'M STARING at a folder with two strange words written on it.

There's a noise behind me—

THE VISION IS over in less than a second.

I try to keep the odd writing I just saw in my mind as I scramble to get a pen and paper.

The first pen I grab is out of ink, so I go into the drawer where I keep my magic props and get a permanent marker. Then I can't find paper and have to take a birthday card I got from Dad.

I'm ready to write; only now I'm having doubts about what I saw.

The first word started with an uppercase 'C' and had two 'a's with a weird letter between them that looked like a flattened 'w.'

I write it as well as I can and rack my brain for the second word.

I think there was an uppercase 'Y,' followed by 'p,' then a '6,' then an 'a,' and then an upper case 'H' but written in a small font for some reason. I write what I recall on the card.

Cawa Yp6aH.

This can certainly be Nero's password—a theory supported by the fact that one of my goals in Headspace was to determine this very thing.

I debate texting a picture of this to Felix, but stop myself.

It can wait until Felix gets home. If Nero is somehow monitoring Felix's phone, I don't want him knowing that I already got his password.

Meanwhile, maybe I can do the Headspace thing again?

I get into the meditation position and focus.

An hour passes.

Two.

Three.

I'm calmer than I've ever been, yet the lightning doesn't show up on my palms.

After I struggle with it for a while longer, I give up.

Visions must be limited to one a day—something Darian didn't mention. Or maybe it's different for every seer, and this is my personal limit. Alternatively, maybe I need more practice before I can enter Headspace twice in a day.

Musing about the limits of my power, I go into the kitchen and eat dinner. When I'm heading back to my room, Felix enters the apartment.

"We've got a lot to talk about," I say instead of a hello, and while he changes his shoes and makes himself a sandwich, I tell him about all the fun he's missed.

"Can you show me the password?" he asks, attacking his food.

I go to my room and get the birthday card.

When I show it to Felix, he raises his unibrow.

"This isn't a password," he says. "At least, it might not be."

"Oh? What do you think it says, then?"

"It says *you*." He points the remainder of the sandwich at me. "It's your name, written with a Cyrillic alphabet—most likely Russian."

"It is?" I look at the paper again, expecting to see the iconic 'R' facing the wrong way.

"Yes," he says. "That 'C' is an S, followed by an 'a' that's similar in both languages. Then that's a single letter for the "sh" sound and another 'a'—all making Sasha. The last name is like that too, where the 'Y' is the 'oo' sound, 'p' is 'r', '6' is a 'b,' 'a' is the same again, and that 'H' is an 'n.'"

Under my scribbles he writes his version: "Саша Урбан."

"Yep." I sink into a chair. "That looks exactly like what I saw in the vision, but why would Nero make that his password? Does he even speak Russian?"

"With a last name like Gorin, he could theoretically *be* Russian, but I agree. I don't think this is Nero's password." Felix attacks the rest of his sandwich.

"But if it's not Nero's password, what is it?" I turn the card upside down, but it doesn't make sense that way either.

"I'm afraid this might be proof that Baba Yaga will get to talk to you after all," Felix mumbles over the food in his mouth. "*She* is definitely Russian, and she might've written your name on that paper. Maybe to force you into a binding contract or something like that."

"Rose warned me not to sign anything for Baba Yaga, but I don't recall a single scrap of paper in her office." I massage my temples with circular motions, trying to think of an alternate explanation. "Why can't it be something else?" I suggest desperately. "A good thing? Like, say, what if I'm going to find my Russian birth certificate?"

Felix wipes his hands on a paper towel. "The men who attacked you on the way to the gym were Russian, so they're probably working for Baba Yaga." He gets up.

"Wait." I also stand. "How do you know they were Russian?"

"The guy you dubbed 'the admiral.'" Felix walks to the living room. "Those epaulettes on his shoulders are something done for high-ranking criminals in Russian prisons. You saw what kind of people hang out at Baba Yaga's establishment. You do the math."

He plops into the recliner and reaches for the TV remote in a bout of husband-like behavior.

I stare at him in disbelief. "Are you seriously about to watch TV right now?"

Felix looks at the remote in his hand, then at me. "What do you want me to do? If I told you not to leave the house—the only way to prevent further Baba Yaga encounters—would you listen?"

"Maybe," I lie. "Though you have to admit, becoming a hermit isn't a solution."

"It's not a good long-term solution, no." He gestures

with the remote. "Alternatively, you *could* swallow your pride and make up with Nero, so that—"

"Forget it." I turn on my heel. "Watch your stupid TV."

I stomp into the kitchen, get the card, and go to my room.

Fluffster is inside, so I show him the card and explain Felix's theory.

He looks at the card, his beady eyes widening. "I possess more memories than I thought. I can read that. Does it mean I can speak Russian?"

"I don't know." I lean in and give Fluffster a side scratch. "Maybe try talking to Felix? If that doesn't work, we should get you a Russian book. Or maybe you can watch something Russian on YouTube?"

"Great ideas, all," he says and runs to the door.

Left on my own, I realize that I can put Felix's Baba Yaga theory to the test. All I need to do is get back into Headspace and run the same vision for a longer duration of time.

Encouraged, I begin meditating.

And meditating.

And meditating.

No matter how hard I try, Headspace eludes me.

My theory about one vision per day must be true.

Before I can think of what else to do, Fluffster runs back into the room.

"I speak fluent Russian," he says in my mind. "Felix said he'll get me some books, and he showed me a Russian search engine called Yandex.ru. We searched about domovoi there. I learned some really interesting things."

Fluffster proceeds to tell me the fairy tales about his kind and describes the plot of a cartoon with a domovoi character.

"Maybe you'll remember more as time goes on, after all," I say when he runs out of steam. "Maybe I should take Baba Yaga's call and thank her."

Fluffster shakes his furry head. "I just read about her in the original Russian. Even if she just borrowed that name, she's bad news."

"I was kidding. Besides, she must think my phone is disconnected—which is probably why she's now sending her goons after me."

"Probably," Fluffster says and yawns. "I'm going to nap, if you don't mind."

"I'm also going to head to bed for the night," I tell him. "The sooner I wake up, the sooner I can try having another vision."

CHAPTER FIFTEEN

I'M awake at six a.m. on a Saturday, for the first time ever. I guess this is what happens when you go to sleep so early.

I go through my morning routine and share an oatmeal breakfast with Fluffster.

"Did Ariel come home last night?" I ask as we finish up.

"No," he says. "She didn't."

"We're supposed to go to the gym today. I hope she doesn't flake on me."

Fluffster shakes his head disapprovingly and joins me when I head back into my room.

He curls up on my bed, and I decide to work on getting another vision.

The meditation goes smoother than ever; I'm clearly getting better at it.

My palms get warm in record time, and lightning hits my eyes.

———

I'M SURROUNDED by a new set of shapes.

How do I—or Headspace or whoever—decide where I end up when I first appear here? Should I pay closer attention to these shapes?

Either way, today I have a different goal in mind. I need to find the Russian writing vision again and figure out if it's connected to Baba Yaga or Nero.

I float forward, doing my best to think of the same things as I did yesterday.

There are hordes of different shapes around me, but none are the impossible-angled ellipsoids that I need. In fact, I don't see a single shape that's even remotely ellipsoid.

I try to focus on the shape itself and will myself to find it.

Nothing happens, and I eventually give up.

The password shapes are clearly beyond my reach.

Maybe you only get one chance to see a vision set in a specific location and time?

If so, I should be very careful with those time intervals in the future.

Speaking of time intervals, I can at the very least test a theory about them. All I need to do is find a shape I like, then zoom out a bunch of times, and see if this will lead to a long vision.

The warm, white, pickle-tasting roundish prisms play a welcomingly safe music, so I settle on them.

I zoom out once.

Twice.

Three times.

On the fourth, I pick a prism at random and touch it.

———

A FIST SLAMS into my face, then into my stomach. Then a leg sweep smacks my back into the ground.

Scrambling to my feet, I block a round kick, try to throw a punch, and fail. An uppercut sends me flying back in a heap of limbs.

"No more Miss Nice Sasha," I grit though my teeth as I block the next punch, uppercut my opponent into the air, and then throw my deadly metal fan at him— drawing rivers of blood.

Closing the distance between us, I unleash a combo —a set of moves I've previously memorized.

When I'm done, he barely has any strength left.

I'm going to win and enjoy wiping that smug expression from his face.

I jump, determined to end it.

He blocks my kick, then sweeps his leg under my feet, sending me tumbling to the ground.

As soon as I try to get up, he freezes me with his special move, walks up to me cockily, and unleashes a series of punches and kicks.

I'm on the ground, health bar empty.

"Finish her," a deep voice says.

In the next frame, I'm standing shakily.

He walks up to me, freezes my midsection, punches a hole in it, breaks my spine as he brings my body over his head, and rips what remains into two bloody pieces.

"Fatality," the deep voice concludes.

"That was much better." Felix selects a female with huge boobs as his next character. "One of these days, you're going to win. You'll see."

I clench my jaw and choose Sub-Zero—his last character.

And lose again.

Then lose even worse.

Then lose without hitting him even once—a state of events the deep voice calls "Flawless Victory."

When it comes to video games, I'm way too competitive. I can't take losing.

We play for hours, and I always feel like I'm on the verge of figuring out Felix's technique, but then he changes something and I lose again. And again.

"You're still playing?" Fluffster asks after another hour of my defeats. "Can you give me my dust bath?"

"Hold on," Felix says. "Let me kill Sasha one more time."

———

I FIND myself back in my room.

Wow.

That was a multi-hour vision—though probably the most useless one I've ever had.

Sounds like Felix is going to ask me to play *Mortal*

Kombat later today, and I'll say yes, just to lose for hours.

Or will I lose? I did see how some of those games had gone. Maybe I can leverage that knowledge?

Either way, I need to act naturally. I don't want Felix to catch on.

I read magic books for an hour, then binge on TV until Felix wakes up and eats breakfast.

Eventually, he knocks on my door.

"Hey," he says when I open it. "Sorry about last night. I should've talked to you instead of watching TV. I was just dead tired—but I'm ready to talk if you still want."

I smile. "It's fine. I was maybe rash too. There wasn't more to talk about. I'm staying in today, as you suggested, and when I do go out, I'll make sure Baba Yaga can't get me."

"Good. I was also wondering how to entertain you —and I have an idea."

"What did you have in mind?" I ask, but of course, I already know.

"Why don't we play some video games?" he says predictably. "We can play *Mortal Kombat*. I know you and Ariel play that all the time."

"Are you sure you'll tolerate all that computer-generated gore?" I ask, inwardly smiling an evil grin.

"I can manage," he says and heads into the living room where we have Ariel's Xbox set up.

As he starts up the game, he grumbles something negative about the console, but I ignore it. He's a huge

Nintendo fanboy and thus unable to have an objective opinion about any other system.

TV on, controllers in hand, we begin to battle.

I start off by losing. We haven't gotten to my vision yet.

Then we finally get to the part I foresaw: his blue ninja slams a fist into my face, then into my stomach, then sweeps my legs, dumping me on the ground.

Now, though, I have the benefit of foreknowledge—and I impress myself with how well I remember what both of us are about to do.

So, I win.

Then I win again.

"Hey," Felix says after his fourth defeat in a row. "Something fishy is going on." He narrows his eyes at me. "Are you using your powers to win?"

"No," I lie. "Are you?"

He reddens, and I want to smack him outside the game.

Why hadn't this occurred to me before?

He's a technomancer, and the Xbox is a glorified PC, so of course he can manipulate it as easily as the other computer stuff.

"No more video games," I tell him. "I can't believe you'd cheat."

"It's only because I cheated that I could catch *you* cheating." He throws the controller on the couch. "Tell me how you did it."

Grinning, I explain, and his anger turns into awe as I go on.

"That's really interesting." He turns off the TV. "Such a long vision. I wonder if there's a cost to it?"

I scratch the back of my head. "I didn't think about cost. I don't feel particularly tired or anything—so maybe the length of the vision doesn't matter?"

"Hmm… You said you can zoom out as many times as you want, right?"

"I only zoomed out a handful of times, so who knows? Maybe there's a limit that I didn't reach?"

"There must be. Otherwise, what stops you from seeing a vision that lasts a year or two? Or a lifetime?"

"I have no idea." I put down my own controller. "Maybe such visions *are* possible."

"That would be amazing," he says. "But in any case, if Headspace is like a computer interface, then I bet the initial size of those shapes is already optimized for the best vision duration."

"Optimized by whom?"

"You?" he suggests. "Or some kind of seer gods. Who knows?"

We sit in contemplative silence for a few moments; then I stand up.

"I should see if I can enter Headspace again," I tell him. "Probably not, but worth a try."

"Good idea." He gets up as well, takes the game out of the Xbox, and replaces it with another. "You do that. I've got this racing game I wanted to try."

I make my way to my room and try meditation again.

It fails, as I assumed it would.

After Felix and I eat an early lunch, I try again but to no avail.

Giving up, I realize that Ariel didn't show up to take me to the gym—and, of course, that makes me really want to go to the gym.

I pick up my phone and dial her number.

A familiar ringtone goes off in Ariel's room.

I go there, and sure enough, her phone is still on the charger.

Why did I let her convince me to delete Gaius's number? If I had it, I'd at least call *him.*

Knowing full well that both Fluffster and Felix would chastise me for even considering leaving the house, I do some pushups by my bed and consider my physical activity done for the day.

After dinner, Felix and I rent a couple of movies, and I head to bed early again.

———

FOLLOWING our unofficial tradition for Sunday mornings, Felix prepares something extremely yummy for breakfast—quark cheese pancakes called *syrniki.*

As we eat, Fluffster informs me that Ariel didn't come home yet again, and I begin worrying about Orientation.

It's today, and if Ariel doesn't show up, I'm screwed.

Returning to my room, I contemplate the practicality of carrying a gun. My last gun lived in a big bag, but I should think of something better.

An idea arrives, and I locate the outfit I designed to allow me to vanish a cellphone.

Yep.

The secret pocket that's key to the method of that effect works well as a holster for the Glock.

In a pinch, I can also use it to make a gun disappear, though the reverse would be much better.

Then I get another idea. Even without Ariel, a vision can help make my trip to Orientation safer. In fact, perhaps I can repeat what happened yesterday and see a multi-hour prophecy.

Yes, that's it.

This way, I could go to Orientation in my vision instead of in the real world—and skip the trip unless the vision shows me getting there and back harmlessly.

Excited about such a workaround, I get into the lotus pose and focus on my ever-slowing breath.

Nothing happens.

I sit, my mind as clear as can be, but the lightning on my palms never materializes.

Maybe this is the cost Felix mentioned?

If so, the guy is a total jinx, but he might be right. Looks like yesterday's longer vision drained me, and I can't reach Headspace today.

Or at least I hope it's just for today. As sweet as it was to beat Felix in *Mortal Kombat*, it would suck to lose my powers for a long time over a video game.

Regardless, I need a backup plan when it comes to Orientation if Ariel doesn't appear at the last minute.

I get dressed, hide my gun in the secret pocket, slide

the admiral's knife into a regular pocket, and walk into the living room.

When Felix and Fluffster notice my arrival, I ask, "What if I take the gun with me and cab it there and back?"

"I'd rather you stayed home." Fluffster half runs, half hops a circle around me. "I don't think you should *ever* leave."

"Great." My tone drips with sarcasm. "Felix?"

He stands up. "I know how important Orientation is. Which is why I'm sharing that cab with you."

"You are?" I look over his thin frame with skepticism. "Actually, no. You're not. Why put you in danger?"

"If you're going, I'm going." In a quieter voice, he adds, "I was actually going to go there anyway, so it would be silly not to go together."

"You were?" Fluffster and I ask at the same time.

"It's not a big deal," he says defensively. "Just chaperoning a friend there."

"A friend?" I look into his black eyes to see if he's joking and find no sign of it. "A friend who isn't me?"

Felix blushes. "It's Maya." He looks down. "She and I made a pact. If the werewolf bitches threatened her again, Maya would text me, and I would take her to Orientation." He takes out his phone and waves it in the air. "She texted."

"Maya?" I repeat dumbly. "You were going to take Maya to Orientation and are only telling me about it *now*?"

Maya is my petite classmate and new friend, who is, and I quote, "turning eighteen in a few months." In part because she's so tiny, she fell prey to Roxy and her b-hive's bullying.

For Felix to make such a pact with her is gallant in the extreme. Except I somehow doubt Roxy would threaten Maya on her way *to* Orientation. It's much more likely the girl is just scheming to spend time with Felix.

And I bet he knows this.

Most importantly, though, I don't think Felix could actually help Maya deal with Roxy if push came to shove. I can picture it now. Roxy or one of her minions turns into a wolf, bites someone; Felix sees blood, faints, and that's that.

"I *can* take care of myself," Felix says, as if discerning my thoughts. "Wait here."

I hear him rummage in his room, then go into Ariel's. When he comes back, he's holding two guns—the one I saw in Ariel's room earlier and a funky-looking contraption.

"This one, I will give to Maya for the duration of our trip." He stuffs Ariel's gun in the back of his pants. "And this one"—he displays the funky gun—"I acquired as contraband after that whole mess with Harper. Mind you, if I get caught with it, the Council will have my head."

Fascinated, I examine the intricate carvings on the side of the weapon, and its odd sights and handle. It looks like someone took a musket, shrank it, and then used it as a basis for a futuristic laser blaster. "What is it?"

"A gun," Felix says. "From Gomorrah."

I examine it with even greater interest.

"Gomorrah technology is ahead of ours," he explains excitedly. "This gun has more computational power than your laptop. It can auto-aim, has a nonlethal mode, is lighter than any weapon made here on Earth, and the coolest part is that I can use my technomancer powers on it. Thus far, I made it so that it only works for me—so even if I lost it or someone stole it, it would be a useless toy for them."

I reach over and touch the gun. The material feels even more plastic than that on my Glock. Close up, it looks more like a toy gun than some toy guns. "But wouldn't it be against the Mandate to brandish that about on Earth?"

"It won't activate the Mandate protection if I pull it out, if that's what you mean." He sticks the weapon in the back of his pants next to Maya's/Ariel's gun.

"But if someone sees—"

"Dead men tell no tales," he says. "Assuming I use the lethal option, that is."

I roll my eyes. "Please. You'll pass out before you shoot that thing. You faint at the sight of blood, remember?"

"I don't always." He confidently walks to the front door and puts on his shoes. "We played that gory game, and I was fine."

"It wasn't real blood," I remind him. "Not like when you actually shoot someone."

He shrugs. "There's always the nonlethal option. If I were to use that, the person would just blank out for a few hours. But even if I had to shoot someone full throttle, this gun shouldn't make them bleed. At least in theory. In any case, I wouldn't pass out *before* squeezing the trigger."

"Riiight. You'd shoot the bad guy, and *then* you'd pass out."

"So what? The bad guy wouldn't be a threat anymore."

"Assuming you killed him with one shot," I mutter. "And assuming there's only one guy."

Felix's jaw is set in a way he must've learned from Ariel. "Do you want to go to Orientation or not?"

"Fine." I put on my own shoes. "Let's go."

Before we leave the building, we summon the car and wait for it to arrive, hands on our concealed weapons.

We get into the car unmolested and head for Maya's place, which is nearby.

"Hi, Felix. Hi, Sasha," Maya chirps excitedly when she gets in. "Thanks so much for coming to get me."

If she's disappointed that I'm here, Felix-blocking her, she's very good at not showing it.

"Here." Felix discreetly slides Ariel's gun across the seat. "Use that in case something bad happens."

Her eyes get so wide they barely fit in the rims of

her stylish eyeglasses. She recovers quickly, though, and hides the gun inside her backpack.

I really hope Felix knows what he's doing, giving the kid a gun. I'll have to remind him to take it away before we drop her off at home; the last thing we want is her parents finding it.

The ride to Queens is slow in traffic, and I let Felix and Maya chat. Their clumsy flirtations are cuter than newborn kittens. Maya is pretty mature for her age, which, combined with Felix's immaturity, bridges their age gap, but they're still adorably awkward together.

Damn, I wish Ariel were here for this. She loves to make virgin jokes at Felix's expense, and this ride would give her a lot of material. Then again, is he still a virgin given the succubus attack?

Probably. It didn't look like he got that far with her.

As we pull up to the Orientation building, I notice a familiar face behind the wheel of the Jaguar that rudely cuts us off at the intersection.

"That's Chester," I hiss at Felix, pointing at the car in question.

Oblivious to any traffic behind him, Chester stops in the middle of the road, and Roxy gets out of his car.

She looks annoyed at something. Maybe she doesn't like Daddy driving her, or maybe she wanted him to park by the curb, like a normal person.

I duck before Chester sees me, because if he does, I'm sure some truck will barrel into our car a few seconds later.

Fortunately, Chester pulls away as soon as his hell-spawn enters the building.

Our driver parks.

We get out of the car, and Felix accompanies us to the classroom. As we walk, I can almost feel Maya wanting him to take her hand—but he doesn't.

"I'll be back in a bit." Felix is looking right at Maya as he says this, and I make a mental note to have a serious conversation with him. In a nutshell, it would be, "Before you do anything, wait at least 'a few months.'"

Maya and I enter the classroom, grab two chairs, and sit together as far away from Roxy and her hive as is mathematically possible.

The Queen B is acting normal—by which I mean she's clearly saying nasty stuff about us to her hive, but in a voice too low for me to overhear.

Whatever Rose told her in the park, she'd clearly wasted her breath.

Maya's hearing must be sharper, because her hand goes into her backpack—but she catches my stern look and doesn't bring out the gun.

Dr. Hekima walks in, and everyone shuts up.

"Hi, all." Dr. Hekima's Einsteinian hair is messier than usual today. "Boy, do I have a great lesson for you."

He walks up and hands me a printout, then gives one to Maya before going around the circle.

The printout is covered in legalese, which, if I understand it right, talks about giving consent to having my mind invaded for the purposes of the lecture.

What?

I must've misunderstood.

"The forms are for later," Dr. Hekima says after everyone has a copy. "To start, I'll just talk, and the topic is something I'm sure you have been eagerly awaiting." He pauses for drama and looks everyone over, his eyes shining. "The Otherlands."

The teenagers show no sign of the eagerness he just implied. No one seems to care, except for me.

I'm ready to jump up and down in excitement.

"Raise your hand if you've heard of the term 'alternate dimension,'" Dr. Hekima says.

My hand shoots up, and a few others gingerly follow my example.

"How about 'other worlds?'"

More hands.

"What about 'parallel universes?' Or 'the multiverse?'"

Pretty much all hands are up now.

"Good," he says. "That will make it easier to explain what the Otherlands are. The first thing you need to know is that there are gates, which are a means of travel to the Otherlands—worlds very different from our own. We'll cover gates in more detail later, as the focus of today's lesson are the Otherlands themselves."

I listen eagerly as he gets up and begins to pace.

"Something you need to keep in mind is that Earth itself is one of the Otherlands," he says, circling around the classroom. "And we, the Cognizant, are not native to it."

He pauses for drama again, and that allows me to realize I've been thinking of the Otherlands as "out there" and Earth as my home. But we are, in effect, aliens here.

Where is our original home?

Does anyone know?

Dr. Hekima keeps pacing and talking, covering some of the things I've learned from Ariel and Felix.

There are an infinite number of worlds, in many of which time flows differently. The gates only lead to a tiny fraction of this infinitude, so there are countless worlds that you can't access by a gate.

There are also worlds that had gates and then died —some from nuclear war the Cognizant couldn't prevent, others from an asteroid or some other apocalyptic catastrophe. His main point, and something Ariel has mentioned already, is that we can't gate willy-nilly to these barren worlds.

It would be like going to Jupiter or the sun itself.

Some of the accessible worlds have humans, while others don't, and whenever humans are missing from a world, the Cognizant have no powers there.

"You see the connection to our prior lecture?" Dr. Hekima's pacing speeds up. "When we talked about what would happen if the Cognizant were discovered by humans?"

Everyone, including me, looks blank.

"Worlds with humans are a precious resource," he

says. "If humans were to kill us, or banish us from their world, that would obviously be bad. But if we were to kill them, it would be its own tragedy. We'd lose another place where we can have powers—and of course, genocide is morally repugnant. This is why the Mandate exists in the worlds where technological and cultural human development made it necessary."

I want to ask him about darker scenarios, like, say, a world where the Cognizant keep humans in some sort of slave-like state just to retain their powers, but then I realize that's why he clarified the part about technological and cultural human development.

Modern-day Earth humans wouldn't allow that without a fight.

Realizing I've missed a few seconds of the lecture, I leave my ponderings for later.

"—carefully reviewed cosmological data on a number of Otherlands, and couldn't find a single star, planet, or galaxy that would be shared between them." Dr. Hekima looks at us conspiratorially. "Some Otherlands even seem to have slightly different laws of physics—though the differences are obviously not severe enough to interfere with life as we know it."

The idea of different laws of physics boggles my mind and makes me wish I'd majored in physics back in school. That way, I could've asked some good questions at the end of the lecture.

Realizing I just spaced out again, I focus back on Dr. Hekima's words.

"—the limited time remaining, I figured I'd use my

powers to show you instead of telling." He sits back down. "This is where the consent forms come into play, so please review them now."

I'm about to study the printout again when Dr. Hekima says, "For those of you who don't know"—he looks at me—"I'm an illusionist. I can make you experience what I wish. This is something I'd rather not do without consent, hence the forms in front of you."

Everyone around me signs the form, and I join them without hesitation. Whatever we're about to see, I'd never forgive myself if I missed it.

Dr. Hekima walks around and collects the forms, then stands in the middle of the class and raises his arms like a conductor.

Pulsing red energy streams from his fingers into the heads of my classmates, one by one, and when it hits me, the dingy classroom goes away.

Eyes widening, I gape at the impossible landscape around us.

CHAPTER SIXTEEN

WE'RE IN THE SKY, on a huge floating island.

Clouds obscure the land below, but more islands are visible in the far distance.

How are these things floating?

I know Dr. Hekima mentioned different laws of physics, but surely he didn't mean gravity misbehavior?

Also not following the laws of physics is the temperature. It should be freezing this high up, but it's pleasantly balmy.

I look around. We're surrounded by gates on all sides. Dr. Hekima brought us to the hub on this world.

The air is crisp with a hint of ozone, and the high elevation is making my breathing noticeably more difficult.

Every building in the surrounding town looks like a cathedral of some kind, only made out of a light-colored, porous material, and with a lot more windows.

Elfin-looking people dressed in togas are walking all around us. I half expect them to start strumming little harps—or whatever else you're supposed to do in Heaven.

My classmates are all sitting in the same chairs as in class—and everyone looks as overwhelmed as I feel.

This doesn't seem like an illusion. I could swear I'm actually here, in the sky.

If I didn't know better, I'd bet my life on it.

"Ready for another example?" Dr. Hekima asks, and not waiting for anyone's reply, he snaps his fingers.

The location instantly changes.

We're in a much darker place.

The air is fresh and salty, like a beach on a summer night.

Above is a giant transparent bubble, like a force field of some kind. And beyond it is something that resembles water.

Are we on the bottom of the ocean?

We must be—unless a sky can have fish-like creatures "flying" in it.

The denizens of this surreal world are dressed in skintight outfits reminiscent of scuba gear, but no breathing apparatus is anywhere in sight, nor are gills.

I guess they don't go beyond their bubble habitat.

The kids around me are oohing and aahing, and even Roxy and her hive look impressed.

Dr. Hekima smiles. "More?"

Without waiting for our agreement, he changes the scene again—and this time, I recognize where we are.

This is Gomorrah.

I'll never forget the moonless sky with the telltale nebula that brings to mind fire and brimstone—or the sprawling supercity that dwarfs all the cities of Earth combined.

Without a word, Dr. Hekima changes the scenery again.

The new place is all gorgeous greenery and hills, reminding me of the Shire from *Lord of the Rings*—though, I guess, we could easily be in New Zealand.

The next world is familiar again. The fluorescent purple sky, pink clouds, two moons, the Saturn-like ring, and the unusually thick, sweet air belong to the world Ariel and I passed through on our way to face Beatrice in Las Vegas.

Dr. Hekima's fingers start to snap faster.

I glimpse worlds I could've only dreamed of, and worlds that remind me of every fairy tale I've ever read.

Then examples of Otherlands show up even faster.

They flit through our awareness too quickly to fully register, but still deepen the overwhelming sense of awe.

If Dr. Hekima's goal was to make us feel small and insignificant at the prospect of these countless worlds, he's succeeded admirably. Even self-centered Roxy looks subdued by the wondrous parade.

Until the Copernican Revolution, people thought Earth was the center of the Universe. Learning otherwise must've been as humbling of an experience as this.

The scent of burned coffee hits my nostrils, and I know I'm back on Earth—in the least interesting room of the least interesting Otherland among the multitude I've just witnessed.

"We'll continue this topic next week," Dr. Hekima says, glancing at his watch. "Please save your questions for then."

Wait, what? No questions?

I expect my classmates to revolt, but they just start putting their stuff in their backpacks.

Before I can speak up, Dr. Hekima vacates the room.

I prepare for Roxy and her hive to start something, but they leave very quickly too. Maybe they're getting a lift and are late for it?

Either that, or Rose and Vlad did have some kind of influence on Roxy.

Maya takes out her phone and sends a text.

A second later, her phone dings in reply.

"Felix should be here in a few seconds," she says.

As the last of the students leave the room and I dig into my pocket, I ask, "Can you use your psychometry on this?"

I take out the admiral's knife and show it to Maya.

"Sure." She takes it from me. "Want to do it now?"

"Yep, as we wait for Felix."

"Felix is here," says a familiar voice from the doorway. "But please continue."

Maya gives the arriving Felix a wide grin and sits on the floor, holding the knife handle tightly. A glowing, purple-tinted energy seeps from her skin into the object, and Maya's expression turns trance-like.

"He's cutting her face," she chants under her breath. "Her blood mingles with her tears, but that just heightens his arousal. He tells her what he's going to carve up next, and she screams louder—" Her eyes roll behind her head for a moment; then she exhales, and her eyes go back to normal as she drops the knife on the floor as if it were a snake.

"His name is Innokentiy Charnetskavoy," she says, opening her eyes. Her voice is unsteady as she continues. "He's a human monster of the worst kind. Part of the Russian mafia. You should stay away from him." She visibly shudders.

A Russian connection.

Felix was right about those epaulettes.

"That name is a mouthful." I hide my terror by bending to pick up the knife. "I think I'll keep calling him 'the admiral.'" I straighten, pocketing the knife. "As to staying away from him—I'd love nothing more, but unfortunately, someone sent this guy after me, so I don't have much of a choice."

I look at Felix to see his reaction to all this and notice how pale he is. "Dude, are you about to faint?"

"No." His voice is hoarse. "I just don't like hearing about blood."

"I'm sorry," Maya says. "I don't have control over what I say when I do that."

"It's not you who should be sorry." Felix gives me a meaningful glare, and I look down, away from his gaze.

He's right to be upset.

In hindsight, I shouldn't have asked Maya to use her powers like that. The poor girl might now have nightmares.

I definitely will.

"We better go catch the cab," I say to change the topic and pull out my phone to summon us a ride.

We walk down in uncomfortable silence to find the car already waiting.

As we drive, the conversation resumes, and by the time we enter downtown Manhattan, Felix and Maya are back to their flirting, which relieves some of my guilt.

"Let's drop me off first," I say, suppressing a mischievous smile. To Maya, I add in a low voice, "This way, Felix can collect the gun from you right by your door."

Neither of them questions my dubious logic. They clearly want a chance to be alone.

"Bye, guys," I say when the car stops next to our building. "It was nice seeing you, Maya. Felix, I'll talk to you later."

"Later," he says.

"Thank you," Maya says. "I mean, bye."

Smiling, I exit the vehicle and sashay to the entrance. Mentally planning the rest of my weekend, I enter the building and summon the elevator.

This is when a tsunami of premonition drowns me in dread.

Acting purely on instinct, I turn on my heel to face the building's entrance.

Smiling menacingly, the admiral closes the door behind himself.

CHAPTER SEVENTEEN

I FREEZE as he charges at me.

Even before Maya's reading, this man looked big and scary, but now that I know about his penchant for knife torture, the terror is paralyzing.

Somehow, my muscles unlock and I reach into my secret pocket to grab my gun.

The admiral also reaches into his pocket as he runs, taking out a syringe.

Gulping in a breath, I rip my gun out of its hiding spot and shoot.

My shaking hands must mess up the shot because the admiral keeps coming, seemingly unscathed.

He's so close now that I'd have no problem hitting him with the next bullet—except he moves too fast.

Before I can squeeze the trigger, he chops at my wrists with the edge of his palm, like a karate master attempting to break a brick.

Pain explodes in my arms, and the weapon clatters to the floor.

He kicks the gun away and grabs my throat, almost gently, then lifts the syringe.

Ignoring the pain in my wrist, I slip my right hand into my pocket.

My fingers close around his knife, and in a single motion, I yank it out and press the button to pop out the blade, then slice at his chest.

He grunts in pain, his hand letting go of my throat to grasp the wound.

I stab him in the shoulder.

He screams and backs away, so I bolt for the staircase, leaving the knife embedded in his flesh.

He runs after me.

I sprint faster, pushing my muscles to their limits.

When I reach the stairway, I leap two and three steps at a time as I make my way up, the sounds of pursuit urging me on.

The neighbors must've heard the gunshot. Could one of them be on the way to save me?

Unlikely. If I were them, I'd call the police and stay in.

Two flights of stairs later, my breathing is ragged and the admiral is closing the distance.

How long would it take the cops to get here?

Probably too long to save me.

If I could just make it to my apartment, Fluffster would take care of him.

I can barely breathe by the time I reach my floor,

and the sound of the admiral's footsteps is right behind me.

I smell his garlicky breath as I desperately reach for the door handle, but it's too late.

His hand grabs my shoulder in a vise-like grip.

I pivot, reaching for the knife still stuck in his shoulder when a needle pricks my arm.

No. I can't allow this to happen. I have to stay conscious.

If I pass out, I'll—

———

I WAKE up to pitch blackness. Some kind of cloth is covering my face, my mouth is painfully dry, and my head feels like it's stuffed with rotten cotton candy.

I attempt to move and find that I can't.

Scanning my body, I realize my hands are bound with something metallic—probably handcuffs—and that I ache in places I didn't know it was possible to have aches. The cloth over my face shifts slightly as I try to shake it off.

It must be a bag acting as a blindfold.

There's a sense of movement to my surroundings.

Am I in the trunk of a car?

My breathing speeds up, and I inhale gasoline fumes.

Yes. Definitely in the trunk of a car.

This is not good—especially in light of being cuffed and blindfolded.

I shift my weight around as I would if I wanted to perform a Houdini-inspired escape from a trunk.

My arms are behind my back—not a great start for any escapism demonstration.

Channeling all my recent yoga classes, I slide my bound hands under my butt, then farther down my legs. Nearly dislocating my shoulders, I wriggle my cuffed wrists over my feet to the front of my body.

Now I can deal with the cuffs—

The car stops.

I fake unconsciousness.

Someone opens the trunk, and I see faint light through the thick cloth covering my head.

Garlic breath assaults me again, and rough hands grab me under my shoulders and knees, then carry me somewhere.

Flashing back to Maya's horrific psychometry revelations, I do my best to breathe evenly, as an unconscious person would.

Luckily, my captor hasn't noticed that my cuffed hands migrated to the front.

Unless he noticed and doesn't care.

We enter a new place that smells woodsy—like wet birch trees with a hint of eucalyptus.

The hands place me into a chair, and the bag is removed from my head.

The place is so bright I'm blinded even through the closed eyelids.

"Sashen'ka," says a familiar ancient-sounding

androgynous voice in a heavy Russian accent. "Are you awake, dear?"

I keep my eyes shut, still pretending to be unconscious.

I know what I'd see if I opened them, of course.

Wrinkled face, dandelion-like hair.

Baba Yaga.

A man—the admiral by my estimation—barks something at her in rapid-fire Russian.

"Innokentiy noticed your hands went from behind your back to your front," Baba Yaga says in English. "So you can stop pretending."

"So, he did notice." I open my eyes and swallow to moisten my parched throat. "You can't blame a girl for trying, though, can you?"

As my eyes adjust to the bright halogen lamps, I verify that it is indeed Baba Yaga sitting across the table from me, holding a cup of tea in her gnarled hands.

We seem to be in a restaurant of some kind.

"Actually, I *can* blame you for trying to deceive me," Baba Yaga says. "But I won't. Not yet anyway."

She studies me, and I stare back with the innocent expression I use when someone claims they caught me executing a secret magician move.

"Is this the Izbushka?" I ask to break the silence and do some reconnaissance at the same time.

The place doesn't look like Baba Yaga's fancy establishment and has more of a cafeteria feel, but it's not like I saw every nook and cranny the last time.

The witch sips her tea instead of replying, so I look around.

On the table in front of me is a large golden tea kettle I've seen at Felix's parents' house—a Russian samovar.

To my left is Baba Yaga's right-hand man—Koschei. The usual mischief is absent from his marble-green eyes as he stares blankly into the distance.

To my right is my kidnapper—Innokentiy, a.k.a. the admiral.

A woman in nurse scrubs is putting finishing touches on a stitch job on his shoulder, but he doesn't seem to notice. The full malevolence of his gaze is trained on me.

"She's untouched, right?" Baba Yaga says to the admiral, noticing his stare.

The malice in her voice is unmistakable.

Koschei must pick up on it too, because he steps toward the admiral, who violently shakes his head and pleads with them in Russian.

"Fine. I believe you," Baba Yaga says to the admiral, and Koschei stops. "Get out of here." She regally waves her hand, and the admiral and the nurse bolt out of the room. "You too, Koscheiushka," she adds. "Sasha and I need to discuss feminine matters."

"I don't trust this one," Koschei says, but reluctantly turns toward the exit.

"Leverage is far superior to trust," Baba Yaga says to his back. "You know she'll do as I say when I tell her."

"I'm not sure she's loyal even to her friends," he says

over his shoulder, and before either of us can come up with a rebuttal, he slams the door behind himself.

"Tea?" Baba Yaga grins, exposing the few jagged teeth in her otherwise empty mouth.

"I'd love a cup, thanks," I say, doing my best to keep my voice steady.

Tea is the last thing on my mind, but maybe she'll take off my handcuffs to let me drink?

She pours me tea and moves a saucer with jam and honey toward me, but she leaves the cuffs on.

I take the cup with exaggerated clumsiness, blow on the tea, and take a small sip. Looking up, I toast the old woman with my cup so that my cuffs clank. "This is a very nice tea."

"Flatterer as well?" Baba Yaga picks up her own cup again. "I've never met a seer quite like you before."

Since a reply isn't required, I use this moment to consider my options. Despite her frailty, Baba Yaga is a formidable opponent. The last time we met, she attempted to use a mind control spell on me—and only Rose's counter spell saved me.

Since I don't have such protection today, I need to be on my best behavior and at least consider whatever it is she wants from me. Otherwise, she might try to force me with that spell again—and succeed. Not to mention the other evils she can do to me, like leaving me alone with the admiral and his knife.

What is it that she wants, anyway? I told her I wouldn't do anything illegal when we made the bargain, so how awful can her demand really be?

"Did you look into the future?" Baba Yaga asks, misconstruing my thoughtful expression. "If so, you must've seen how futile resistance would be."

I resist the urge to point out that she's misquoting the Borg. "I did." I blow on my tea, hoping that helps sell the lie. "I'll do what you want, so how about you tell me what that is?"

Baba Yaga cocks her head and studies me, as if trying to see into my brain. "I want a seer of my own," she says as I sip the slightly cooler tea. "Not one in my employ, not one beholden to me, but one who'd treat me like a parent."

The tea goes into the wrong pipe, and I start coughing uncontrollably.

Is she saying what I think she's saying?

When my eyes stop watering and the heaving spasms ease, she continues. "I want you to bear a seer child for me. That is the service I require."

So I did understand her correctly. Red specks dapple my vision, and I slam my cup on the table, using all my willpower not to throw it at the witch's head. "You want *what?*"

"A baby seer," she enunciates. "I assume you know where babies come from?" Her chuckle is a borderline evil cackle. "Just as a hint, there are no birds, bees, cabbage, or storks involved."

A few minutes ago, I'd decided I'd consider what she wants, but this is unthinkable.

The rage that grows within me feels like a living being.

Give up a child?

My hands squeeze into fists so tight my nails stab into my palms.

Have my child be raised by this monster?

I'm itching to leap up and smash things, Hulk style.

Have my child not know her biological mother?

I picture my teeth ripping out Baba Yaga's wrinkled throat.

Then, there's the very idea of getting pregnant—

All blood leaves my face. "You didn't have someone impregnate me when I was passed out, did you?" I don't feel any soreness or anything like that, but—

"How crass do you think I am?" Her lips curl in disgust. "I do not condone rape. Never have. But even if I weren't a paragon of virtue, the father-to-be is extremely squeamish and uncooperative in that department."

"*The father-to-be?*" I contemplate toppling the table and leaping for her. Would she cast her spell in time or have a chance to summon her minions?

As though picking up on my thoughts, Baba Yaga pulls out a gun from under the table, and her thin lips curl in that toothless smile again. "We are in a banya," she says matter-of-factly.

"A banya?" I stare at her, thrown off kilter.

"A Russian spa where you can warm up your bones with wet and dry heat," she explains helpfully.

"I know what a banya is," I hiss, and catch myself before I add that Felix took Ariel and me there once. No need to involve friends in this. Taking in a deep breath, I say in a calmer tone, "What I don't understand is what a banya has to do with this reluctant-to-rape father-to-be?"

She cocks her head. "You know of domovoi, but you don't know about the bannik?"

"Bannik? No, I don't know what that is."

"Not what. Who." She takes another sip of her tea. "A bannik is to a banya what a domovoi is to a home."

I stare at her blankly.

"Slavic mythology." Baba Yaga puts down her cup.

My blank expression gets its own blank expression. Can fury mess with hearing?

It's possible. Blood is still pulsing violently in my ears.

"To make a long story short, banniks are powerful seers with a big limitation." She waves her hands to encompass the cafeteria. "Their power is attached to a banya in the same way that a domovoi's power is connected to their house."

A seer from mythology who's bound to a spa? My brain is on the verge of exploding with questions, but I refocus on my unique predicament. "How exactly is this supposed to work? The domovoi take an animal shape, so—"

"Ah." She looks relieved. "Is that what's bothering you? No furry business, I promise. Conception will not be an issue at all. You won't be disappointed with Yaroslav in that department. No flesh-and-blood woman would be." Her cheeks redden in an improbable blush. "If I weren't so old—"

"That isn't what's bothering me," I snap. More evenly, I add, "I don't know how this sort of thing is done where you come from, but—"

"I'm not asking you to marry him." She takes out a smartphone from under the table and taps the screen a few times. "I'll cover your medical bills, protect you for the nine months in question, and even throw in a nice cash bonus."

That she thinks she's being reasonable makes me want to pick up the samovar and pour the boiling tea on her head, slowly.

Before I can act on this, or other similarly violent urges, the door behind me opens.

"So?" Koschei prompts. "The *parilka* is ready, and I have to leave to take care of our guest."

"Parilka" is what Felix called the super-hot steam rooms in the banya, I recall.

"Innokentiy or one of his men can take her to the parilka if you're so busy, but speaking of guests"—Baba Yaga waves the phone—"I was about to make Sasha an offer she cannot refuse."

This is the second time she's quoting the Godfather, but I don't point it out, because the idea of an offer I cannot refuse can only mean one of a few things—none of them good.

"I'm ready," I lie. "Take me to the bannik."

My plan is simple and desperate. Let them take me to this seer who allegedly has something like a conscience—if "squeamishness" about rape can be said to be that. Hopefully, he'll be easier to escape from.

Baba Yaga looks at her screen, then at me.

It's almost as if she has some horrific image on there that she wants to show me—like, say, the last girl who refused to accommodate her, with some limbs missing from her torso.

"There's no need for more threats," I say as coolly as I can under the circumstances. "I'd rather go with Mr. Koschei than be near that Innokentiy character ever again." I let some of my true feelings for the admiral show on my face as I add, "He gives me the creeps."

Baba Yaga looks confused for a second. Then a toothless smile spreads across her face. "You already knew." She waves the phone excitedly. "You foresaw?"

"Did I know or foresee that you're a sociopath?" I'm tempted to ask, but instead, I say, "Let me meet this chick-magnet bannik and get this over with."

"Take her," Baba Yaga tells Koschei, almost giddily. "Looks like I still have a knack for these old-fashioned deals."

Koschei helps me get up from the chair and leads me out of the cafeteria into a large hall.

In the middle of the space is a pool, a Jacuzzi, and a giant bathtub with ice floating in it. These must be the source of the chlorine smell hitting my nostrils.

Guards—or at least I assume that's what the half-naked dudes are—are frolicking everywhere.

Ignoring everyone, Koschei leads me down a couple of labyrinthian corridors filled with shower stations and wooden doors.

In the occasional window, I see big sweaty men

sitting in the varied parilka rooms wearing towels and funny hats on their heads. Occasionally, they spank one another with bunches of birch branches—a dubious relaxation treatment I'd also seen in the banya Felix took me to.

This banya is ten times bigger than the one I visited, though—especially if every one of these wooden doors leads into a different steam room.

After we make a sharp right turn, we face the biggest wooden door in the place.

Koschei opens the door and gestures for me to enter.

I walk in.

The large windowless room seems empty, and the heat inside is so intense it momentarily takes my breath away.

Is this what Hell would feel like?

Felix's banya was way less hot, and Ariel nearly passed out anyway—though that was in part because she refused to properly rehydrate between sauna sessions.

Vodka isn't water, after all.

Koschei looks around, doesn't seem to find what he needs, and frowns.

I break into a serious sweat.

Seemingly oblivious to the heat, Koschei bends over a wooden bucket of water, takes a large wooden ladle that hangs next to it, and pours water on the nearby rocks.

The rocks hiss angrily, like a giant snake, and the

room gets enveloped in burning water vapor—which makes the heat triple in intensity.

Is this Baba Yaga's idea of hot and steamy, or is this a new form of torture?

In seconds, I sweat out enough water to drown an elephant. If I pass out from a genuine heatstroke, is that going to be an excuse not to make a baby, or could this bannik consider passing out in his domain a form of consent?

More importantly, is this heat a ruse to make me want to get naked?

If so, it's kind of working.

"Yaroslav," Koschei says from the vapor. "She's here." Realizing I'm hard to see, he leans so close he becomes visible again. With a creepy smile, he says, "I'll let you two get acquainted."

Before I can retort with something witty, Koschei leaves, slamming the wooden door behind himself.

A gallon of sweat later, I feel a presence in the room. At least, that's the best I can describe it.

I frantically look around, but the vapor makes it impossible to see if there's anyone else present.

Well, if I can't see them, they can't see me.

Wiping the sweat from my eyes, I walk through the vapor to cover my smaller movements. Reaching into my mouth, I turn my tongue-piercing gizmo into lockpicks, pull them out, and make short work of the handcuffs.

The sensation of the presence intensifies.

Ignoring the hair rising on the back of my neck, I

gently place the cuffs on the wooden bench and hide the lockpicks back in my tongue.

My completely soaked-through clothes make it hard for me to creep stealthily for the exit, but I give it my best shot.

When I see the door in the haze, a mere four steps away, a sense of deep foreboding stops me in my tracks.

"That's right," says the vapor around me in a melodious, Russian-accented masculine voice. "You can't leave yet."

CHAPTER EIGHTEEN

IS the heat playing tricks with the acoustics?

"Who is there?" I drag the scorching air into my lungs. "Show yourself."

"My name is Yaroslav," the vapor says in the same soothing baritone. "I am—"

"The bannik and the father—or more accurately, the rapist—to be," I say, ignoring the frantic hammering of my pulse. "Except, that's not happening today. Or ever."

The temperature in the room seems to rise a few more degrees. If it weren't for the humidity, the wood benches might start to spontaneously combust.

With a whoosh, the surrounding vapor gathers in a single spot a few yards away from me.

I wipe another stream of sweat from my eyes in order to see, and by the time I complete the gesture, the vapor is gone.

A man covered only by a small towel around his

waist stands in the exact spot where the vapor condensed.

A very impressive man.

Baba Yaga wasn't kidding. The guy looks as though the heat of the banya has melted away every ounce of fat on his tall body, leaving behind the kind of lean and muscular perfection you only find in Photoshopped magazines. Only those too-perfect pictures don't typically have the long, tangled blond hair and wild beard that frame the gorgeous features of this specimen.

I'm not a huge fan of the stranded-on-a-deserted-island look, but on him, it's beyond hot—pun intended.

He meets my gaze.

His eyes are a light shade of gray, almost as though they're made of vapor.

My heart hammers faster in my chest. Can all this heat give me a heart attack?

It's possible. There *was* a warning sign for people with heart conditions in the banya Felix took us to.

Desperate to clear my thoughts, I violently shake my head. Beads of water fly all around me, as though I were a wet dog.

The gesture helps. I'm reminded that it doesn't matter what the bannik looks like. I wouldn't let him impregnate me even if he was the god of lust incarnate. He might as well be a necrophiliac, in fact, because if any baby making is going to happen today, it will be over my dead body.

Apparently, I win our little staring contest because he looks down and softly says, "I know you're angry."

"You don't say." I back away from him toward the door.

"I've foreseen your anger." He walks over to the wooden bench and picks up the cuffs I left there.

"You what?" I take another step back.

"I have the same power as you." He puts one of the cuffs over his wrist and locks it into place. "I can see the future."

Is that his plan? To cuff us together?

That's clever. That way, I'll be within grabbing—

He puts the second cuff on his other wrist and snaps it shut.

There goes my understanding of his actions. Is he insane? Does he think that if I said no to vanilla sex, I might be more amenable to something kinkier?

Is this a judgement on my Criss Angel-inspired style of dress?

He raises his cuffed hands. "Does this make you feel safer? I want you to feel safe when we're closer together."

I take another step back and feel the too-hot wooden door at my shoulder blades. "We're not getting any closer. Stay where you are." I take care not to lean against the door lest it burn through my clothes.

"I need you to hurt me," he says, kneeling on the floor. "In some of my visions, you kick me. In others, you punch—"

"What?" I wipe the river of sweat from my eyes

again, beginning to get an inkling of where this is heading.

He's either about to help me escape, or he needs this intricate setup to get aroused—which would make him the world's lousiest rapist.

"If you don't hurt me, Baba Yaga will not believe my story, and the consequences for me will be dire." A quick flash of thunder shoots from his palms into his eyes, and he looks distant for a moment.

Refocusing, he visibly shudders.

Did he just glean the future?

"What story?" I ask, just to be sure.

"When Innokentiy searched your unconscious body, he missed some cleverly hidden lockpicks. When you entered this room, you used said lockpicks to escape your handcuffs," he says with the certainty of someone who's rehearsed a lie to the point of almost believing it himself. "You pretended to comply with Baba Yaga's instructions until I got close to you—at which point you snapped the handcuffs on me. Once I was helpless, you savagely hit or kicked me, and ran for the door."

"That's a decent plan," I say. "Maybe I should've done exactly that."

"You did," he says. "In one of the futures I gleaned."

For the first time, I notice that he's not sweating at all; despite the heat, his delectable naked torso is impossibly dry. "So." I clear my newly parched throat. "You are helping me. You want me to escape."

"Of course." His back straightens. "I'm not a rapist."

"It seems that you're not," I say cautiously. "But how do you know Baba Yaga isn't watching us through some hidden camera right now?"

"The heat and humidity," he says, and the temperature in the room seems to increase again. "I make sure no cameras can survive in this room."

I slick back my sweaty hair. "If she's not watching, how can she make sure we don't lie about sleeping with each other?"

"All she needs is the leverage she holds over us." He looks around the room, his face darkening. "She'd hold you hostage until a positive pregnancy test—and for nine months after. If you were slow to get pregnant, she would apply pressure… and it would be highly unpleasant."

My knees feel weak, and I wonder if he'd make the room cooler if I admitted that I'm on the verge of a heat stroke.

"I think it's time you hurt me." He looks at me, squaring his shoulders. "Sometimes, waiting for pain is worse than pain itself."

I stare down at the kneeling bannik.

This could still be a strange trick, but I don't think so. And if he's truly trying to help me, the least I can do is be merciful and make this unpleasant part quick.

I rush at him.

His eyes widen.

Using all my momentum, I attempt to kick him in the ribs.

Except I slip on the wet floor, and my leg goes off target.

Instead of his ribs, my steel-toed boot slams into his face.

I land on my butt, my tailbone screaming, but his head crashes into the wooden bench.

Burning my palms on the surrounding wood, I crawl toward him as he groans like a wounded animal, shakily lifting his bound hands to his matted tangle of hair.

His nose doesn't look broken, but it's bleeding profusely all over the place, as is the spot where he hit his head.

"This"—he pulls his bloody hands away—"means we're in one of the more dangerous futures I've seen. But there's still a chance—if you do exactly what I tell you."

"I'm sorry," I say, my stomach twisting as I take in all the blood. "I slipped."

"The more you hurt me, the less Baba Yaga will," he says, painstakingly gathering himself into a crouch. "Worry more about your injured posterior messing with your ability to sneak around and concentrate."

He's right. My tailbone is a literal pain in the butt as I stand up and take a few steps.

"I should be fine," I say, determined to be stoic.

"Good." Bleeding all over as though on purpose, he sits up. "We will kick the entry door as hard as we can exactly twenty seconds and two milliseconds after 6:55 p.m."

"We will?" I look at the door in question, pull out my phone, and wipe the fog from the screen. I'm impressed the thing hasn't died in the heat. Did Felix boost it with his powers before giving it to me?

Speaking of Felix, I have a bunch of missed calls and worried texts from him. Ignoring it all, I look at the clock.

We're twenty-five minutes away from the deadline.

"Yes," he says. "And here is what you will do after that." He proceeds to tell me his plan—and despite the scorching air, my hands and feet grow icy as I picture the million ways this can go wrong. He must not like the lack of confidence on my face because when he finishes, he says, "Now repeat it all back to me."

I do.

He corrects a few minor details and goes over the plan once more before ending with, "If you're off by a second at any point, it will all be for naught."

I look at my phone again.

Given that we have plenty of time before the first step of the plan, I ask, "Why are you really helping me?"

He walks over to the bucket with water, takes the wooden ladle, and clumsily dips it in.

"Drink this." He thrusts the ladle at me. "You're getting dehydrated."

I look inside the ladle. By some miracle, he managed not to bleed into the water, so I take a careful sip.

The water is near boiling, yet it's as refreshing as

soda commercials always try to make their products seem.

"You're dodging my question," I say after I make a tiny dent in my thirst.

"Our futures are entwined." He sits down on the nearby bench and smears some blood onto it. "By helping you now, I open a set of possibilities that might lead to my freedom later."

"Care to elaborate?" I try to take a seat on the bench opposite him—only to jump up in pain. My tailbone is still unhappy, and the wood is too hot to sit on.

"The more I say, the higher the chance you will do something to thwart my visions." He wipes at the blood running down his chin. "That is just the nature of our powers."

"Ah." I pace the length of the parilka. "It's like when I was dodging threats I saw in my own visions."

"Exactly." He moves down the bench, leaving more blood in his wake. "One of the main reasons the future doesn't always go as seers foresee it is because of the scenario you describe—the seer who saw the vision doesn't like it and uses his foreknowledge to change his fate." He looks at the blood streaks, shakes his head minutely, and slides farther down the bench. "The second biggest reason the visions don't manifest is when another seer comes into the picture and, on rare occasions, when a trickster does."

The stuff he's doing with his blood would make an abstractionist painter proud. He really wants Baba Yaga to think he fought for his life.

"A trickster?"

"Yes." His chiseled jaw tightens. "I don't hate easily, but I do hate them for this." He waves his hand around us. "At least I hate one in particular."

"It was a trickster who got you under Baba Yaga's thumb?"

"Yes." The temperature in the room jumps yet again, and his eyes seem ready to spew out vapor. "The trickster *mraz'* told Baba Yaga whom to put pressure on, and the old owner sold the banya to her. No doubt the trickster extended probability manipulation to benefit the witch so I'd be blind to the whole scheme."

"Was it Koschei?" I ask. "Is he a trickster?"

"No," the bannik says in a calmer tone, and the heat lowers back to simply intolerable. "Koschei is something else entirely. If you don't mind, I prefer not to even utter the trickster's name. There are rumors that just thinking or mentioning one of their kind can expose you to bad luck. It could be superstition, but better safe than sorry—given how much luck you're about to need."

Oops. Seems tricksters are just like Voldemort. Going forward, I shall rename Murphy's/Chester's Law back to just Murphy's Law—just in case.

But then again, didn't I just think the name I wasn't supposed to think?

Does it mean my luck might be worse?

I look at the phone again.

We're still a few minutes away from my mission

impossible, so I say, "Can you teach me a little bit about being a seer in the time we have left?"

"Sure." His eyes gleam excitedly. "Why don't we start with what you already know? This way, I can fill in the gaps for you."

I swiftly tell the bannik everything related to my powers, starting with how good I've always been at stock picking and other similar activities. I then explain the TV power boost and the unconscious prophesies that followed, move on to the two unsolicited awake visions, and finish with my recent Headspace experimentation.

"I must say, I'm extremely impressed," he says when I stop talking. "You've made many years' worth of progress in a short time. You might well be on your way to becoming one of the most powerful seers."

"That's great, but how do I take it to the next level?" I walk to the bucket and use the ladle to get myself another scorching drink.

"Keep practicing. And try to understand what really brings on Headspace—because it's not meditation as you seem to think." He crosses his legs as though planning to meditate. "Not really."

"It's not? Then what is it?"

"Focus." He closes his eyes, his expression serene. "Meditation is one path to it, as is spending time in the banya, or climbing mountains, or rigorous sport conditioning—just to name a few options. The key is that you empty your mind and focus in just the right way."

As though to illustrate his point, lighting dances on his palms, then shoots toward his eyes but stops before reaching its destination.

Wow.

I wipe a new rivulet of sweat and try to imagine using the banya as a way to reach Headspace.

It could work. Not in my current adrenaline-pumped state perhaps, but normally, when it's used as intended. In fact, when Felix showcased the banya in Manhattan and had us do the whole hot-room, cold-dip routine, my mind did clear admirably—

"Eventually, reaching Headspace will get easier and easier, and you'll be able to do it without any aid," the bannik says as lighting appears on his palms once more.

Show-off.

"For now, I can't reach Headspace even with meditation," I complain.

"Right." He opens his eyes and swings his legs down. "You should be careful with vision length going forward. Longer visions indeed drain your powers."

"I saw a vision that lasted many hours. How long will it take me to recuperate?"

"Depends on your power." He gingerly stands up and takes a careful step toward the door. "The recovery time improves as you get more control over your abilities—so you can expect the wait time to be less and less as you practice. For now, I'd make your visions short."

"Assuming I survive long enough to practice," I

grumble and look at the clock on my phone. "It's almost time."

"Indeed." He walks toward the door, and I follow.

He stands in an exaggerated kicking pose, and I do my best to mimic the strange posture.

"In three, two," I whisper. "One."

Moving like mirror images, we kick the door.

CHAPTER NINETEEN

MY FOOT BELLOWS in pain from the impact.

The cops on TV shows make this look too easy.

The door doesn't break or fly off its hinges, but there *is* a thud of a body hitting the tiled floor outside.

"Go." Yaroslav drags the body of the unconscious admiral into the room. "Keep an eye on the time and do exactly what I said."

"Thank you." As though possessed by an evil spirit, I lean in and peck him on the cheek.

He stares at me like I kicked him in the face again.

"It's time," I say and jump over the body as I bolt from the room.

The air-conditioned air outside the parilka is the most refreshing thing I've ever experienced. Behind me is the thud of Yaroslav kicking the admiral in the head to make sure he doesn't come to his senses anytime soon.

I rush down the corridor and stop next to the wooden door of a parilka with a window.

Plastering myself against the edge of the door, I attempt to even out my breathing.

There are vague muscular shadows in the vapor inside the room, but I hope they won't see me.

Four more seconds like this.

An armed guard rounds the corner.

He's about to turn my way.

Did I already mess up the bannik's vision by thinking about Chester (and thus courting bad luck)? In a moment, the guard will see me standing here like an idiot, and after that, Baba Yaga will no longer play Mrs. Nice Witch.

The door next to me opens at the exact moment it's supposed to, blocking me from the guard's view.

I allow myself a quiet sigh of relief.

"*S lyohkim parom,*" the guard says to the guy opening the door.

According to Yaroslav, that means "with a light steam"—a traditional banya greeting that roughly translates to "hope you had a great time at the banya."

I look at my phone and swiftly walk sideways with my back pressed against the wall, heading away from the speakers.

The guy who exited the door expresses gratitude to the guard in a deep voice.

Someone from inside the parilka complains in Russian about something. Maybe about the door being open and the heat getting out?

I move faster, glance at my phone, and leap for the next corner.

If I'm off by even a second, the guard will spot me.

Given the lack of shouts, I assume he doesn't.

I don't have time to congratulate myself, though, because I have to implement the next step of the plan —disguise.

Walking as softly as I can, I approach a shower stall.

The shower is running, as Yaroslav said it would be, and I hear a deep voice humming some Russian song over the running water.

The large bathrobe Yaroslav mentioned is on the wooden hook, as is the towel.

Shoving aside concerns about hygiene, I grab the robe and put it on over my sweat-dampened clothes.

The guy must be a giant because the thing covers me to my feet.

I then grab the damp towel and wrap it around my head.

I count two seconds in that spot and run for the door at the end of the corridor.

There's a bucket of water with a broom-like bunch of birch tree branches soaking.

I grab the bunch, inhale as much of the cool air as I can, and enter the parilka, just as a guard turns the corner and sees my back entering the room.

He doesn't raise an alarm.

The disguise must've worked.

A large hairy guy is lying face down in the distant corner of the room. He says something in Russian.

According to Yarolsav, he just said, "Please add some heat."

I grab a nearby ladle, dip it into a water bucket, and pour water into a stove-like contraption nearby.

Ignoring the hissing, I add water again and again, until I produce enough steam to run an ancient locomotive.

"That's enough," the guy says—again according to Yaroslav. "Now, spank me."

Making my way through the thick fog by memory, I loom over the man and raise the birch-tree torture device in the way Yaroslav explained.

Flicking my wrist, I grab a bunch of hot air with the wet leaves and channel it at the hairy dude's back as I give him a wet smack.

He grunts in pleasure.

The door opens.

I repeat my odd action again.

The hairy guy starts to moan inappropriately.

Maybe if I'm really strapped for money, I could moonlight as a high-end dominatrix.

The newcomer says something congratulatory in Russian.

I spank my victim a few more times.

My arm is getting tired pynd the extra layers of clothing conspire with the heat to make me sweat out what little moisture I had left in my body.

There goes my new career idea. Spanking people is *hard*.

Ignoring all discomfort, I keep on going.

My victim's enjoyment is decidedly disturbing, especially for such a public place, but since it helps my cover, I don't complain.

The door opens the third time, and the newcomer asks if he should add some vapor.

Everyone except me shouts approval.

As soon as the hissing ends and a cloud of thick steam permeates the room, I stuff the birch bunch under my armpit and run for the door.

Yaroslav's power doesn't fail.

Not a single banya enthusiast stops me.

I exit, drop the torture equipment into a bucket, and walk briskly to the end of the hallway as I check my phone.

It's almost time.

I peek around the corner and see a guard's disappearing back.

I sprint.

This part of the banya has cameras, but my robe and towel should make me blend in.

Hopefully.

This is the least certain part of the plan.

I walk swiftly for the prerequisite number of seconds and then duck into a special "cold room."

The chilly air is pleasant, but I only get to spend a few seconds here before I resume my quest.

Leaving the cold room, I speed-walk for a couple of seconds, then duck into a Turkish-style sauna. It's so full of steam that it's hard to breathe in it. I wait the one and a half minutes as instructed, getting thirstier by the second. By the time I leave, I'm on the verge of licking the droplets of condensed water from the walls and the ceiling. I don't, though. Because *yuck.*

Exiting the Turkish room, I sprint into the next corridor.

Now is the trickiest part of the whole escape.

At the end of this hallway is a set of doors that lead to the backyard of the place.

I exit.

The backyard is a nice touch. If I'd come to this banya as a customer, I'd enjoy chilling on one of the lounge chairs. The surrounding wooden fence creates decent privacy, and the fall air is pleasant after all that heat.

Two guards are here, smoking as predicted.

The smoke gets into my face as I inhale a lungful of fresh air, and I fight the urge to cough.

I'm supposed to go around the corner where they can't see me without drawing any attention to myself.

Desperately trying not to cough, I walk past the guards, doing my best to stride with the confidence of someone who totally belongs here.

My mind too focused on the smoke, I trip on the nearby lounge chair.

Shit.

That will draw attention.

The guards say something to me in Russian.

I grunt in as deep a voice as I can manage and keep walking.

"*Stoy!*" one of the guards shouts.

That's completely off the script.

Damn it. I was so close.

I sprint desperately for the fence.

There are shouts in Russian behind me.

I rip the towel from my head, sling it over the top of the splinter-filled wood fence, and pull myself up.

A gunshot rings out.

The fence next to my arm explodes into pieces.

I fall down on the other side and roll.

The bathrobe and my jacket slightly dampen the impact on my ribs, but I still lose all air from my lungs and want nothing more than to lie here for a few months.

Fighting the deadly impulse, I scramble to my feet, throw off the robe, and dash toward a nearby building, recognizing it as the one that Yaroslav had described to me.

I hear a thud of boots landing on the pavement behind me and more Russian shouts.

The guards must've cleared the fence.

Another gunshot rings out.

A window on the first floor of the building shatters into tiny shards.

Are they crazy?

What if that stray bullet had killed someone?

More importantly, don't these guys realize my uterus is important to their employer? Baba Yaga's creepy Sasha's-baby idea wouldn't work if the mother-to-be gets a bullet in her brain.

I run into the dingy building lobby and slam the 11F button on the intercom.

This was part of the original plan too, except I'm much too early—which means this might not work.

Another gunshot.

Someone is bound to call the cops.

The door opens.

Whoever lives in 11F is either really brave or is really desperate to get a UPS package. If I heard gunshots outside, I wouldn't open the building door for a few years.

I run in and make a sharp right, letting the faint smell of garbage guide me.

My nose doesn't fail.

It takes me a few seconds to locate the side entrance where the building's superintendent dumps the waste from the whole building.

Jumping over the black bags, I keep following my nose, this time focusing on the fresh smell of the ocean.

Without looking back, I reach the boardwalk in two minutes.

There are large crowds here, so I do my best to lose myself among them.

Walking along with the leisurely strolling people, I spot the Coney Island rides in the distance.

Weaving my way through the crowd, I run for the park.

When I pass the Thunderbolt and the Astro Tower, I hide in the line in front of one of the food vendors. If

I don't take care of my dehydration, I might collapse, and at the moment, there are no guards anywhere.

Then again, that doesn't mean they're not lurking around.

As the line moves, I use my phone to summon myself a cab ride.

When it's my turn, I buy two overpriced water bottles, open one with shaking fingers, and chug it down in one long, greedy swallow.

People around me eye me with amused expressions.

"Worth every penny," I say to them as I leave.

As I navigate through the festive crowds, my phone tells me that my ride is already waiting for me near Nathan's Hotdogs, so that's where I go.

The Cyclone roller coaster creaks in the distance as I approach the street and locate my cab.

A wave of sudden dread overcomes me.

I gape at the other side of the wide street in front of me.

The two guards are looking at me menacingly from across the road.

CHAPTER TWENTY

I SPRINT FOR THE CAB.

They leap into the traffic.

Would they dare shoot me in front of hundreds of witnesses?

They dodge cars as they run toward me.

To onlookers, it might seem like they want to steal my cab—a common sin in New York City.

I reach the cab, rip the door open, and dive inside.

There's a glimmer of metal in one of my attacker's hands.

"I'll give you a hundred-dollar tip if you hit the gas right this second," I tell the older woman behind the wheel. "And I'll write you the most glowing review you've ever gotten."

I'm not sure if it's the money or the promise of a great review that does it, but we rocket forward— nearly running over both guards in the process.

I duck so they can't see me in the rearview window.

No one shoots at us.

Five blocks later, I sit up and look back.

No pursuit.

In another mile, I uncap my second water bottle and take a relieved swig from it.

Still no one behind us.

When we turn onto the highway, I allow myself to relax.

No one is following me.

I managed to escape.

Unless someone is waiting at my building entrance again.

My heart jumps.

I take out my phone and dial Ariel to ask her to escort me up.

Her voicemails answers, and a strange, unsettling feeling comes over me.

Shaking it off, I dial Felix next.

"Sasha," he says, picking up on the first ring. "What the hell happened? I got home, and you weren't here. There were police next to the building, and the neighbors said there was gunfire. I've been crazy worried, thought the worst happened."

"The worst pretty much did happen," I tell him. "Our old friend from Brighton Beach forced me to have a chat that almost led to an atrocity. I'm lucky to be alive."

"Baba Yaga? What did she do?"

"I'm in a cab," I say. "Let's talk when I get home." I

hope Felix understands that the Mandate makes it very hard for me to explain anything in front of the driver.

"Of course. Anything I can do?"

"I need to be sure no one jumps me on the way to the apartment," I say. "Is Ariel home?"

"She's not. But I can walk down and get you."

"You might not be enough. No offense."

"None taken," he says. "When are you arriving? I'll find an excuse to get the police here. I could tell them there was another shot fired or something like that."

I launch the GPS app on my phone and share the estimated arrival with Felix.

"I'll be ready," he says. "Though, have you considered getting in touch with Nero? He could—"

"No," I say irritably. "What Nero needs to do is hire a security person for this building to make sure what happened to me can't happen again. Ours is probably the *only* downtown building without a doorman or a guard."

"In Nero's defense, the lack of a doorman might be so that a human isn't sticking his nose into Cognizant business," Felix says. "Our building is teeming with our kind."

"Are you actually defending Nero?" I squeeze the phone tighter.

Felix sighs. "Let me make the arrangements for your safe arrival."

"Thanks," I say and hang up a little too forcefully.

For the rest of the ride, I attempt to meditate, and

though I don't reach Headspace, I'm much calmer by the time I arrive.

I spot Felix talking to police officers as I leave the car.

He winks at me as I pass by them. Then he says something to the cops, and they follow me into the building.

I summon the elevator.

"Did you find any bullet casings?" I overhear Felix ask as I get into the elevator.

The doors slide closed, so I don't hear the police reply.

I hope they find the bullet and link it to the admiral. Since he's not Cognizant, the police can deal with him as they do with any human criminal—and I doubt Baba Yaga would help a mere lackey.

When the elevator arrives at our floor, I leave the safety of the car and run straight for our door.

Entering, I close the door behind me, and when I lay eyes on Fluffster, I finally breathe out in relief.

I'd dare anyone to try to kidnap me *now.*

My furry protector would annihilate them.

"Felix told me something happened." Fluffster's mental message brims with worry. "Something about Baba Yaga capturing you?"

"I'll explain in a minute," I say, heading to the kitchen. "When Felix gets back."

I rummage through the freezer and get a pack of frozen peas. Then I take the ice tray and fill two glasses with water and ice.

"Did Ariel come home?" I ask. Putting the peas on the chair, I plop my still-aching tailbone onto the icepack as I gulp half a glass.

"No." Fluffster tilts his head in an almost dog-like fashion when I nearly choke on an ice cube in my eagerness to rehydrate.

Huh. Ariel wasn't just late to take me to Orientation. She never showed up at all.

That's not like her.

Figuring I could use some pet therapy, I gesture for Fluffster to jump on my lap. He does, and I proceed to mindlessly stroke his fur.

We sit like that until the front door squeaks, and Felix walks into the kitchen.

"Spill," he says.

"It happened when I entered the building," I start and tell them both about my encounter with Baba Yaga.

"I wonder if she was telling the truth about needing a child seer. In some Russian fairytales—no doubt apocryphal—she spends all her time eating little kids," Felix says when I'm done. "Also, those same fairytales often feature owing someone your firstborn, but not this directly."

"You don't say." I gulp down more water. "There are no fairytales where the princess—and I want to be the princess—is bred like a cow?"

He blushes and shakes his head.

"I hate to say it, but I told you so," Fluffster informs

me. "Hopefully, now you will listen to me and give up the annoying habit of leaving the house."

"Well, you win this time." I pick up the second glass. "I'm staying in until I solve this issue."

"Will you reach out to Nero?" Felix asks.

"No. Maybe." I down the glass, then say, "If I do, it will be as a last resort. First, I'd like to talk to Rose and Vlad." I take out my phone, pull up the calendar app, and locate Vlad's nearest mid-day visit. "He'll be visiting her in three days. I was going to ask about vampire relationships anyway, but now I'll also talk to him about this. Maybe the Council or the Enforcers can help me."

"I doubt it," Felix says. "It's as likely as world peace, or Baba Yaga growing a conscience—"

"If they can't help me, then I'll sit home until I master my powers." I get up, put the half-melted peas back into the freezer, and pour myself another glass of water. "If I learn to do what the bannik did, I'll be able to tell when it's safe to go out and when it isn't. I think my power can be used to become almost invisible to my enemies."

"That's not a bad plan," Felix says. "Do you want me to make you something to eat?"

"Please," I say gratefully. "Something with lots of electrolytes."

Felix makes us both asparagus-and-ham-stuffed potatoes, and I wolf down dinner before giving in to my exhaustion and heading to bed.

———

THE NEXT TWO days I spend as a shut-in—mainly ordering groceries online, watching TV, and meditating.

Unfortunately, none of my meditation attempts lead to Headspace.

At least I'm getting better and better when it comes to the prerequisite clearing of my mind.

I also develop a technique that should come in handy when my powers do come back.

Every time I can remember, I check my phone's clock, in an OCD-like fashion.

My thinking is this: if I do this religiously, when I eventually get visions where I have my body, I'll always know what time it is—because that future self will check her phone.

I've gotten very good at this practice in as little as two days. There is a negative side effect, however.

Constantly checking the time has made the two days at home crawl by even slower.

On the third day, I sleep almost until noon, stumble into the kitchen, and check my phone's clock as part of my new OCD-like practice. When I find none of Felix's leftovers, I grudgingly prepare the pan for cooking and get some eggs from the fridge.

"Hello, sleepy head," Fluffster mentally says as he walks in.

"Hey." I look down at him. "Did Ariel come home last night?"

"No," he replies worriedly. "Not once this week."

Pursing my lips, I angrily crack an egg into the sizzling pan.

When Ariel does eventually show up, we're going to have a talk.

Fluffster drills me about my futile job search as I eat, and when I'm almost done, the phone in Ariel's room starts ringing.

I bolt up and nearly trip as I rush to the source of the noise.

Maybe Ariel has realized she's left her phone here and has decided to get in touch with me by calling herself.

The anxiety hits me just as I grab the ringing device.

I know this number.

It's Baba Yaga.

I reject the call, but the caller doesn't leave a voicemail.

So, I'm still on Baba Yaga's mind. No surprise there.

I take Ariel's phone with me as I clean up the kitchen, then make my way back to my bedroom and dress in a more presentable outfit.

According to my calendar, today is the day Vlad is at Rose's apartment, so that's where I'm heading.

"Will you have your powers in the hallway?" I ask Fluffster as I take my gun and switch off the safety. "I'm worried someone is waiting for me to leave the apartment."

"No," he says. "I once almost got eaten by that hellish cat when I made the mistake of venturing out."

"This will have to do, then." I wave the gun. "I'll also prop the door open, so if someone is there, I'll shoot them and run back in."

Matching actions to words, I grab a giant "Global Economics" textbook from my shelf to use as a door stopper.

"I'll be here," Fluffster says and makes himself comfortable by the entrance. "Also remember, if you scream, Vlad will probably hear you."

I nod, then take a calming breath and exit the apartment.

CHAPTER TWENTY-ONE

NO ONE BOTHERS me as I sprint to Rose's apartment.

Ringing the bell, I hide the gun.

The door opens, revealing Rose's smiling face.

"Sasha." Her makeup is extra meticulous, and her summer dress looks like it came from a trendy fashion magazine. "Please come in."

I step in. The apartment smells like Chanel perfume, fresh flowers, and exotic tea.

Rose leads me into the living room.

Vlad is standing by the window. The sun rays falling on his skin fully dispel one prevalent vampire myth—their UV light sensitivity.

Unless he has SPF 5000 on?

"Hello, Sasha." The corners of his pitch-black eyes crinkle with a suggestion of a smile—which then instantly disappears, leaving behind the usual brooding mask.

Lucifur raises her head from the large pillow on the

couch. Her flat face is a mix between grumpy and sleepy. She seems to want to say, "You? What is it with all these peasants disturbing Our Majesty's tenth royal nap?"

Ignoring the cat's glare, I walk to the couch and sit next to her pillow.

She dangerously vibrates when I dare to rub under her chin.

Can cats purr in indignation?

"So." Rose sits down next to me, a cup of tea in hand. "What trouble have you gotten yourself into now?"

I raise my eyebrows. "You can see it on my face or something?"

Vlad grunts something unintelligible while Rose just looks at me, unblinking.

Sighing, I tell them about my forced visit to Baba Yaga's banya.

"You have to reconcile with Nero," Vlad says when I'm done. "He can put a stop to this."

"Nero and I are irreconcilable," I say firmly. "I was hoping there's some kind of police-like group in the Cognizant society that can help me instead?"

I flap my eyelashes innocently, as though I've forgotten that Vlad is the head of the Enforcers—a group that definitely sounds police-like. Or maybe SWAT-like. Or are they more like the type of secret police that dictators employ?

"I'm afraid the Council wouldn't concern itself with your troubles," Vlad says, sounding genuinely apologetic. "Especially in light of the fact that Baba Yaga was on the Saint Petersburg Council in the past and has ambitions to be on the New York Council when a seat opens up." He shrugs regretfully. "I'm afraid you're on your own."

"Though, of course, we are happy to help you in our unofficial capacity," Rose says, giving Vlad a stern glare.

"Right," he says, a bit too quickly. "In my *unofficial* capacity, I'd be happy to help you. I just don't know how." He looks like he's about to swallow fermented cockroach larvae as he offers, "Perhaps I can escort you to Orientation?"

"Ariel can help me with *that*," I want to say. But then I recall her absence and decide it's time I learned more about vampire relationships, so I blurt instead, "What's a blood whore?"

Tea spews from Rose's mouth, and Vlad looks like he did swallow that larvae.

"Chester called Ariel by that term at Earth Club," I hurriedly explain. "I think he was referring to her relationship with Gaius."

"Oh," Vlad says, the broody unreadableness back on his face. "I see."

Rose also regains her composure. "Sasha was asking about vampire relationships, and I told her to come back so we could discuss it when you're here," she tells Vlad.

"And my query just became that much more urgent." I mindlessly stroke Lucifur's almost-chinchilla-soft fur and, surprisingly, don't lose any fingers in the process. "We haven't seen Ariel for days now. Her behavior has been erratic. She—"

"Gaius took a personal leave of absence from his duties." Vlad stalks over to a chair and takes a seat, his back stiff. "He went to do something in Russia. Perhaps he took her with him?" It doesn't sound like he believes the answer to be yes.

"I think Ariel would tell me if she was going on a trip, especially somewhere as exotic as Russia," I say.

Rose pointedly stares at Vlad.

He grudgingly pulls out his phone and sends a text in that ultra-fast way that only vampires and teenage girls seem able to do.

The reply is instant.

"Ariel isn't with Gaius." Vlad locks eyes with Rose, and I wonder if he has Fluffster-like ability to have a secret telepathic conversation with her. "Gaius also said they're not in a relationship." He looks down at his phone. "He said, and I quote, 'It's just a casual, mutually beneficial arrangement. She means nothing to me.'"

Rose's features darken.

"They are consenting adults," Vlad tells her apologetically.

"Gaius is lying." I fight the urge to get up, grab Vlad's phone, and text that smug asshole some choice insults. "Ariel has been hanging out with him for the last—"

"Following someone around like a puppy does not a relationship make," Vlad says, then looks at Rose's even more furious expression. "I'm sorry, but it's true."

"This sort of thing happens to some who taste vampire blood." Rose glances at Vlad, as if for some confirmation. When he nods, she says, "The experience is… extraordinary."

"So… what? Are you saying Ariel is hooked on Gaius's 'extraordinary' blood?" I look at Rose, then at Vlad.

They both dodge my gaze.

My worry intensifies. "Is she like a heroin addict or something?"

"More like a sex addict than a drug addict." Vlad finally meets my gaze.

"It should be in a category of its own," Rose says with a faint blush. "But suffice it to say that you need tremendous willpower if you're going to imbibe such a strong substance. It also helps when you're in a loving relationship with your drug of choice." She gives Vlad such a heated stare that I half expect her to jump to her feet and start making out with him in front of me. Again.

"I don't like this." I give the cat another stroke. Magnanimous purring and my continued existence are my rewards. "Could it be that Ariel found another vampire to get blood from?"

Vlad shakes his head. "She drank from Gaius," he says. When I look at him blankly, he explains, "His scent will be on her for weeks. It ruins the… appetite."

"Riiight. We wouldn't want sloppy seconds from another vampire."

Rose chokes on her tea, and Vlad just shakes his head again.

"If she isn't with another vampire, I have no idea where she could be," I say.

"She could be in a human hospital." Vlad pinches the bridge of his nose and frowns deeper than usual. "Depending on how much she's been indulging, the withdrawal symptoms could be quite severe."

"Withdrawal?" I suppress the urge to shout obscenities. "You said it was like sex." I almost add, "I haven't gotten any for two years, and I have no withdrawal symptoms, aside from occasional crankiness," but this would be TMI.

"She could've checked herself into rehab," Rose says soothingly. "There's an excellent facility in Gomorrah that specializes in all manner of Cognizant addictions."

"I don't believe it." Frustration enters my voice. "Wouldn't she tell me if she was going to rehab?"

"She might've felt ashamed," Rose says. "But you have a point. She'd at least concoct some story to explain her absence."

Vlad stands up. "Can you bring me some of her hair? It's time to put this question to rest."

"Her hair?" I stare at him. "That might be hard to locate."

"I could triangulate her whereabouts if I had her genetic material," Vlad grudgingly explains. "It's something my kind can do."

I recall the lock of hair Gaius ripped from me at our initial meeting, and how he then found me in Vegas after the fight with Beatrice. This must be how he was able to do that—and why Ariel insisted he give the hair back.

Thinking about those events floods me with guilt. My misadventures are the reason she'd first tasted Gaius's blood.

Putting these unhelpful thoughts aside, I focus on the practical implications of Vlad's revelation. I now remember hazily contemplating shaving my head when I learned about this hair business, but Gaius's glamour must've made me forget all about it.

Not that I would really shave my head, but maybe I'd get as OCD as Ariel about leaving my hair lying about.

Except she might not have OCD. Her hair might not break due to her super strength.

"I doubt I'll find anything," I say and explain Ariel's hair situation. "But I will go look. It can be any DNA, right?"

I picture Vlad holding a used feminine hygiene product and find it difficult to keep my face straight.

"Yes, it can be anything." Vlad walks up to the window and stares at the park below.

"Okay." I launch to my feet. Having something to do gives me a small boost of energy. "Give me a minute."

Rose walks me to the door.

"I'll be back," I whisper to her. "As soon as I can."

"I'll make sure Vlad stays here until you get back." She squeezes my hand reassuringly and opens the door.

"Thanks," I say, exiting the apartment.

"No problem." Rose smiles and closes the door.

Given that she doesn't know Ariel that well, I'm extremely grateful she's nudged Vlad to help.

I start walking toward my apartment, then hear the elevator arrive.

Crap.

In my worry about Ariel, I've completely forgotten about my own vulnerable situation.

The elevator doors slide open.

I pull out the gun.

CHAPTER TWENTY-TWO

"SASHA." Felix's face is white, his eyes bulging. "Don't point that at me."

I quickly hide the gun.

This situation is making me too jumpy. If Felix had turned out to be a neighbor, he might've called the cops on me after such a stunt—and I don't think I would enjoy begging Vlad to get me out of that debacle with his glamour.

"You okay?" Felix steps out of the elevator.

"Let's talk in the apartment," I say and dash for the door.

Felix follows.

I pace the living room as I tell him and Fluffster what I just learned.

"The blood must've helped her deal with her PTSD," Fluffster mentally says when I finish. "Must've worked better than those drugs she occasionally takes. At least this means she's not bipolar."

"Yeah," Felix says, looking at Fluffster. "Blood addiction *does* explain a lot. The highs and lows of her mood. The disappearing act."

"Except the latest disappearing act isn't that." I face Felix. "Can you please help me find her hair or any other DNA for Vlad?"

I don't tell him about my earlier futile hair search. It might bias Felix to give up too easily, and besides, it's not like I was especially thorough.

"I'll do that." Felix walks over to the couch and looks in the crease. Over his shoulder, he says, "Meanwhile, I think you should try using your powers again. Do your best to get a vision about Ariel."

"I don't know if I'll be able to concentrate with all this going on." I catch myself chewing on my nails and stop.

"You can't expect to always have visions in a relaxed atmosphere." Felix turns over another couch cushion. "I'm sure you'll figure it out. For Ariel."

"Fine," I say. "I'll be in my room. Please don't bother me for a while."

"I'll help Felix search," Fluffster says.

"Just a second," I say, then pick him up and hug him like a teddy bear.

Some of my tension seems to get absorbed by his heavenly fur, so I put him down and head to my room.

Are his soothing effects a domovoi power, or is every chinchilla like this?

When I get to my room, something that Yaroslav, the bannik, said resurfaces in my mind. A thought that's been waiting for a quiet moment when something isn't going wrong.

Meditation is just a means to an end. The key to reaching Headspace is a special type of focus.

Does that mean I can bypass meditation and jump right into that special focus?

It seems unlikely.

Then the word "focus" triggers another idea.

Right before I discovered I'm Cognizant, Nero had me research a company called Rapid Rabbit Biotech and their soon-to-be announced product, a drug called Focusall. Though my presentation about this company at the Alpha One conference turned into a fainting disaster, maybe something good came out of that whole affair.

After all, I still have some samples of the drug—and it has the word "focus" right there in its name.

The more I think about it, the more excited I get.

When I was on Focusall, I was able to finish my work in a fraction of the time it usually takes, and more importantly for Headspace, no matter what I was doing or how much pressure I was under, I was as focused as a Zen monk.

I rummage through my desk drawer and locate the sample bottle.

Hand unsteady, I dry swallow one of the green pills.

According to the company, this medication takes about two hours to kick in, but in my experiments with it, I'd felt it sooner.

Not willing to waste time just waiting, I assume my

meditation pose and attempt to get the information I need the old-fashioned way.

I pay attention to my breath and try not to think about all the different ways I can fail. For example, my powers might still be out of commission, thanks to that long vision about gaming with Felix. Or Ariel might be in trouble and get seriously hurt in the time it takes the drug to kick in. Or Focusall might not help me get into Headspace; it wasn't designed for that. Or—

I banish all the negative thoughts from my mind and make a herculean effort to only pay attention to my breathing.

After a few minutes, my mind clears.

I guess all this meditation practice I've been doing is paying dividends now.

In another minute, I'm shocked to feel my palms get warmer.

There's no way this is Focusall helping.

This is all me.

Of course, the excitement over the palms warming makes the feeling dissipate.

Redoubling my efforts, I completely empty my mind again and breathe.

My palms heat up, and the lightning finally hits my eyes.

———

I'M bodiless in Headspace again.

Ignoring the safe shapes around me, I think of nothing but Ariel as I migrate forward.

Following some instinct unique to this realm, I stop when I reach a gaggle of warm, purple, popcorn-tasting roundish octahedrons.

Unfortunately, the music coming from these shapes is the most foreboding I've ever come across.

"I'm not leaving Headspace until I see this," I mentally state, though I'm not sure to whom I'm giving this ultimatum.

Before I even attempt the vision, though, I have to make an important decision.

How long should the prognostication be?

If this shape truly sheds light on Ariel's situation, I want the vision to be as long as possible as a form of reconnaissance. But if this vision is *not* about Ariel, then I might want it to be extra short, so I can enter Headspace again in the near future.

In fact, could I have two visions in one day if I made one of them as short as possible?

That vision with my name written in Russian was short, and I couldn't get into Headspace later that day, but that was when I was just starting out. My powers may have grown since then, and two tries would definitely be better than one longer vision.

Thus decided, I start to zoom in on the shapes, over and over.

Given my prior experience with zooming in, this vision will be a couple of seconds, at best.

Assuming it happens at all, that is. I've never been able to activate shapes that were *this* frightening.

Metaphysically gritting my nonexistent teeth, I reach out to touch the shape.

It doesn't work.

I do it again.

And again.

And again.

And twenty more times.

Does time flow normally in the real world as I exist in Headspace? If so, if I keep trying this long enough, the Focusall might kick in.

But would that even help in here?

Unlikely, I decide.

Then again, the very idea of time passing normally "outside" as I float here is unlikely. The couple of times I've witnessed other seers have a vision, it happened instantly. At most, they momentarily looked distant.

So, I doggedly keep trying to touch the shape.

Over and over.

On what is likely a millionth attempt, something finally gives, and the shape violently sucks me into itself.

———

I PLACE my palm on the doorknob.

Before walking in, I can't help obsessively checking my phone again. Maybe it wasn't the best idea to develop this habit after all. Oh, well. At least I know that it's 3:24 p.m.

OCD appeased, I open the door and step in.

The windowless and barren giant room is illuminated by halogen lamps from a nearly forty-foot ceiling.

There's a woman sitting in a chair in the center of the room. Though aviator sunglasses obscure much of her face, I have no doubt this is Ariel. No one else has those perfect cheekbones.

She's holding a wooden bowl and a matching wooden spoon. The steaming liquid spreads fumes of chicken soup throughout the large space.

With erratic, exaggerated motions that remind me of a marionette, Ariel ladles the soup and places the spoon into her mouth.

Why is she acting like that? Could it be a side-effect of her withdrawal?

"Ariel," I whisper loudly and take a step forward. "It's me. Sasha."

There's a crack of neck vertebrae as Ariel jerks her head toward me.

Before I can ponder this new bit of odd behavior, someone to my left clears his throat.

Pulse jumping, I raise my gun as I spin around to face the new danger.

I recognize him immediately.

This is Innokentiy, the admiral.

Muscles bulging under his wife-beater shirt, he stands there, his knife out and ready.

The expression on his face is savage. He must be upset over all the cuts, bumps, and bruises he's gotten because of me.

I aim the gun between his eyes and squeeze the trigger.

Without the gun range muffs, the bang stabs at my eardrums.

My marksmanship is clearly crap. Instead of his head, the bullet goes into his shoulder like a hot spoon into ice cream.

He yells something incoherent in Russian, nearly dropping the knife, but catches it with his left hand at the last moment.

I aim at his head again.

With a practiced flick of his wrist, he throws the knife at me.

I squeeze the trigger, but it's too late.

His knife enters somewhere just below my chin.

The pain is like swallowing pepper spray at first. Then it's more like choking on magma.

I attempt to scream but end up spewing out blood with a horrific gurgle.

The admiral looms over me with a sadistic grin. Grasping the knife handle, he rips the weapon out.

I fall to my knees, clutching at the fountain of blood from my neck as he stabs me again and again.

CHAPTER TWENTY-THREE

I COME BACK to my senses with a gasp.

No wonder so much fear-music surrounded this vision back in Headspace.

Evening out my breath, I sit still as the implications and revelations explode in my mind.

Ariel was in some warehouse—with the admiral.

She must've been kidnapped.

Of course. That's why she hasn't been home these last few days.

And given the admiral's presence, it doesn't take Sherlock Holmes to figure out who's behind it.

Baba Yaga.

This makes so much sense.

Some of the things the witch said when she had me at the banya now fall into place.

"Leverage is far superior to trust," she said. "You know she'll do as I say when I tell her."

She must've been talking about Ariel. I didn't want

to hear her threats and thus pretended to give in, and she must've thought I knew about Ariel's situation from a vision.

This is also why Koschei said, "I'm not sure if she's loyal even to her friends."

He wasn't making a generic insult. He was very specific.

I smack myself in the forehead as I recall something else he said: "I have to leave to take care of our guest."

I bet he meant Ariel.

And Baba Yaga replied with something like, "Speaking of guests"—and tried to show me something on her phone.

It was probably a picture of captured Ariel. She was the key to the "offer you can't refuse."

Now that I know, I can't believe I didn't guess it back at the banya.

In my defense, I had just been knocked out with who-knows-what chemical and was brimming with adrenaline to boot.

Or maybe I was willfully blind? After all, if I'd known that Ariel was in trouble, it would've been inexcusably cowardly for me to escape alone.

No.

I wasn't deliberately obtuse.

Still, a small voice in the back of my mind can't help but wonder: if I'd known about Ariel's situation, would I have let Baba Yaga force me to have a kid and let her grow up without me?

To let history repeat itself with *my* child?

Then I realize I should give myself a break.

According to my vision, I'm going to be brave. I was clearly trying to rescue Ariel when I paid the ultimate price.

Ignoring the existential dread that this train of thought generates, I jump to my feet to go locate Felix.

"Are you okay?" he asks when I find him in Ariel's room, next to a very dusty Fluffster. "You look like a ghost."

"Please tell me you found Ariel's hair?" My query comes out hoarse.

Felix shakes his head. "I looked everywhere seven times."

"I looked under the beds," Fluffster says mentally. "No luck. And you guys should really vacuum better."

Ignoring that jab, I storm into the bathroom and rummage through the garbage there.

Nothing with DNA. Not even something gross.

I glance around the room, a hint of an idea nibbling at the back of my mind as my eyes pass over the sink, but then someone places a hand on my shoulder.

My resulting squeal is most unladylike.

"I'm sorry." Felix yanks back his hand as though he got burned. "Didn't mean to scare you."

"It's okay. I'm just jumpy. I had a vision back in my room." Feeling a little faint, I lower the toilet cover and sit on it. "Baba Yaga kidnapped Ariel."

Human and rodent eyes stare at me in stupefaction, so I haltingly tell them about my vision.

"There's a bright side." Felix perches his butt on the

edge the bathtub. "We know she's alive right now. And will be at 3:24."

"We also know that you will somehow figure out how to locate her," Fluffster mentally adds. "Otherwise, you couldn't have been there in the future."

I nod.

"Did you happen to look at the GPS on your phone when you were in the vision?" Fluffster asks. "If so, that might be how we'll find the place."

Before I shake my head, I see Felix shaking his. "I doubt she found the place based on a vision," he says. "That would be a causal loop."

Fluffster looks at him blankly.

"A predestination paradox?" Felix tries again, but Fluffster's expression remains unchanged.

"Allow me to explain," Felix says with mock patience. "If the vision tells Sasha where to be, but the only way Sasha can be there is to learn the location from a vision, you get information from nowhere. A type of paradox."

"Please stop." I rub my forehead. "I *didn't* look at the GPS so this is a moot point." The reminder about my new habit forces me to pull out my phone and check the time. OCD satisfied, I say, "I probably should get into the habit of also checking my location when I do this—paradoxes be damned."

"So we have no clue where Ariel is?" Fluffster asks.

"Not necessarily." I stand up and resist the urge to massage my behind. The toilet cover isn't the most comfortable seating arrangement in general, and is torture for someone with a hurt tailbone. "Given that Ariel is under Baba Yaga's control, we already have two options for where she might be—the *Izbushka* restaurant and the banya. The room she was in was really big and had enormous ceilings, but maybe it's a storage room at one of those places?" I look at Felix's animated unibrow and say what he must already be thinking, "Can you hack into their cameras and see if you can spot Ariel?"

Felix jumps up and rushes from the bathroom.

"Turn off the lights," Fluffster reminds me as I hurry after Felix.

Muttering under my breath about Fluffster's priorities, I nevertheless do as he says. Then we both make our way to Felix's room.

We find Felix typing away on his laptop.

"Nothing in the banya," he says, turning the laptop toward us. On the screen are a bunch of security-camera views that show the banya I so recently escaped.

Felix then turns the laptop away, points at the screen, and directs a stream of magenta energy there.

Looking satisfied, he bangs away at the keyboard with an enthusiasm of a five-year-old playing Whack-A-Mole.

To prevent myself from chewing my nails in suspense, I pick up Fluffster and scratch behind his ear.

"Nothing in the restaurant," Felix says after a few very long seconds, then lets us see the results.

Just like before, there are a number of security

camera feeds on the screen, but no Ariel in any of them.

"This is inconclusive," I say, examining the screens carefully. "There could be no cameras in the storage area where they keep Ariel. I don't see Baba Yaga's wooden-hut-inspired office, for example, or some of the sauna rooms."

"You're right," Felix says, his post-hacking glow noticeably dimming. "Whatever they're doing in that room, they probably wouldn't want recorded evidence."

We stare at each other in an uncomfortable silence, everyone no doubt imagining worst-case scenarios of what might be happening to Ariel. After all, she's in the room with the admiral and his knife. Then this train of thought reveals a logical flaw, so I say, "Guys. Ariel wasn't tied up in my vision. So why didn't she just deal with the admiral using her super strength?"

Before anyone can answer, Ariel's phone rings inside my pocket.

I snatch the device and stare at it.

I know this 718 number.

"It's Baba Yaga," I hiss at Felix. "Can you trace this call to her location?"

"Yes," he whispers—as though she can overhear us. "Pick up the phone and talk to her until I'm done."

As I press on the screen to accept the call, Felix shoots an arc of his magenta mojo at the phone, then frantically types away on his laptop again.

"My friend's phone is nearly dead, so please make

this quick," I lie and put the phone on speaker. "Who is this?"

"It's me," the witch says in her androgynous voice. "Are you trying to play dumb?"

"Baba Yaga?" I say as cheerfully as I can. "Is that you? Koschei told me you never speak on the phone to anyone."

"I've made a rare exception," she says evenly.

"Looks like it." My cheerfulness is getting harder to fake, but I give it my best as I say, "I didn't realize you and Ariel knew each other—but here you are, calling her phone."

There's silence for a couple of seconds. Then Baba Yaga says, "So, you didn't know?"

"Know what?" Someone should give me an Oscar for the innocence I feign.

"Here's the deal," Baba Yaga says matter-of-factly. "I have Ariel."

"You *what*?" The outrage in my voice is *not* fake.

"She is my leverage," she says. "I figured you wouldn't live up to your side of the bargain, and I was right."

I wave a hand in front of Felix's monitor. He looks up, shakes his head, and resumes typing away.

"Now hold on a second," I say indignantly. "Our bargain called for a *service*. Getting you groceries is a service. Delivering your mail is a service. What you asked for is far, far more than that."

"Semantics," Baba Yaga says. "You agreed to do what I asked, and now you will."

Felix is still busy; else I'd shout obscenities at the witch. As is, I take a calming breath and say, "Please. Ariel has nothing to do with this. She didn't make any deals with you. You've got to let her go."

"I will," Baba Yaga says. "Once I have what I want."

I find it harder and harder not to smack the phone into the wall, but damned Felix is still doing his thing. "We agreed that whatever the service is, it would be legal," I say, stretching the words. "Forcing me to sleep with someone against my will is illegal. So is selling babies."

There's a moment of silence when all I can hear is Felix's fingers dancing on the keys of his laptop.

"Americans," Baba Yaga finally says with a sigh. "Such a puritanical nation."

I look at Fluffster, and he shrugs his furry shoulders. Felix raises the right side of his unibrow but keeps typing.

"Thanks for that insight," I say. "Do you have any more useful social commentary?"

"I will ignore your sarcasm because I like you," Baba Yaga says. "Did I mention that to you before?"

Second half of Felix's unibrow goes up, and Fluffster looks flabbergasted.

"If this is how you treat someone you like," I say, "I'd sure hate to be your enemy."

"You would," Baba Yaga says, and though there isn't any malice in her voice, cold chill dances up my spine. "But since I do like you, I'm willing to be reasonable. Accommodating, even."

I return confused glances from Felix and Fluffster and stay silent, unsure what to say.

"Instead of coitus and the subsequent birthing and all that, all I'll ask you to do is donate one of your eggs to me," Baba Yaga says. "I can then use in-vitro fertilization to get what I want, and everyone walks away happy."

Struck speechless, I just watch Felix's unibrow breakdancing as he keeps on typing.

"Hello?" Baba Yaga says. "Did you not hear my extremely generous offer?"

"I'm here," I manage to say. "You caught me off guard with your 'generosity.'"

"Obviously, a surrogate would carry the child," Baba Yaga says calmly; she clearly didn't notice the air quotes I accidentally put around the word "generosity." "All you'd need to do is get a few hormonal shots and a tiny procedure to get the egg out."

My momentary stupor gone, I get a mischievous idea, so I grab the phone, run to the kitchen, and open the fridge.

"So," I say. "Just to be crystal clear. I give you one of my eggs"—I pick up one organic free-range specimen and hold it in my hand—"and we would be even, right?"

"That's right," she says. "Except I might ask for a few eggs, as IVF doesn't always work on the first try."

"Okay." I reach into the fridge and pick up a few more chicken eggs. "I'll get you what you want shortly. For now, can you please let Ariel go?"

"What kind of idiot do you take me for?" Baba Yaga asks as I start wrapping the eggs in paper towels.

"I thought it would be a nice gesture if you let her go." I stuff the wrapped eggs into a plastic container. "As I said, she has nothing to do with this."

"Even if I were so inclined, which I'm not, I don't think you actually would want me to let her go yet," Baba Yaga says.

"Oh?" I place the eggs into a box from one of our recent deliveries and head back into Felix's room.

"Your girl still has major withdrawal symptoms," the witch says. "She'll be a danger to you and herself, but I can keep her clean for the few weeks she needs to get over it."

"Sure," I'm tempted to say. "The famous Baba Yaga rehab. Homicidal rapists as staff and an insane baby snatcher in charge. Who wouldn't want to get better there?"

With anger putting a spring in my step, I rush back into Felix's room.

He looks up from his work, gives me a lukewarm thumbs-up, and mimes hanging up the phone.

"Oh crap," I say with exaggerated worry. "The phone is dy—"

With huge enjoyment, I hang up on Baba Yaga. For good measure, I then remove the battery from Ariel's phone and even consider stomping the device to death. I decide against it, since that would be a lot like killing the messenger.

Felix gives me a strange look.

"Where is she?" I ask, resisting the urge to snatch his laptop away.

"This whole thing was a bust." He looks down at the recently scrubbed floor. "Baba Yaga was calling from her restaurant, but I examined the blueprints for that place, and there isn't a room there with ceilings as high as the room from your vision. Same goes for the banya."

I sit on his bed and wrap my arms around myself. "There's still a bright side. If Baba Yaga isn't where Ariel is kept, it will make the rescue that much easier, won't it?"

"Except we don't know where Ariel is," Fluffster chimes in.

"But we will," I say. "According to my vision."

Felix gives me that odd look again. Is he gathering the courage to say something unpleasant?

"I've got to ask," he says, confirming my suspicion. "And please understand this is just me playing devil's advocate, almost literally." He inhales and in one breath says, "Have you thought about doing what she asks?" Reddening, he adds, "I mean, if she wanted my sperm to save Ariel, I'd j—"

"Stop." My hands ball into fists, but I try to keep my voice even. "Any children of mine *will* know their biological parents. They will not be raised by an evil witch from Russian legend. They will not—"

"I'm sorry." Felix looks ashamed. "Please forget I even asked. I was being stupid."

"It's okay," I say, though all I want to do is scream

that yes, he'd been uncharacteristically stupid. "This is a difficult subject for me." I take in a big breath and let it out. "If nothing else works, I think I'll *pretend* to go along with Baba Yaga's plan. Maybe I can use my sleight-of-hand skills to swap the IVF medicine for a saline solution or do something else to stall the whole process while we look for Ariel. But, again, my last vision indicates a way to save Ariel *today*, so that's where I'm putting all my hopes."

"And you're not worried about what happened to *you* in that vision?" Fluffster asks mentally. "Getting stabbed in the neck isn't exactly the best outcome."

"Our rescue plan will get adjusted to prevent that." I rub my neck with frozen fingers. "For example, if I don't go into that room, I should be fine. Hopefully."

"Sounds like we really need that DNA." Felix closes his laptop. "Any ideas?" He looks from me to Fluffster and back again. "Maybe we can call the place where she did her manicure? What are the chances they keep old nail clippings?"

"Zero," I say. "Let me look for some of her DNA around the apartment again."

I get up and scan all over, then again, then once more.

When nature calls, I walk into the bathroom, do my business, and check there for the umpteenth time.

Not even a stray toenail or a dirty Q-tip. (Does ear wax have DNA?)

When I'm washing my hands, my gaze falls on the sink and an earlier vague idea solidifies.

There, standing in the cup, is Ariel's toothbrush. The poor thing is ratty and torn, as usual. Is Ariel's super strength this hard on the plastic, or did she keep this toothbrush from childhood instead of a comfort blankie?

A toothbrush—especially this one—scrapes one's mouth, which sounds like it should yield DNA.

Then again, does the toothpaste wash it off?

Taking out my phone, I check if a toothbrush can be used for DNA, and all the websites answer a resounding *yes*.

Of course, none of the sources—and that includes the craziest parts of the internet—can confirm if a vampire can locate someone with a used toothbrush.

Grabbing a plastic bag and rubber gloves from the kitchen in order to not contaminate the sample, I go back to the bathroom and secure the toothbrush.

I then run into Felix's room, wave the bag excitedly, and explain.

"You're a genius." Felix bangs himself on the forehead with an audible smack. "Why didn't I think of that?"

"Yeah," Fluffster says mentally. "In the TV shows, they always get DNA by scraping someone's cheek."

"I'm going to talk to Vlad," I say to Felix. "Can you please prepare for a rescue mission in the meanwhile?"

"Sure," he says.

"Also, as the lowest priority, hire a bike messenger, or something equally fast, to deliver a package I left by the door. It's got my chicken eggs for Baba Yaga," I say. "She agreed that we'd be even if she gets my eggs."

"That will only antagonize her," Felix says.

"I don't care," I say, with perhaps too much forcefulness. More calmly, I add, "Once Yaga gets those eggs, my conscience will be clear."

A small smile tugs at the corners of his mouth. "Because in your devious mind, you will have fulfilled your agreement with her."

I shrug. "She said we'd be even if I gave her my eggs. It's not my fault she wasn't careful with her words."

"I'll do as you ask," Felix says. "And I'll record the feed from Baba Yaga's office as she gets your package. I'm sure you'd like to see the look on her face when she opens it."

"Now you're getting into the spirit of it," I say and walk out of the room, with Fluffster tagging along.

"I'm going to leave the front door ajar again," I tell the domovoi as I match actions to words.

"And if anyone *is* there, you scream so loudly that Vlad will hear," Fluffster says.

"Yep," I reply as I take out my gun.

Am I always going to feel so paranoid about leaving my apartment?

Oh, well.

I step out and sprint for Rose's door.

CHAPTER TWENTY-FOUR

I AGAIN REACH Rose's apartment without misadventures.

After she lets me in, I tell her and Vlad about my vision and Baba Yaga's phone call, then hand the bag with the toothbrush over to Vlad and hold my breath in anticipation.

He grabs the bag with the tips of his fingers, as though it were a frog and he were a squeamish Victorian lady. Sniffing the contents, he wrinkles his nose just as the aforementioned lady would, and says, "Yes. I can use this."

He then turns away, and all I see are a few sparks of silvery energy blocked by his broad shoulders and back.

Did he put that toothbrush in his mouth?

Curiosity is killing me.

"Brooklyn." He turns on his heel, pulls out his

phone, and taps the screen a few times. "Here." He steps closer and shows me a GPS app.

The pin he dropped on the map is somewhere in Sunset Park, Brooklyn, not far from Costco.

That area is teeming with warehouses, and though some got leased to trendy businesses as part of renovating Industry City, plenty are still decrepit and would make a perfect place to keep one's victim. Or to run a black site, or shoot a torture porn flick—if you were so inclined.

Of course. That explains the huge room with the high ceilings.

It's in a warehouse.

"If we take the tunnel, we can be there in fifteen minutes," Rose says.

"We?" Vlad tosses the toothbrush aside and frowns so deeply that his imposing brow threatens to jump off his face and choke somebody.

"If Sasha goes against Baba Yaga alone, she's as good as dead," Rose says, putting her hands on her hips. Her voice is surprisingly calm.

Vlad stares broodily at her.

She stares back, her face unreadable to me—but it must be readable to Vlad because his frown deepens.

"Sasha is like family to me," Rose says, and this time, there's a detectable threat in her calm tone.

Vlad seems to deflate at first, then takes a deep breath and through his teeth says, "*You* are not going."

Rose takes a step toward her beau. "I thought I made myself—"

"What I meant is, you're not going because *I* am," Vlad says, his voice clipped.

"But—"

"No," Vlad says. "If you want to help, you can give me a boost."

"Just a boost?" Rose frowns. "But I want to help more."

"After the last time, I wouldn't even ask for a boost, but I know it's the only way to make sure you don't go." He sighs. "This way, you know you'll be helping a great deal."

"Fine," she says testily. "There's no time to argue. Come here."

He steps toward her.

She closes the distance, and they sensuously embrace.

I look at Lucifur in confusion. The cat gazes back at me with an expression that seems to say, "We know, vassal. Humans are disgusting, filthy creatures whose behavior is impossible for Our Majesty to comprehend."

I look back at Vlad and Rose.

Instead of making out with the vampire, Rose is shooting a blush-pink stream of energy at him, and in a moment, her power covers Vlad from head to toe.

He seems to grow a few inches—though it might be a visual illusion.

With a blinding flash, the energy dissipates.

Rose sags in Vlad's embrace, so he gently picks her up and puts her down on the couch.

"Leave us," he says, and before I get a chance to say anything, he's already slashing his wrist with his suddenly extended fangs and putting the bloody result to Rose's mouth.

Though I swiftly make my way to Rose's kitchen, it's not hard for me to figure out what's going to happen next.

Rose will drink his blood. His heroin-like blood that she compared to sex.

Pushing aside my concerns about her possible (and Ariel's definite) addiction, I focus on another aspect of what I saw.

Vlad called whatever Rose just did for him "a boost."

Does that mean she enhanced his vampire powers?

As I ponder that, Vlad enters the kitchen with broody steps.

"Is Rose okay?" I ask swiftly.

"I will not kill any Cognizant as part of this so-called rescue," Vlad says, his face an emotionless mask.

I blink. "Who said you need to kill anyone? Now, can you please answer my question?"

"Being the Leader of the Enforcers puts other limitations on my conduct," he continues in that automated way cucstomer psyrvice representatives insincerely apologize to irate callers. "If my duties interfere with your goals, you will *not* raise any objections."

"Understood," I say. "What about Rose?"

"If I ask you to jump—"

"I'll ask how high," I grit out. "In millimeters. I got it. Can you please just tell me what happened to Rose?"

"I'm fine." Rose shuffles into the room, holding a cane.

The new paleness of her face and sunken eyes seem to contradict her words.

Then I realize something.

This is what she looks like sometimes, on those bad days that I used to attribute to old age.

Vlad looks her over, frowns, and gives me an accusatory glare. "I want Rose to stay in your apartment," he says. "Your domovoi will keep her safe."

"Of course," I say. "That's a great idea."

"If I go, Luci has to come with me," Rose says weakly.

"Must she?" I wince, recalling how the cat nearly ate Fluffster the one and only time they met in the hallway. "We'll be back in a few hours at most. Can't you—"

"If she doesn't go, I won't either." Rose's chin comes up.

Vlad gives me a look that seems to say, "If Rose doesn't go, I won't help."

"Fine," I say, eager to start the rescue. "Take her and let's go."

Vlad takes the carrier and walks into the living room to get the cat. There are sounds of a struggle, and Lucifur hisses like a rabid cobra a few times, but after a minute, Vlad returns to the kitchen with the cat in her carrier.

Lucifur looks furious. With a tiger-like pounce, she claws at Vlad's wrist through the plastic bars.

His skin heals instantly.

"Must be nice to be a vampire," I mutter under my breath. Then I look at Rose. "Why isn't Vlad the designated cat washer?" To Vlad, I explain, "Washing her is how I got the scar on my arm that I had to cover up with the Queen of Hearts tattoo."

Vlad mumbles something unintelligible in reply.

"The poor thing is scared of him." Rose snatches the carrier from Vlad, and Lucifur instantly calms down. "She likes you much better."

I look at the cat, wondering how she would behave if she *didn't* like me.

The cat gives me her usual baleful glare that seems to say, "Anyone Our Majesty doesn't like tends to beg for merciful death."

I shake my head and lead Vlad and Rose to the still-open door of my apartment.

When I enter, Rose walks in, but Vlad stops at the doorway.

I debate inviting him in, but the point is rendered moot when Felix and Fluffster join us by the door.

"Rose, wait," I start saying, but she opens the carrier and lets her rabid beast out.

Predictably, the first thing the damned cat does is leap toward Fluffster. The look on her face seems to say, "At last. The furry noble feast grown for Our Majesty's pleasure."

This encounter, however, unfolds differently from when she met Fluffster in the hallway.

Since everyone watching is Cognizant, the domovoi isn't bound by the Mandate and doesn't have to pretend to be a chinchilla. More importantly, he's on his home turf now.

There's a mental shriek in my head, and from Rose and Felix's expression, in their heads too.

For a moment, the horrific monster shape that killed Harper appears where Fluffster stands—only marginally smaller, about the size of a Great Dane.

Lucifur stops her hunt instantly, and the shape disappears.

The cat turns toward Rose with a look that seems to say, "Our Majesty has realized overgrown rats such as this might have cooties."

And ignoring Fluffster completely, the cat rushes past him to explore the apartment.

There's a sound of pottery hitting the floor.

Felix cringes and mutters, "I think that was my favorite vase."

"I'll get you a new one," I say. "What's important is that Vlad figured out where we're going. And 'volunteered' to come with me."

"Come with *us*," Felix says confidently.

I look at him as though he's about to sprout shoelaces from his nostrils.

"I'm going with you," he says, slightly less confidently.

I cross my arms. "No, you're not."

"Am too." He mirrors my posture.

"No way."

"Yes, way."

"Children," Rose says. "Time is of the essence."

"Yeah." Felix bares his teeth. "What she said, plus you need me."

"We do?" Vlad asks from the hallway.

"My powers can come in handy," Felix says defensively. "Also, I bring firepower that only works for me." He takes out his futuristic musket/blaster.

"You're not supposed to have that," Vlad says, frowning.

Felix winces. "Right, sorry. I'll get rid of it after this. You won't report me to the Council, right?"

Vlad's frown deepens. "No. But make sure you do get rid of it."

"Yes, sir." Felix salutes smartly.

"Fine, you can come with us," I say, dubiously studying the Gomorrah gun. "But I'm only agreeing because I don't want to waste any more time arguing."

"I prepared these for us." Felix takes out a dozen headphone earbuds from his pocket and hands one to me.

"We're not listening to music during the rescue," I say. "Not even if the songs are really cool."

"No, silly." He rolls his eyes. "I turned these into communication devices." He puts one in his own ear. "Like the Secret Service."

"Oh." I take one and say, "Give one to Rose too.

She's staying behind, and Vlad might appreciate being able to stay in touch."

Felix hands an earbud to Vlad and Rose. "If Rose is staying behind, I have an idea. Be right back."

He runs to his room, and I use the delay to run into Ariel's room and get her M9 knife. The weapon fits well in the hidden pocket where I usually conceal the gun, and the gun itself goes into the waistband of my pants—gangsta style.

Coming back, I find Felix holding a tablet, with a small webcam sticking out of his shirt pocket.

He hands similar cams to Vlad and me, and we also attach them to our clothes.

"This"—he gives Rose the tablet—"will let you see what we see." He throws his magic at both devices, plays with the tablet for a moment, and three video feeds of the room we're standing in show up on the screen.

"I want an earbud," Fluffster says mentally.

"Sure." Felix picks the smallest one and inserts it into the domovoi's cute ear. "Yours and Rose's earbuds should be picking up the mics in the web cams in our pockets. Can you hear it?"

"Yes," Fluffster says. "I hear you twice, in the earbud and in the real world."

"That's fine. Once we leave, it'll only be your ear," Felix tells him. "Just keep in mind, you won't be able to speak with us—unless you can do this mental communication thing over long distances."

"No long distances." Fluffster's head droops.

"I'll work as a go-between," Rose reassures him. "Now, really, you all better get going."

"Rose is right," I say and head for the door.

Vlad is already summoning the elevator, and Felix quickly catches up with us both.

Our silent elevator ride is as comfortable as sleeping on the ceiling, and as soon as the doors open, Vlad strides out into the parking lot without looking back.

"Is it my imagination, or is Vlad acting pissy?" I whisper to Felix as the vampire uses his supernatural speed to put some distance between us.

Instead of saying anything, Felix takes out his phone, types something, and shows it to me. The text says, "Vampires have super hearing."

"Oops," I say disingenuously.

"You've got to give him a break," Rose chimes in through the earpiece. "He doesn't like this situation."

"She's right," Vlad says when we finally catch up with him. Staring at me with his black-hole eyes, he says, "Enforcers aren't supposed to get entangled with mundane personal disputes between the Cognizant."

"Right," I say. "If—or when—Ariel is killed, then you can 'help' with a clear conscience."

Vlad doesn't reply. Instead, he reaches into his pocket, yanks out a keychain with a bundle of keys, picks a gizmo that looks like a black toy car, and presses it.

A nearby black car that looks just like the toy beeps.

"You drive a Tesla?" Felix enviously asks Vlad. To

me, he explains, "This is their top-of-the-line model. It self-drives, though that feature is still slightly limited. It has ultra-high energy efficiency, though—"

"Inside." Vlad opens the DeLorean-like, upward-moving back door and gestures for me and Felix to get in.

After we promptly obey, Vlad sits behind the wheel, and the electric car glides out of its parking spot.

Sharing yet another unpleasant silence, we drive down the street.

"Why electric?" I ask after we pass the fifth intersection, mostly to see if Vlad is speaking to me.

"Better for the environment," Rose says in my ear. "Vlad tries to have a low carbon footprint."

"Oh?" I look at Vlad's stormy countenance in the rearview mirror, but he ignores my query. "Do you also drink blood exclusively from free-range, grass-fed people?"

Felix chuckles, and though Vlad still doesn't reply, I think I detect a hint of amusement in his eyes.

"Longevity and caring about the environment go hand in hand," Rose explains professorially. "Once you've seen your favorite forest disappear, or a favorite species of bear go extinct, or if you're just observing the islands of plastic accumulating in—"

"We get the picture," Felix says. "But we still reserve the right to find the idea of a tree-hugging vampire amusing."

"I wonder if this is what Nero's obsession with the

paperless office is about," I muse under my breath. Louder, I ask, "How old is Nero?"

"Old," Vlad and Rose say in unison.

"How old does someone or something have to be for you two to consider it 'old?'" I'm tempted to ask, but before I get the chance, the car's high-end speakers start playing a loud tune.

"This is 'The Future' by Leonard Cohen," Felix says over the clamor. "We heard it in that *Natural Born Killers* movie Ariel made us watch."

I remember that night. It's when the gore on the screen made Felix faint. It stands out in my memory because I wanted to wax the middle of Felix's unibrow while he was passed out. We magnanimously decided to abstain from that prank in the end, though Ariel said, and I quote, "We're postponing this, pending Felix's future behavior."

"Darian," Vlad says, jolting me back to the present. "To what do I owe this pleasure?"

"A mere courtesy call," Darian's voice says through the car speakers, his British accent extra strong as he ceremoniously enunciates the words. "You've never been one of those who doubt the usefulness of seer kind, but I'm still going to remind you how instrumental we can be."

"You saw a premonition involving me?" Vlad's tone is skeptical.

"Indeed," Darian says. "And thus, I decided to impart on you some words of warning and wisdom."

There's a long silence. Vlad, like the rest of us, must

want to hear said words of alleged wisdom, while Darian is clearly milking the situation for all the theatricality he can squeeze out of it.

Vlad audibly clears his throat.

"Right," Darian says. "Here goes." His voice takes on an Obi-Wan-like quality as he says ponderously, "Beware the red light. Use the—"

"—force, Luke," Felix and I finish in unison.

Vlad gives us a dark look in the rearview mirror, so I speak for both of us. "Come on. That British accent and that segue—"

"Sasha." Vlad's eyebrows merge together tightly enough for Felix's unibrow to claim trademark infringement.

"Did you say 'Sasha?'" Darian sounds so concerned I'd give him a Golden Globe for pretending not to know I'm in the car.

"Yes." Vlad looks confused.

Darian hangs up with a loud click.

Vlad looks even more confused as he swerves onto a large street.

"Nero forbade Darian from speaking to me on the pain of death," I explain after a moment of silence. "I bet Darian knew I was in the car but pretended he didn't."

"Plausible deniability," Felix says. "Clever."

"But wouldn't he have seen this episode play out exactly as it just did?" Rose asks via the earbuds. "This is Fluffster asking, by the way," she adds.

"Exactly," I say. "I bet this is exactly what he wanted

to happen. I'm sure we heard enough to help us. Or more likely, enough to help *him,* as this will undoubtedly benefit some long-term agenda of his."

What I don't add is that said long-term agenda could be to shack up with me.

I'm distracted from my "Darian plus Sasha" musings when my road-awareness Spidey sense suddenly tingles.

We're flying toward a large intersection, and the bout of anxiety—or whatever this is—seems focused on the quickly approaching street light.

Only the light is green, not red.

In that very instant, the green turns to yellow.

"This seer stuff can give even a vampire a headache," Vlad mutters and presses the gas to speed up so he can pass the yellow light before it turns red.

"This is a good way to get a ticket," I distantly hear Rose complain in our ears. "This is Fluffster speaking," she adds. "He says the ticket would be Vlad's responsibility to pay."

A ticket is not why my intuition is revolting.

It must be the upcoming red light itself.

"Stop!" I shout in panic.

I'VE GOT to give vampire instincts their due. Vlad slams the brakes before I get the word out.

I've also got to hand it to Elon Musk and the rest of the folks at Tesla. The car stops before we cross the striped pedestrian lines at the same time as the light above us turns red.

A huge garbage truck barrels across the intersection at race-car speed.

I exhale a breath I didn't realize I was holding. "This must've been the reason for Darian's call."

"Yes," Rose says, sounding shaken. "If you'd gone ahead, that truck would've hit you."

"I was aware of it," Vlad says defensively. "We would've made it."

"Maybe," Rose says. "And *you* would've been fine if the collision had occurred."

What she doesn't need to add is that Felix and I would've been turned into medium-rare humanoid burgers.

"You'd survive that?" Felix looks at the quickly disappearing truck and the thin car frame around us. "I didn't think even a vampire could live through something like that."

I want to tell him that Rose gave Vlad some kind of a magic boost but decide against it; Vlad may want that info kept secret.

The light changes back to green.

Vlad expresses his feelings about the whole red-light incident by slamming on the gas so suddenly that the g-forces press me into the seat.

We get to the highway in silence.

I decide to lessen the tension in my favorite way, so I say, "Do you guys want to see something cool?

"A trick?" Rose asks excitedly. "Can you do something that I can see through the camera?"

"Vlad," I say, fighting the urge to chastise Rose for calling it "a trick" instead of "an effect." "Do you want to participate in this?"

Vlad half grunts, half hums in reply, which I take as an agreement.

Reaching into my pocket, I bring out a deck of cards. Leaving Felix's FELLATIO gizmo in the card box, I take out the cards and hand them to Felix to examine and shuffle as I pocket the box.

When I get the cards back, I say, "This effect will test the connection between Vlad and Rose, to see how well suited they are."

Rose squeals in glee, and even Vlad looks more interested in the rearview mirror.

"If this works, it means you two were always meant to be together," I say. "But if it doesn't, it just means that I need more practice."

Everyone chuckles.

"Let me make sure there are no jokers in the deck," I say and spread the cards to have a quick look through them.

"Now," I say when I square the cards. "I want Rose to name a card value, without a suit."

"Seven," Rose says.

"Great," I say, and almost imperceptibly wink at Vlad in the rearview mirror. "Vlad, name a suit."

"Clubs," Vlad says, and it could be my imagination, but I think he winks back at me.

"Great." I spread my hands as far apart as the car allows. "Watch this."

Angling my hands so that they can be seen by Rose through the camera, I spring the cards from hand to hand—a classic card magic flourish.

Most magicians do a "waterfall" in this type of situation—where cards go from top to bottom, with the help of gravity. Springing the cards—especially my version of it—is trickier, particularly at the distance at which I'm holding my hands, but I'm *very* good at springing cards. Given how much of my youth I've sunk into practicing this—and we're talking gruesome practice that involves gathering cards from all over the floor when you mess up—I *better* be good.

I'm happy with the result. There's a triumphant whoosh, and every single card looks like it developed superpowers as it makes its way from my right hand to the left with a gravity-defying jump.

Felix and Vlad look impressed—which is great, given that the actual impressive part is coming up *next*.

"Notice that I have a single card left in my right hand," I say and show them the truth of my statement.

In my right hand, I'm holding one card.

"No way," Rose mutters in the headpiece.

Slowly, I turn over the card in question to reveal that it's the card Vlad and Rose jointly named—the seven of clubs.

Rose shouts something unintelligible.

Though he doesn't say anything, Vlad looks very pleased in the rearview mirror. He must like the proof that he and Rose have a strong connection, even if he knows how I did what I just did—assuming I'm right in thinking that he does.

Felix keeps staring at the card. His usual "I know how you did that" smug expression is missing, which makes me want to cackle from glee.

"That was great," Rose says. "Both Fluffster and I think so."

"I agree," Vlad says as he swerves off the highway. In a much more serious tone, he adds, "We're almost there."

I pocket the cards without even bothering to stick them back in the box. Quickly taking out my Glock from my waistband, I check to make sure it's loaded.

Following my example, Felix plays with the controls of his Gomorrah weapon.

A big futuristic screen shows up above his gun—a screen that looks to be a hologram from some sci-fi flick.

I rub my eyes.

The transparent screen keeps hovering in the air.

"Wow," I say. "You weren't kidding. Gomorrah technology *is* way ahead of ours."

"Yeah." Felix studies his gun so lovingly Maya would be jealous.

"It's here." Vlad points at a giant rundown warehouse building on the right.

Two big dudes wearing suits are standing by the entrance to the place. They look like clones of the guys who tried to kidnap me when Ariel and I were heading home from the gym the other day.

Actually, they could be the same guys.

Vlad turns a corner and parks the car.

"I'll take the lead," he says, unlocking the door and springing into action.

With supernatural speed, he disappears around the corner before Felix and I even exit the vehicle.

I get out and sprint after Vlad, with Felix huffing and puffing on my tail.

I turn the corner just in time to see Vlad's eyes turn into reflective pools of mercury as he stares down the two guards.

"You're getting sleepy," I hear Vlad mutter in the

earpiece, the words dripping from his tongue like honey from a spoon. "Very sleepy."

Really? Hypnosis is one branch of mentalism that I haven't explored, but everyone knows that line.

Vlad's glamour voodoo works without a hitch. By the time I catch up, the two dudes are taking a nappy-nap on the pavement.

"This might go easier than I thought," Felix whispers and looks at his gun with disappointment.

"Don't jinx it," I whisper back, but I'm also feeling hopeful.

Maybe all I need to do to thwart the horrid vision is to let Vlad go into the fateful room and deal with the admiral.

Vlad lightly taps the seemingly locked door with his open palm.

The door flies in as it would if a SWAT team breached it with a battering ram.

He steps inside.

"I thought his kind had to be invited in," I whisper to Felix, and he shrugs.

"I guess this is not anybody's home."

We follow Vlad in.

There are six more suited goons inside. They all look shocked to see us—until Vlad catches their gaze, that is.

"Sleep," he says in that same hypnotic tone. "Now."

The six dudes instantly go catatonic.

This is definitely going well.

We step over the sleeping guards and walk up to a door that says, "NO ENTRY."

"So illogical," Felix mutters. "The whole point of the door is to allow entry."

"Yeah," I agree, straight-faced. "This lazy door is almost a window."

With another tap of his palm, Vlad proves to the door that it can indeed allow entry—at least if a vampire is in the picture.

As the door flies off its hinges, a small red light above turns on to show us the door's displeasure.

Apart from that faint red glow, this room is dark.

Felix clicks something on his gun, and the hologram screen shows the room in ultra-high-def night vision mode.

There are ten green-tinted goons spread all around us. They are armed with assault rifles and have night vision goggles on.

They must've donned that gear and killed the lights in order to catch us by surprise.

"Will the dark or the goggles interfere with Vlad's powers?" I whisper to no one in particular.

"You'll see," Rose whispers back.

"Guns down," Vlad demands in that same glamour voice.

The men put down their guns.

"Pass out," Vlad orders, and they instantly oblige, falling down with ten juicy smacks.

Vlad walks to a large set of doors that slide upward and kicks them in.

The doors fly open, and Vlad goes inside.

Felix and I exchange an impressed look as we follow him.

The new room is also dark, but thanks to Felix's gun, I can see inside of it very clearly.

Seeing and understanding what I'm seeing are two different things, however.

The dozen gunmen here are not like the ones we've met so far. For starters, not a single one looks Russian. Instead, these guys are a melting pot of criminal types you'd expect to see on most-wanted posters from all over the globe. They're also not wearing formal suits—and what they do have on is the weirdest part.

They're wearing johnnies. As in, those hospital gowns that leave your butt exposed. And they do not have anything underneath those johnnies, not even the customary hospital booties.

Last but not least, they're all wearing sunglasses. Not even cool sunglasses but cheap-looking shades… in a pitch-dark room.

Is the sci-fi gun screen making this up?

"Drop the guns," Vlad commands them.

They do *not* do as they're told.

I blink in confusion.

With eerie choreography, each of the oddballs raises his gun—aiming directly at Vlad's head.

CHAPTER TWENTY-SIX

THE ADRENALINE in my system focuses my mind. "Shoot!" I shout at Felix and aim my own gun at the nearest hospital-gown-clad dude—codename Johnny One.

There's a horrified scream in my earbud.

It's either Rose or a banshee with a pearl diver's lung capacity.

Doing my best to ignore the noise, I pull the trigger.

All the Johnnies must've pressed their triggers at the same time; the resulting noise is deafening.

Johnny One hits the ground but tries to crawl. I must not have hurt him badly. Still, maybe numbering them isn't such a good idea.

To my relief, Vlad's head doesn't look like a pasta drainer; he must've anticipated the gunfire because he's moving like a blur on Felix's gun's screen.

Is Vlad's speed too fast for the night vision camera

to properly capture, or is he really giving the Flash a run for his money?

Whooshing by a Johnny nearest him, Vlad rips his head off as though executing a Fatality move in a *Mortal Kombat* game. Then he stomps on the head of the still-crawling Johnny One.

The crunch of bone and skin breaking is the most disgusting sound I've ever heard.

Yep. Definitely not going to number them. Whatever these vampire-glamour-immune Johnnies are, their heads are as detachable and crushable as a regular person's.

Though maybe not.

The Johnny with the head ripped off keeps trying to claw at Vlad, even as blood gushes from his neck like water from a broken fire hydrant.

What is that guy that he can move after losing his head? A zombie? Is that the deal with the hospital garb?

No. The zombies I've encountered didn't bleed this much—and they smelled very distinctly.

Unless it's simple biology? There is the proverbial chicken that runs around with its head allegedly cut off. Can people do that?

The banshee sounds in my earbud intensify, and I debate getting rid of the device to make it stop.

Vlad throws the headless Johnny against a wall, and that puts an end to the weirdness as the guy slides down in a limp heap.

I'm certain Felix is about to faint.

Even I, usually not squeamish, feel woozy at the carnage.

Felix surprises me, however. Instead of fainting, he shoots one of the Johnnies who's aiming at me.

The Gomorrah gun makes a soft beeping sound but doesn't seem to expel any projectile—though something like a blaster beam shows up on the holographic screen and hits Felix's target in the chest.

The Johnny instantly collapses, which is interesting. The Gomorrah gun must be more effective than a beheading.

Meanwhile, Vlad whirls by five more Johnnies and rips off five more heads, then proceeds to pound the moving headless bodies to the ground.

The air permeates with the coppery stench of blood and death.

Our attackers must not be Cognizant. Vlad said he wasn't going to kill any, and he very much killed these peeps.

Realizing that Vlad is too much of a moving target, a Johnny in the corner of the room aims his gun at Felix.

Once more, the adrenaline in my blood seems to aid my focus.

I can see that Vlad won't rip this one's head in time, so I raise my gun and squeeze the trigger.

The gunshot is so loud that I wonder if we fired together.

The panicked wail in my earbud is joined by what sounds like a wounded cat.

Maybe even a bathing cat.

The guy plops on the ground, his gown soaked in blood. He tries to crawl toward me for a moment, but then relaxes forever.

I must've hit his heart.

Unblinking, I stare at the dead man, then at my hands clutching the gun.

This is the first human who's died by my hands.

Assuming he *was* human, that is—though that shouldn't really matter as any sentient being is equally worthy of life, and these dudes do seem somewhat sentient.

It's shocking how little remorse I feel.

Is the adrenaline making me numb?

What's worse is that I actually feel ready to defend my friends and myself further. I will kill as many as I need to accomplish that goal.

Was I secretly a sociopath all this time and never realized it? Or is it that I made the gown-clad dudes into monsters in my head? On a purely logical level, I don't see a problem with what I did—this was a simple case of self-defense.

Either way, it doesn't matter. If I have to, I can get therapy with Lucretia to sort all this out later. The goal is to survive long enough to need said therapy.

In shocked fascination, I watch as Vlad rips off the remaining heads from their owners' shoulders.

Felix looks around the room through his screen, as though to confirm there is no more danger.

All the hospital-gown dudes are goners.

Rose's screams in my earbud cease.

Looking up from the screen, Felix theatrically covers his mouth with his palm, as though he's about to barf. Then he falls on the ground without any warning.

My heart drops.

Did that last guy's bullet hit Felix after all?

CHAPTER TWENTY-SEVEN

TAKING OUT MY PHONE, I use it as a flashlight to check on my friend.

I don't see any blood and find his pulse strong and breathing even.

"He finally fainted," I whisper, relieved.

"Poor dear," Rose says, her voice hoarse. "Vlad did make a big mess there."

"Understatement of the century," I say, looking around at the massacre.

Turning my attention back to Felix, I slap him on the cheek.

He doesn't rouse.

"I should've brought smelling salts," I mutter under my breath.

"Or left him at home," Rose replies.

"Let me try," Vlad says, leaning over Felix.

His gaze turning mirrored, Vlad forces Felix's

eyelids open and stares into my friend's rolled-back eyes.

"Up," Vlad orders.

Felix stirs.

"Good job," Vlad says, getting back to his feet.

"Give me a moment," Felix croaks out. "Sasha, can you check if all the enemies are dead?"

Is he kidding about that?

How could anyone be alive?

Then I get it. Felix probably wants a moment of privacy to wipe away drool, or something equally embarrassing.

Stepping over severed heads and puddles of blood, I walk up to the only guy who doesn't have any apparent wounds—the one hit by the Gomorrah gun.

No pulse, no breath.

The Gomorrah gun must send out some death ray or something. Creepy, but perhaps the perfect weapon for Felix's delicate sensibilities.

"Are you okay?" I call out without turning.

"Solid as a cucumber," Felix says, his voice sounding stronger. "We should proceed."

I turn just in time to see Vlad remove his helping hand from Felix's shoulder.

"Are you sure you want to keep going?" I ask, coming toward them. "If you faint in the middle of—"

"I will not faint again," Felix says, his hands clenching determinedly. "Let's go."

He marches toward the next door.

Vlad and I exchange impressed glances.

Felix rattles the door handle.

The door doesn't bulge.

Felix kicks it, the way cops do in TV shows. The door tauntingly stands as it was, but he yelps in pain, mumbling what must be Russian cuss words under his breath.

"Let me deal with it," Vlad says and lightly taps it as he's been doing all along.

The door flies in as though it was never shut to start with.

"Before we proceed, can I ask about the horrible screaming in my ear?" I say. "It was almost scarier than those Johnnies."

"Johnnies?" Vlad raises an eyebrow.

"I bet she means the hospital-gown people," Felix says nervously—clearly trying to keep his mind off the massacre of said Johnnies behind us. "I think they call a hospital gown a johnny because they make it easier for patients to use the john. Now the reason the toilets are called johns has to do with Sir John Harrington—"

"I'm sorry about that screaming," Rose chimes in via the earpiece. "When I heard the gunfire and saw—"

"It was pretty distracting, dear," Vlad says gently. "Any chance you can abstain from doing it again?"

"I'll try to control myself," Rose says. "I even scared Luci with my outburst."

I knew I'd heard a cat in there somewhere.

"Tap on the earbud to mute it or turn it on," Felix suggests a bit too forcefully. "I'll also mute the mics on our webcams, so you don't hear those gunshots." Felix sends arcs of energy at our cameras. "Our earbuds are already muted." He taps his, and the static comes on. "See?" His voice echoes in the room and in my ear. He taps his earbud again, and the static goes away.

"I see," Rose says. There's a moment of static in my ear, and after a pause, it repeats again.

"Did you hear me just then?" Rose asks.

"No," Felix says. "Looks like you got it."

The static repeats, and the earbud goes blissfully silent once more.

Vlad gives me a look that seems to say, "And you wanted to take Rose with us."

"She wanted to go herself," I'm tempted to reply. "I'd never bring her—especially now."

We walk into the new room in sullen silence, and I feel uneasy right away.

There's a red light at the end of the room.

"Another lazy door?" Felix mutters.

"Too bad some people's mouths don't have a convenient mute button," Vlad whispers.

I ignore them because my sense of foreboding kicks into the stratosphere, and adrenaline makes the puzzle pieces fit together in a flash of insight.

"On the ground," I hiss at my allies. "Now!"

CHAPTER TWENTY-EIGHT

MATCHING ACTIONS TO WORDS, I drop into a pushup position on the floor.

Vlad does the same, his movements so fast it looks like a CGI effect.

Felix follows suit, grunting as he hits the floor. His landing might not have been as graceful as mine.

At the same instant, machine gunfire bursts out, like some heavy-metal drums from hell.

Thank goodness Rose is on mute right now. If *I* feel like screaming, she's probably waking up the dead with her panicked yells.

Felix points his gun up like a periscope. The screen shows the door and the wall behind us riddled with bullets.

I swallow my heart back into my chest and exchange a grim glance with Felix.

If we hadn't ducked in time, we'd be dead—and even Vlad would be inconvenienced, at the very least.

But then, could I have actually died here instead of from the admiral's knife in my throat as my vision foretold?

It's possible.

By blabbing about my vision to everyone, I could've easily created another one of those butterfly effects and changed the future I foresaw.

"I'll get them on the reload," Vlad shouts into my ear over the noise. "Cover me!"

The machine guns keep firing, so I have to yell into Felix's ear. "Get ready for cover fire as soon as—"

The gunfire stops.

Vlad blurs into motion.

I shoot into the darkness—aiming mainly at where Vlad shouldn't be.

Felix follows my lead, firing his weapon in the vague direction of our enemies.

Before I can shoot again, I hear the sounds of spinal cords ripping, followed by blood gushing like a spray from an overzealous five-year-old's water gun.

The sickening copper smell is back, so I look at Felix for signs of fainting.

I find him looking determined instead.

"All clear," Vlad says, appearing out of nowhere.

We jackknife to our feet, run toward the faint red glow, and examine the carnage.

All those bullets came from more Johnnies. Going by the severed body parts, there must have been seven—unless one of the heads rolled away into the dark.

What I took for machine guns turn out to be AK-47

assault rifles—not that this would make us any less dead if we hadn't hit the ground.

"This was why Darian called," I say, my voice unsteady as I explain my earlier eureka moment. "That's the red light we were to be wary of." I point at the bulb above the "NO ENTRY" door the dead guys molested earlier. "The whole 'Use the force' bit was advice for *me*. Darian wanted me to trust my seer intuition—which went through the roof when we entered this room."

"It fits," Felix says, his words barely audible. "Seems like we wouldn't have crashed at that red light, as Vlad said."

There's a sound of hissing static. "Darian could've just said 'watch out for AK-47s when you enter such and such room,'" Rose says in my ear, her voice now like sandpaper. "This is Fluffster complaining, and I agree with him."

"Seers," Vlad says with exasperation. "They are an infuriating lot."

I choose not to get offended and instead ponder if I should swap my gun for an assault rifle.

"They don't have any more ammo," Vlad says when I share my idea with him.

"Crap." I look at the rifle next to my feet with disappointment. "I only have the one magazine."

Vlad shrugs as a hiss of static informs us that Rose is back on mute.

I do a quick mental count. I have thirteen out of my fifteen rounds left, which isn't *that* bad.

"Do you have to make this much of a mess?" I ask Vlad, mostly to lighten the somber mood. "Felix is trying not to faint."

Before Vlad can reply, halogen lights come to life in the neighboring room.

Someone decided the darkness isn't an advantage against us, after all.

We exchange grim looks and cautiously enter the stadium-sized, lit-up room.

"What the hell?" Felix asks, articulating my thoughts exactly.

The room is filled with hospital beds. Hundreds of them. On each bed is a Johnny hooked up to an IV, with a feeding tube going up his nose and sunglasses covering his eyes.

"All men," I whisper. "Someone is not an equal-opportunity employer. Assuming the Johnnies are actually employed to be on life-support, that is."

There's sudden static in my earbud. "Maybe this is where Baba Yaga keeps her wounded minions?" Rose suggests. "Though that doesn't explain how the ones who shot at you ran about." The static repeats.

"How big would her organization need to be if they get so many injured as part of their day-to-day operations?" Felix replies. "Unless they're at war with a bunch of other gangs?"

The static comes on again. "Fluffster thinks the room looks like a hospital housing an aftermath of a war between a bunch of *different* gangs," Rose says, "and

I agree with him." The static shows up again, silencing Rose's earbud.

This static situation could get as annoying as her screaming.

Vlad stops walking and stares at the far corner of the room, his posture suddenly tense.

A slender, dangerously handsome man is whooshing toward us—with a speed that rivals Vlad's. His shoulder-length jet-black hair rustles behind him as he glides in our direction, and his marble-green eyes glint maliciously.

I stop in my tracks. "That's Koschei. He's Baba Yaga's lieutenant."

Static shows up again. "Are you sure he works for her, and not the other way around?" Rose asks. "Fluffster says Koschei features in as many Russian fairy tales as Baba Yaga."

"I know who and what this is," Vlad says grimly, stepping in front of us. "You need to run. Right now."

"Where?" I look around the room. There are many doors around the giant space.

"Use your power to figure it out." Vlad blurs into motion in the direction of Koschei.

I hesitate, unwilling to leave an ally to fight alone. Given his Mandate aura, Koschei is clearly one of the Cognizant, and Vlad said he wouldn't kill our kind, which might give Koschei a huge advantage in this fight.

Since I made no such pledge, I aim my gun at Koschei

and see Felix do the same in my peripheral vision. Like me, Felix must've realized we could shoot Koschei before Vlad has to deal with him. I just hope Felix also realizes we'll be in trouble with the Council if we succeed.

I shoot.

Rose yelps like a stabbed pig. She's clearly forgotten to mute her gizmo.

My bullet hits Koschei in the chest.

The thin man doesn't even slow down.

Felix shoots next.

On the screen of his gun, the blast hits Koschei in the head, but this doesn't slow him either.

In an eyeblink, Vlad and Koschei face each other chest to chest, like two roosters ready for a fight.

I lower my gun; I'd risk shooting Vlad if I continued.

Koschei punches Vlad in the chest, and the vampire slides back a few yards from the impact, though he remains on his feet.

I aim for Koschei, but Vlad leaps back at him before I can fire.

Moving like a video on fast forward, Vlad closes the distance and punches his opponent in the face.

Koschei's head snaps back as though it met Mike Tyson's and Muhammad Ali's fists at the same time—which isn't surprising when I think about what happened to all the doors Vlad had merely tapped.

Moving faster still, Vlad whooshes behind the dazed Koschei and grabs him in a headlock.

With a crunch, Koschei's head twists in the most

unnatural direction; if he were able to look down again, he'd see his own back.

Vlad lets go of his now-limp opponent, and Koschei slumps to the ground like a sack of rotten potatoes.

"So much for not killing another Cognizant," I mutter as I watch Koschei's aura flicker and disappear.

"What are you still doing here?" Vlad says without lifting his gaze from the dead man's body in front of him. "I told you to—"

A flash of purple energy surrounds Koschei, and when it dissipates, his Mandate aura is back.

CHAPTER TWENTY-NINE

I RESIST the urge to rub my eyes.

The head that was twisted backward only a second ago starts to turn back with a nauseating creak. Then a bullet falls out of Koschei's chest and hits the ground with a metallic clink.

"Was that my bullet?" I ask in disbelief. "And did he just come back to life?"

"They call him Koschei the Immortal for a reason," Rose whispers in my ear. "You better leave. Vlad might be busy for a while, and Ariel still needs to be rescued." The static shows up this time.

Good. She remembered to mute herself.

Before I can reply, Koschei gets back on his feet, his movements eerily reminiscent of old-movie Nosferatu rising from a coffin.

Out of the two of them, shouldn't it be Vlad doing that?

As soon as Koschei is on his feet, he swings a fist at

Vlad. Vlad dodges the punch, grabs his opponent's wrist, and snaps his arm in two.

Something in my peripheral vision catches my attention.

One of the gown-clad goons must've come out of his coma because he's sitting upright in his bed. Moving with jerky, exaggerated motions, he tears the IV from his vein. Then, seemingly oblivious to the blood streaming from his arm, he rips the feeding tube from his nose and swings his bare feet to the floor.

Though his eyes are blocked by sunglasses, he seems to be looking my way.

In an adjacent bed, another gown-clad guy does the same thing, except once he's up, he runs in Vlad's direction.

"Vlad, watch out!" I yell. "Felix, let's go." I grab Felix by the arm and pull him with me as I start to run.

The adrenaline in my system seems to sharpen my intuition. I become certain which door to take— though, unfortunately, it's one of the farthest ones.

Naked feet slap against the floor behind us.

I turn to see the first-to-get-up goon chasing us and shoot him in the torso.

He falls, but two more goons get up from their hospital beds ahead of us, their uncut toenails scraping across the cement floor.

I shoot one, and Felix takes care of another.

Sparing a glance at Vlad, I catch him ripping a leg off of his gown-clad attacker and clubbing Koschei over the head with it.

Koschei staggers, and Vlad leaps at him, ripping his heart out.

Literally.

Somehow, the guy who lost his leg has a high enough pain tolerance and immunity to blood loss to try to claw at Vlad from the floor. Vlad tosses Koschei's heart at him, then follows with a few devastating stomps that turn the man into a mound of gore.

At the same exact time, Koschei's aura dims as his body slumps to the floor.

A second later, the purple shimmer surrounds him again, and this time, I know he won't stay down for long. "Don't look there," I warn Felix as I look away myself. "Vlad is doing his thing."

Felix doesn't look anywhere but the door as we pick up our pace.

A couple of bare-assed Johnnies get in our way, and we shoot them almost at the same time.

Felix's Johnny falls down.

The one I shot loses a part of his face, but keeps running for us.

I shoot him again—and Felix does as well.

The man falls down.

What *are* these guys? And if they're human, what was in those IV bags? Pure meth?

Jumping over the two bodies, Felix reaches the door first, pulls on it, and grunts in frustration. "It's locked."

Should I shoot the lock?

I have nine rounds left, but even without my powers, I suspect I might need every single one. There are hundreds of hospital beds around this room alone, and each body on them is a potential threat.

"Cover me," I tell Felix, and without waiting to see if he will comply, I pull out the picks from my tongue and start working on the lock.

The door yields quickly, but Felix still manages to put down a couple of attackers in the time it takes me to jimmy the lock open.

We go through the door and find ourselves in a long hallway.

A Johnny runs into the hallway after us, gets Felix's death ray in the head, and falls down.

Another one takes his place, and Felix and I aim at him.

The door at the other end of the hallway screeches open, so I let Felix take care of the other attacker and spin on my heel to confront the new threat.

As I feared, another Johnny storms in from the other side of the hallway.

"Back to back," I command and press my sweaty back to Felix's even sweatier one.

Felix's back muscles spasm, and the Gomorra gun beeps softly.

I raise my gun.

The guy in front of me speeds up.

With no time to aim, I point at him and squeeze the trigger.

The bullet hits my attacker in the eye. What's left of his sunglasses flies to the side, exposing something odd.

The eye I shot is gone, which is disturbing but understandable. However, I can't think of a reason why the other eye looks as though it's filled with black energy. There's no white in this eye at all.

He keeps running.

How does this guy see where I am with those messed-up eyes?

For that matter, how is he still running?

Not waiting for the universe to answer, I shoot again.

The bullet hits his leg.

Blood gushes from the wound, but my attacker keeps moving forward—now with a limp slowing his progress.

I spasmodically squeeze the trigger once more.

This bullet hits him in the stomach and rips through the intestines. Some of them come out, but he still keeps coming at me, leaving a bloody trail in his wake.

Gasping out a breath, I press the trigger.

No new wounds.

Adrenaline focuses all my attention on aiming the gun. The hallway seems to turn into a tunnel as I channel all my recent target practice into this shot, pointing the gun at where I hope his heart will be.

I shoot again.

CHAPTER THIRTY

I HALF EXPECT Rose's muted screams to carry all the way from Manhattan to Brooklyn. Maybe I'm projecting, though. I'd love to scream my own lungs out, but I contain the urge.

The Johnny falls—a new red stain in the middle of his gown.

I wait a beat to see if he will get up, Koschei style.

He stays dead.

Felix's gun beeps again; he must've shot at another target.

"Let's move!" I yell at him and hurry down the hallway.

His back sticking to mine, Felix follows me, only stopping to shoot three times.

From the hallway, we enter a small room.

Felix smacks the door behind us to close it, turns on his heel, and shoots a Johnny running at us from the south corner of the room.

Without hesitation, I get my lock picks ready and work on the door, hoping that locking a door is simply the reverse of picking a lock to open it.

There's a thud of a body hitting the floor.

I manage to jam the lock.

Instantly, there's a scraping of Johnnies' nails on the other side.

"It won't hold for long," Felix says. "Where to now?"

Aside from the door I just locked, there are three more doors.

My adrenaline-spiked intuition leads me to the farthest one to the right.

Felix follows me.

Just as I reach the door, dread swamps me like a tidal wave. And this isn't the usual "Baba Yaga calling" dread, either. It's more targeted and is clearly associated with the room beyond this door.

Pushing aside the feeling, I check the door but find it locked.

The hallway door creaks like it's going to break at any moment.

I use my lock picks to defeat the lock without making any noise. As I work, the proximity to the damn door makes my insides feel like an underground glacier.

This must be where they're keeping Ariel, and the psychic angst must be due to my vision.

It's about to come true.

"If I walk into that room, I'm dead," I mutter, mostly to myself.

"So don't," Felix says. "We'll walk in together. You were alone in your vision; now there are two of us."

As soon I register his suggestion, the dread intensity changes for the better.

Does that mean he's right?

Strategically, it might make more sense to leave Felix here in the hallway to deal with the enemies who are about to break through, but his presence *would* throw a monkey wrench into my earlier vision.

Yet something about his offer to go together doesn't feel right. In fact, an intuition similar to my road awareness tells me it's a terrible idea.

Since I'm trying to trust my powers, I can't ignore feelings such as this.

But if we don't go together, what do we do?

Should Felix go alone?

No, that generates an even worse anxiety.

Damn it.

The indecision is killing me.

Ariel is just beyond this stupid door, and Vlad is fighting for his life out there.

If only I could have a vision to see what would happen if Felix and I go in together—seemingly our best plan of action at the moment. But seeing a vision would require me to meditate amidst all this insanity. I might have an easier time sprouting a tail.

Then again, the bannik said there are other ways to gather the prerequisite mental focus…

This is when a realization hits me like a punch from Vlad.

The constant bouts of focused thought I've been enjoying throughout this rescue, the ones I attributed to adrenaline—it was not adrenaline at all.

Or at least not adrenaline alone. It's Focusall—the drug designed to make one feel exactly as I've been feeling. If I'd had a moment to think, I would've realized it sooner. I took a pill, and it has now fully kicked in.

I take in a deep breath and let it out.

Was the bannik right? Are there other ways to get the focus necessary for a vision?

More importantly, can I use the focus from this drug?

"Give me a moment," I tell Felix and close my eyes.

Putting all the noises and the thoughts of my imminent demise out of my mind, I even out my breathing.

So many things can mess this up—like the fact that I already had a vision today, albeit a short one. I've never been able to reach Headspace twice in one day before, but I ignore this fact and breathe slower still.

Now that I know to look for it, I can feel the drug in my system. The "centering" that usually takes many minutes of meditation is on the cusp of my mind.

My palms get very warm.

"Are you okay?" Felix asks, messing up my game.

"Dude." I resist the urge to strangle him. "I need a few seconds of silence. I want to summon a vision to see what we should do next, but I can only do it without distraction—if at all."

"I'm sorry. I just thought it was obvious that we go together."

"We will," I say. "After I do this. The sooner you let me focus, the sooner we can proceed."

"Fine." He looks at his phone. "You have two minutes."

Ignoring that, I close my eyes once more and attempt to focus.

My breathing evens out again, and my mind clears even quicker, but seeking out that special focus for a few seconds yields no results.

I relax my breathing further and let go of the worries about failure.

My palms get warm, and before I can lose focus, lightning explodes in my vision.

CHAPTER THIRTY-ONE

I FLOAT in Headspace for a moment, as though catching my nonexistent breath. Then I bring my attention to the surrounding shapes.

They're the familiar warm, purple, popcorn-tasting roundish octahedrons that brought me the vision of my death before.

How kind of them to be right where I need them.

Maybe Felix was right when he thought that the visions I need might be the very first shapes I encounter upon entry. But if so, how does that work? How do they know I need them?

Setting aside my analysis of Headspace metaphysics, I note that these shapes are subtly different from the ones before.

In fact, even their music is slightly less foreboding than the last time.

"I'm not leaving Headspace until I see this," I

mentally state, as I did the last time, in case an ultimatum helps in any way.

Recalling that excursion, I decide that I need to determine the vision duration.

If I'm to have a second vision in one day, it will need to be short. Yet, if I make this *too* short, it might be as useless as the vision where I saw my name written in Russian—and nothing else.

No.

The vision has to at least be as long as the one in which I died.

Thus determined, I zoom in on the shapes over and over.

Rolling up my imaginary sleeves, I reach out with my nebulous appendage and will it to touch the nearest shape.

It doesn't work, but I've been here before, so I try again.

And again.

And fifty more times.

Have I reached my daily limit after all?

I zoom in once more on the shape. Maybe if the vision is a tad shorter, it will work after all?

I reach out.

Once.

Twice.

On my third try, some kind of metaphorical ice breaks, and I tumble into the shape, like Alice into Wonderland.

FELIX PLACES his hand on the doorknob and determinedly opens the door.

I put a hand on his shoulder to stop him from going without me. Recalling the last vision, I check the clock on my phone. It's 3:27 p.m. It was 3:24 the last time, which is good. The more differences between vision and reality, the better.

Nodding to Felix, I let go of his shoulder.

There's a crack of a door breaking behind us. We look back to see a horde of Johnnies pouring into the room.

Ignoring them, we barge into the room I just unlocked.

Felix locks the door behind us as I verify that the windowless and barren giant room is indeed the one I saw in my vision.

And it is, down to Ariel, who's sitting in the middle eating soup.

We pay no attention to her, however, and point our weapons to the left—the place where the admiral was in my vision.

Muscles bulging under his wife-beater shirt, the admiral is exactly where he should be.

Unfortunately, so is his knife.

I aim the gun at the admiral's frowning forehead and squeeze the trigger.

A glimmer of the hologram screen informs me that Felix aimed his Gomorrah gun at the admiral as well.

Our adversary throws his knife just as I press the trigger.

Felix's gun makes that soft beeping sound that indicates it's been fired.

The admiral's shoulder goes bloody, proving once again that the future likes to follow certain patterns.

It's made me miss his head in exactly the same way again.

This time, however, the admiral doesn't yell something incoherent in Russian.

Instead, he drops dead.

Score. Felix's gun strikes again.

What about the knife?

I'm alive, so it can't be in my throat.

No, wait…

There's a horrific gurgle at my side.

My heart sinking through the floor, I look at Felix.

He's clutching at the fountain of blood pouring from his neck as he collapses to his knees.

"No." I lean over him. "This can't be—"

CHAPTER THIRTY-TWO

I'M BACK in my body.

My neck is knotted tight, and I wish I were in the meditation position after all.

The Focusall in my blood causes my thoughts to race at supersonic speed as I analyze what I just witnessed.

I was in a vision, that much is obvious.

Felix is alive—also obvious.

What I don't get is why the admiral threw the knife quicker this time around. Was it because we wasted a moment locking the door? Or was it because he felt more threatened facing two opponents instead of one? Maybe he was less wary of me in my original vision because I'm a girl?

Opening my eyes, I stare at Felix's worried face.

I want to hug him and shout how glad I am that he's alive, but I resist. He might not care about my vision and insist on coming with me into that room.

That's what I would do in his place.

In fact, that *is* what I am going to do, in a way.

I'm going to go face certain death in that room alone, instead of having Felix die in my stead.

"Did you have your vision?" he asks, his unibrow bunching tighter by the second.

"Yes," I say. "It was trippy—I knew about that previous vision while I was inside *this* vision, but I didn't know I was *having* a vision, which kind of made it seem more real."

That last bit was a lie.

His death was what made it seem all too real, but I'm not going to share *that*.

"Wow," he says. "That is trippy. Now if you managed to do it again, you'd know you had a vision that featured a vision. In general, how do you know that you're not in a vision *right now*?"

"I know," I say, part of my awe not an act. "How do I know my whole adult life isn't some super-long vision the teenage me is currently having on her couch?"

Felix's eyes are wide. "We'll need to discuss this further the next time I take psilocybin. Now isn't the best time."

The clawing and banging on the hallway door intensify, as though in reply to Felix's words.

"Right," I say, continuing to act nonchalant. "Stay here and deal with the Johnnies when they break the door." I nod toward the source of the noise. "I'll go—"

"Wait, what about going together?"

"Can't. Firstly, as I said, that door is about to break

—I saw that in my vision. Second, since I knew I had the prior vision inside this vision, I was able to defeat the admiral without trouble."

Felix frowns.

Is he not buying my story?

Lying is a necessary skill for an illusionist, so I'm very good at it, but Felix has always been a difficult spectator—

The door to the hallway breaks apart, like in my vision.

"Don't let them get into that room!" I shout at Felix. "Else my last vision is useless."

Determination replaces doubt on Felix's face as he aims his gun at the newcomers.

This time, I don't check my phone.

I just place my palm on the doorknob and open the fateful door.

CHAPTER THIRTY-THREE

I BARGE into the same room, again.

I guess it was too much to hope that the room would be different than in my visions.

Raising my gun, I pivot to the left.

The knife is in the admiral's hand. Again.

Instead of shooting at his head, or even aiming, I point the gun at his torso and instantly squeeze the trigger.

Acting differently from the way I had in my visions is my only hope—albeit a faint one.

To that end, I next perform a maneuver I've only seen in movies—the one where a G.I. Joe type throws himself to the side and rolls to avoid enemy fire.

The admiral's knife slices through my ear, cleaving it nearly in half.

I land on the floor, all air escaping my lungs as my vision blurs with black-and-white blotches.

The only thing that rolls is my gun—away from me.

I do my best to suck in some oxygen.

The admiral is yelling something incoherent in Russian again.

I must've shot him, like in my visions, but didn't kill him. If I were a betting woman, I'd bet the bullet hit his shoulder again—stubborn future being what it is.

Ignoring the agonizing stinging and burning of my cut ear, I force a few breaths into my damaged ribcage.

Breathing hurts worse than my ear. My ribs must either be cracked or broken.

Clenching my jaws, I take in another breath.

When the blotches slow their dancing in my vision, I glance at the admiral and grunt in frustration—which causes my ribs to scream once more.

The wounded asshole is walking my way, a knife clutched in his undamaged left hand.

I was right about his shoulder injury.

At first, I wonder if this is a second knife, but then I see a bloody trail on the floor. He went to pick up *this* knife—which somehow seems extra sinister. Then again, at least he didn't pick up my gun.

Then I recall what Maya said he likes to do to women with this very knife, and I gulp in another agonizing breath.

No.

I didn't beat my original crap future just to die from that stupid knife a little later and a lot more painfully.

If I *am* going to die, I'd rather he choke or shoot me.

A crazy plan congeals in my mind, and I pretend to meekly crawl away from him. In reality, I use the bigger motion of crawling to cover the two smaller movements of my hands going into my pockets.

With my still-bleeding ear stinging and my ribs howling in pain, acting pathetic is extremely easy.

My performance must impress the admiral. Grinning menacingly, he looms over me with his knife outstretched and his pants bulging for reasons I'd rather not think about.

I crawl another inch and moan proportionally to my pain.

His grin widens as he bends lower, and a whiff of garlic hits my nostrils as he rolls me over.

I rip my hands from my pockets and spring the cards into his face.

My gambit works. As the cards fly at his face like starving butterflies at nectar, he tries to swat them away.

Which is why he misses it when I slash his weapon-wielding arm with Ariel's M9 knife.

My disgust mixes with satisfaction as the knife slices through meaty flesh and crunchy tendon.

The admiral's animalistic cry of pain is music to my ears.

I slash at his leg, then raise my knife higher and stab his foot.

He starts to topple onto me.

No, not topple.

Despite his wounds, he's trying to perform a wrestling maneuver.

My ribs revolt as I throw myself to the side.

His elbow lands an inch away from my chin.

He grunts but recovers surprisingly quickly, reaching for my throat with his injured hands.

If he came down to the ground on purpose and not because his injured leg couldn't hold him, it was a strategic mistake.

Now that I can reach it, I stab his torso with my knife, avoiding his grasping hands.

The blade penetrates something squishy, and there's much more disgust in my satisfaction this time as he cries out in pain.

Gritting my teeth, I recall what happened to me in my first vision, and stab the admiral again.

His yelping stops, but his hands are still twitching, as if reaching for me.

I remind myself what he did to Felix in my second vision, and stab him again, driving the knife deeper this time.

He goes limp.

Ignoring the anguished screams of my ribs, I stab him one last time—just in case.

A soup bowl hits the floor in the distance.

At least I assume that's what the sound is, since Ariel was eating soup in my vision.

Did all the bleeding and stabbing finally ruin her appetite?

Leaving the knife buried in the admiral's chest, I struggle to my feet and face my friend.

My ribs hurt so much I'm sick and dizzy from the

pain—though it could be the blood loss from my cleaved ear.

Ariel is walking toward me briskly, her expression unreadable under those aviator sunglasses.

"What's with the sunglasses?" I ask loudly, even as an awful intuition grows in my gut.

She doesn't reply.

Instead, she picks up her pace and rushes at me, her movements erratic and exaggerated, just like in my prior vision.

"Ariel, stop." I back away.

She moves even faster, swiftly closing the distance between us.

Reaching me, she slams her palms into my chest with all her super strength.

As I fly back, my Focusall-enhanced perception informs me that this is it.

Once I hit the floor at this speed, I'm dead.

CHAPTER THIRTY-FOUR

FOR THE FIRST TIME TODAY, I get lucky.

Instead of a cement floor, the admiral's bloody corpse breaks my fall.

The agony from my ribs, though, makes me wish I weren't so "lucky."

In the next moment, Ariel looms over me.

My survival instinct kicks in, and I grasp her glasses, ripping them from her face.

Ariel's eyes are filled with the same black energy I saw in the intact eye of the Johnny in the hallway.

I now recall where else I've seen this kind of energy, and all the pieces of this twisted mosaic click into place.

"You need me alive," I say on a hunch.

Even if my theory is correct, I have no idea if talking to Ariel will work.

"It's not personal, Sasha," Ariel says, and her usually sexy lilt sounds androgynous and ancient, the words pronounced with a thick Russian accent. "It's strictly business."

To emphasize that message, Ariel's hands grab my throat.

Another person looking to strangle me?

Did I bring this on when I thought that I'd rather be choked than stabbed to death?

I try to pry the strangling hands away, but I might as well try to bend steel pipes.

"Was that another one of your quotes from *The Godfather*?" I say, figuring if I keep her talking, maybe she won't squeeze. "If this is about those eggs I sent via the messenger, I'm very sorry."

What I don't add is that if it *is* about the eggs, it *would* be personal.

"I can't be seen as weak," my enemy says through Ariel's mouth. "That can be deadly in my world."

"Letting me live won't make you look weak," I say, and for all I know, this might be true.

"You've made a fool of me, repeatedly," she says as her fingers tighten on my throat. Glancing at the admiral, she mutters, "He was the human figurehead of my operation."

"You could knock me up and keep me in a comatose state for the duration of the pregnancy, like those gangsters you've been using," I choke out as I continue to tug uselessly at the strangling hands. "Don't you think that would be a fate worse than death?"

"You're a smooth talker." She squeezes harder as I kick out, struggling despite the futility of it—and my natural reluctance to hurt my friend. Grinning, she pins my kicking legs down. "Too bad I don't have any more patience for you."

I want to tell her that the Council won't like me getting killed, and that Nero might be slightly irked as well, but I can't reply as my air supply is now completely cut off.

Maybe it's good I didn't raise that objection. She might then decide to do a major cleanup once I'm dead, killing Vlad, Rose, Fluffster, Ariel, and Felix as potential witnesses.

And if she did that, it might work. Nero and the Council might never find out what happened.

The fingers squeeze harder, but clearly not super-strength-hard, as that would crush my neck.

Is she trying to make my death slower?

Not personal, my foot.

My struggling body convulses as my vision goes white and my lungs feel like they're about to burst.

I thrash harder, even as my body weakens.

There's a sound behind us—though it could be an auditory hallucination of my oxygen-deprived brain.

"What are you doing?" a voice that might be Felix's says or screams in some faraway land.

Ariel's mouth tightens, and the pressure on my throat intensifies.

"You're going to kill her!" Felix shouts. "Stop, now!"

She doesn't.

My consciousness begins to float away.

There's a distant beeping sound, and the strangling fingers loosen on my throat.

I gulp in an agonizing breath as Ariel slumps to the floor next to me, exposing a view of Felix clutching his Gomorrah gun with shaking hands.

"No," I want to scream, but I don't have any air to do so. "You killed Ariel."

CHAPTER THIRTY-FIVE

MY NEXT FRANTIC inhale hurts so badly that it reminds me of the time I breathed in New York Harbor water. I ignore the physical pain, though.

The emotional one is so much worse.

Felix runs up and crouches next to me, worriedly looking me over.

"Please let this be another vision," I want to say, but nothing comes out of my swollen throat.

Ariel can't be dead.

I wouldn't be able to bear it.

Wishing I could rub my eyes, I suck in another excruciating breath and try to roll onto my side.

Shouldn't this much pain short-circuit a vision?

Uncaring, the nightmare continues unabated.

I want to shout but still can't.

How could Felix do this? Granted, it probably looked like Ariel was killing me—which she was—so he made a terrible choice.

A part of me wants to pity him, while another part wishes I could punch him in the face.

"Why was she doing that?" Felix says, as though echoing my earlier train of thought.

His voice sounds hollow, but he doesn't seem shaken enough, given the severity of the situation.

I drag in another torturous breath.

Some of my lightheadedness and nausea abates, so I double down on oxygen despite the pain.

"How could you?" I finally manage to croak out. "You should've let her kill me. Anything is better than—"

"What are you talking about?" He peers into my eyes. "She's not dead."

I stare back uncomprehendingly.

"This gun has a nonlethal mode." Felix offers me a hand, and I grasp it, squeezing his palm like a woman during labor as I struggle to a sitting position.

"She's alive?"

"She's going to be out of commission for a few hours, but then she'll come to her senses—and hopefully explain what the hell she was doing with her hands around your throat. Is that how bad her blood withdrawal is?"

"No." My breaths suddenly seem less painful. The good news must be flooding my body with the much-needed endorphins. "It was Baba Yaga who was doing that," I croak out. "Remember when I told you about how she tried to use some black energy to take over my mind when I went to see her with Fluffster?"

Felix nods.

"Well, I was protected at the time, but Ariel wasn't, so Baba Yaga must've used that trick on her."

"That makes so much sense." Still holding my hand, Felix stands and tries to pull me to my feet. "Those gangbangers in hospital clothing must be in the same boat."

"I suspect so." I shakily stand, stifling a yelp of pain. After I catch my breath again, I rasp out, "They probably started off as enemies of the Russian mob, but then Baba Yaga took over and turned enemies into mind-raped helpers." As I speak, I sway on my feet. Standing is feasible, but just barely.

"It all makes sense now," I continue hoarsely. "The glasses were hiding the black mojo in their eyes. I bet it's so that Baga Yaga's human goons don't realize that her brainwiped minions are obeying her due to supernatural means; she'd be breaking the Mandate in that case."

I let go of Felix's hand to see if I can stand on my own.

It works, but it's torture.

I take a small step.

Nope.

This is torture.

My ribs seem to be poking the pain center in my brain with a hot iron, and my throat feels like I've swallowed an obese porcupine.

"That's all great, but we better get out of here." Felix gives the door he came through a paranoid glance.

"Right," I croak, and take another careful step. "How do we do that?"

"You take her legs, and I'll take her arms," Felix says and grabs Ariel's wrists.

Do I tell him that I'm barely standing?

First, I should at least try his plan.

I bend over and can't help but gasp in pain.

I change my mind again. *This* should make it onto the list of things forbidden by the Geneva Convention.

"You okay?" Felix asks. "I can—"

"You can't carry her by yourself." Gritting my teeth, I steel myself against a wave of nauseating agony and grab Ariel's ankles. "Let's go."

As soon I lift my end, I have to bite my tongue in order to stay silent.

"What's the plan?" I rasp out when the worst of the pain and dizziness subsides. "Please tell me you have one."

"We take her to the car?" he suggests uncertainly. "Maybe figure things out from there."

"What about Vlad?" Biting my cheek, I lower Ariel to the floor and tap my earbud. "Vlad, we have Ariel. How are things going on your end?"

There's a hiss of static in my ear, followed by a noise that brings to mind Dante's Fifth Circle of Hell—the one dedicated to the sin of wrath. Things crunch and rip, and liquids gush on the other end of the line before Vlad says, "I'm busy. Get her out. That's why we came."

"You want us to leave you?" Felix says, pale from the hellish sounds.

"We're not leaving anybody," I say firmly.

"Get out," Vlad says. "It's an order. You're supposed to only ask 'how high,' remember?"

Another hiss emanates from the earbud. "Vlad," Rose croaks out, sounding like she's the one who's been choked. "You *have* to come back to me."

"I will, my love." The gentleness of Vlad's tone contrasts with the sounds of ongoing decapitations in the background. "I have to keep Baba Yaga's army in this room while Sasha and Felix make their escape. Once they're out, I'll have more options."

"In that case, we go." Ignoring my growing need to pass out, I lift Ariel's legs again. "Vlad, sorry for the delay. I'll keep this line open so we can tell you we're out as soon as we leave this cursed warehouse."

"Good," Vlad says, and a bout of static tells me he's muted his end.

Rose mutes hers too; not that she can say much, having damaged her vocal cords with all that screaming.

With painful, shuffling steps, I make my way to the door and lead with my back as we exit.

The room is littered with unmoving Johnnies.

"Did you use the nonlethal mode on *them*?" I ask as I step over one bare-assed body.

"No," Felix says without meeting my gaze. "Nonlethal eats up ten times the battery power, and I wanted to make sure I didn't run out of juice in the middle of everything."

"That's cold," I croak admiringly and put Ariel down to catch my breath. "Where do we go now?"

Felix puts his side of Ariel on the floor and pulls out his phone. He taps at the screen for a few seconds, then shoots it with his power and shows it to me.

There's a schematic of a warehouse on the screen.

"I think we should go this way," Felix says, and a red line appears on the map.

"Let's get going then." I bend over to pick up Ariel's legs again.

My earbud hisses, and Rose's barely audible voice says, "Hurry."

"Of course." I grab Ariel's ankles.

"Felix, what are you doing?" Rose mutters.

My heart rate speeding up, I look up at Felix.

Eyes wide, Felix is pointing his gun at me.

CHAPTER THIRTY-SIX

ACTUALLY, he's aiming at something above me, I realize when he squeezes the trigger and I don't lose consciousness.

I turn to see another Johnny plop onto an already-huge pile of hospital-gown-clad corpses.

We grab our burden and resume our escape, with Felix leading the way.

The door he wants to take is locked, so we set Ariel down again and I use my lock picks to open it.

There's a noise behind us.

We turn to see another Johnny burst into the room.

He trips over the corpses of his colleagues and goes splat.

Felix finishes the man off, then grabs Ariel's legs, as though putting down attackers is old hat to him.

"If we survive, remind me to tell Ariel to lose some weight," he mutters as we lift her again.

"You wouldn't dare say such a thing to her," I rasp out in mock horror. "Besides, she's in perfect shape."

"That was a joke." Felix stops next to another door. "Can you open this?"

"A lady's weight is not a joking matter." I use my lock picks to defeat another lock. "Nor is her age."

"Got it." Felix grabs Ariel, and we proceed through a hallway until we face another lock.

I defeat the door and look behind us.

My bleeding ear has left a macabre trail behind us.

Can Johnnies—or Baba Yaga—take advantage of that?

I rip off a sleeve and wrap it around my head in an effort to stop the bleeding.

There better be some gain from this pain.

Felix goes into the room first and clears it of a couple of Johnnies.

We resume carrying Ariel until we reach the door, which I open as I have the others.

Two more rooms, three hallways, five locks, and seven dead Johnnies later, we face a door that says "EXIT" in big neon-green letters.

"The car is here." Felix shows me the schematic on his screen, with a dotted line leading from the parking lot to the door we're about to use.

"You didn't have to map that. It's just a few yards."

But he's not listening. "Are you hearing that?" he asks with a deep frown.

I strain both my injured and my undamaged ear.

There's a noise that sounds like the pitter-patter of bare running feet.

Must be a bunch of Johnnies approaching us. Is Vlad having trouble keeping them all in that room? Assuming Vlad is still alive, that is—a terrible thought I put aside for the moment.

"Let's run," I say and open the door.

The bright afternoon sun momentarily hurts my eyes, and the sounds of the approaching horde of Johnnies are more noticeable now.

We grab Ariel and haul ass.

As I huff and puff the short distance to the parking lot, my pain reaches the Mandate ceremony levels—and this time, I can't afford to pass out.

"Should we take Vlad's Tesla or steal one of these?" I wheeze-pant, pointing at a bunch of less fancy cars sprinkled around the parking lot.

"You don't care that those belong to the Russian mob?" Felix pants back. "Some of them might be stolen, and the last thing we need is to get stopped by the cops."

"Tesla it is," I gasp out.

"Yeah." Felix sucks in a breath. "It will also be the easiest for me to—"

He stops talking as the stampede of Johnnies streams out of the warehouse like hungry locusts attacking an uncut lawn. Their hospital gowns are covered in blood, supporting my earlier suspicion about them coming from that horrible room where Vlad is fighting Koschei and the rest of the Johnnies.

At least their sunglasses fit their environment now; I could use a pair myself.

An arc of Felix's magenta technomancer energy slams into Vlad's Tesla.

Channeling Frankenstein, the car violently comes to life, leaving skid marks on the pavement as it speeds toward the Johnnies.

There's a look of intense concentration on Felix's face.

The Johnnies scatter like paranoid quail, but the car runs over a couple. Instead of staying down, they crawl toward us on their broken limbs.

The Tesla makes a sharp, two-more-Johnnies-destroying turn and rushes at us.

Resisting the urge to drop Ariel and run, I stand still as the car speeds up and stops a heart-attack-inducing inch away from us.

"Let's get her in," Felix says, and the back doors of the Tesla automagically rise.

Getting an unconscious friend into the back of a car is harder than it sounds, and we waste a few precious seconds making sure we're not about to kill Ariel after going to all this trouble to save her.

I spare the remaining Johnnies a glance; they've regrouped and are almost upon us.

Felix jumps into the passenger seat, so I take the driver's side.

Before I can buckle up or put my hands on the wheel, the car jerks forward of its own—or rather, Felix's—volition.

The electric car is eerily silent considering the speed with which we rocket out of the parking lot.

A revving of engines behind us breaks the silence.

Since I'm not actually driving this thing, I look back.

Every car that was previously standing in the parking lot is now following us—at least one Johnny in each.

Ignoring Baba Yaga's mind-puppets for the moment, I tap the earbud and say, "Vlad, we left the building."

No response.

"Vlad?" I say. "Rose?"

There's a hiss of static, and I hear Rose try to say something, but her hoarse words are unintelligible with the noise of our pursuit and the beating of my pulse in my ears.

"Take over the driving," Felix orders and shoots his magenta energy at the big screen in the dashboard.

"Wait!" I shout as our car swerves—and barrels straight at the nearby streetlamp.

CHAPTER THIRTY-SEVEN

I GRASP the steering wheel so hard my ribs scream in pain. Pulling the wheel all the way to the left, I slam on the brakes.

We skid and just barely miss the obstacle.

In the back, Ariel rolls from the seat onto the floor with a loud thud.

A car with a Johnny careens at the streetlamp I dodged, and turns into a pancake.

I get our car under control, and when both it and my heart rate even out, I see why Felix nearly killed us.

He put the view from Vlad's webcam on his gun screen, and it is indeed like the Fifth Circle of Hell.

Koschei is missing both arms, but he's trying to bite Vlad with his teeth—so Vlad punches him so hard the teeth fly in every direction. Koschei then tries to headbutt Vlad, so Vlad rips his head off—though, of course, it's too much to hope that Koschei will stay down for long. With a practiced viciousness, Vlad proceeds to kill a slew of attacking Johnnies while Koschei is resurrecting.

Vlad must've done this over and over. Shreds of hospital gowns and a variety of Koschei and Johnny body parts cover every surface—making the battlefield look like the playroom of a serial killer surgeon with a penchant for modern art.

Even the ceiling is covered in blood.

What I can see of Vlad's arms through the camera is also not looking great.

His clothes are torn and his pale skin is covered with multiple layers of viscera—hopefully none of it his.

A muscle-bound Johnny tries to get uppity and grabs Vlad's shirt, so Vlad rips into his throat with his teeth.

"Is he drinking blood in the middle of all this?" Felix mutters, his face pre-fainting pale.

"He might need the extra calories or whatever it is the vamps need from blood," I reply. "Turn that off or you'll faint."

Felix dismisses the grisly feed but still looks like he might pass out at any moment.

"Where are we headed?" he asks, probably to distract himself.

"Vlad clearly lied about the ease of escaping that room to make us leave." I take a deep breath. "So, though I hate to have to do this, I don't see any other choice." I decelerate and make a sharp turn. "I'm going to ask Nero for help."

Felix exhales a relieved breath, and I debate if I should call him a traitorous Nero sympathizer or a—

A Johnny uses my decrease in speed to his advantage and bumps us from behind, giving my already miserable neck whiplash.

"Hit the gas," Felix says and shoots his energy at the upcoming red light.

I do so, and the stoplight changes from red to green.

"Shouldn't it be called 'the buzz' in an electric car?" I ask, mostly so that I myself don't pass out from the pain in my ribs.

"The official term is 'the accelerator,'" Felix says, and makes the streetlight turn red behind us.

The Johnny—or Baba Yaga controlling him— doesn't heed the red-light and promptly gets skewered by a huge truck that was probably headed for the many warehouses surrounding the place.

"Dude." I give Felix a worried glance. "Don't hurt innocent bystanders."

My friend takes out his phone, does some technomagic, and says, "The driver is fine. He has good insurance. We can send him a big check later as well."

"Good," I say. Then to my own phone's AI assistant, I reluctantly issue a verbal "Videocall Nero" command.

Felix is so eager for me to talk to Nero that he moves my call from the phone onto the dashboard screen.

The phone rings and rings.

Oh, no.

When I stormed into Nero's office the last time,

Venessa said he was in Europe for a few days. Is he still there?

Racking my brain for a plan B, or even C, I come up with bupkis.

The engine-revving sound is back.

I go on full alert and spot two Johnnies in two different muscle cars, one in each rearview mirror.

"Use your gun," I tell Felix. "It's silent."

"But deadly," he says, pulling out his Gomorrah weapon.

I floor the buzz/gas pedal.

Felix rolls down his window.

A Johnny tries to slam into us on the right.

Felix's gun beeps.

The death ray must hit the rightmost Johnny; his Jaguar slams into a row of parked rental bicycles.

"Duck!" Felix yells.

"How can I duck and drive at the same time?" is what I want to say, but I comply instead.

The leftmost Johnny bumps against our side.

If we survive all this, will Vlad kill me for the damage to his fancy car?

Felix's gun beeps again.

I lift my head and spare the leftmost Johnny a glance. He slumps onto the steering wheel, his sunglasses gone.

The driverless car goes wild, veering toward us.

I accelerate.

There's a screech of metal and plastic as it scrapes our back flank.

Yep. Vlad will not be pleased.

Flooring the accelerator again, I fly onto the highway ramp and dodge a Toyota Camry as I switch into the middle lane.

"I'll take over driving for the time being," Felix says, his tone subdued. "You might want to actually talk to your Mentor."

I'm glad Felix takes over, because what I see on the dashboard makes me let go of the wheel.

It's Nero, his face dark with fury.

"You're bleeding," he says in a voice that brings to mind a hangry Tyrannosaurus.

"Worse than just bleeding," I croak out. "I need help."

"First things first." Is that worry on Nero's features? I must be concussed. "Detail your injuries."

"My ribs hurt," I rasp out. "My ear is cut and my—"

"That's enough," Nero says. "Where are you?"

"Driving on I-278 East."

"Let me rephrase," Nero says impatiently. "Where are you going, and when will you be there?"

"Our apartment, and we're fifteen minutes away, depending on traffic," Felix says. "But we could come to your—"

"Go home. I'll meet you there," Nero says sternly. "And make it ten minutes." He locks eyes with Felix.

"Yes, sir," Felix replies immediately. He visibly concentrates for a moment, and the car torpedoes forward.

"I need to get some things in order," Nero says. "Will call back as soon as my arrangements are made."

"Wait—" I start, but the call is already disconnected.

"Don't kill us," I whisper to Felix as I watch the other cars and the trees whoosh by.

Ignoring the stabbing sensation in my ribs, I buckle my seat belt.

Felix doesn't slow down. Whatever threat he saw in Nero's eyes must scare him more than the prospect of a mere car crash.

At least the road is clear; otherwise, we'd crash for sure. As is, we just have a ninety-five-percent chance of crashing—give or take a few percent. Mostly give.

When we whoosh by the toll station before the tunnel, I fully expect to slam into one of the booths, but Felix somehow manages to pass by them.

In the rearview mirror, I spot a sports car with three Johnnies passing the turnstile without paying.

Unfortunately, no one stops them—though whoever owns the car will get a juicy ticket in the mail.

"I can lose them in the tunnel," Felix says, shooting the Gomorrah gun at the pursuers without much luck.

My phone rings. It's a video call from Nero, which I accept.

Felix puts the call on the screen again.

"Hello?" Nero says. "Sasha?"

"We're in the tunnel," I say. "Might get disconnected at any moment."

"Sasha?" Nero says louder. "Tell me how you got hurt. Who do I—"

He gets cuts off, so I have no idea if he was about to say "kill" or "call" or "thank."

"Baba Yaga," I reply, just in case he can still hear me. "Did I lose you?"

Nero doesn't reply. His video image is pixelated and frozen on the screen.

Judging by that one frame of the video, Nero is inside a limo with two people: a man and a woman. The unfamiliar man is pale and wearing all black with sunglasses that I've come to associate with Vlad's Enforcers.

Is Nero bringing a vampire to help clean up my mess?

The woman, on the other hand, looks familiar, though all the adrenaline makes it hard for me to recall where I've seen this bewitchingly exotic beauty.

Then it hits me. She's the doctor (or maybe nurse) who always comes to the fund during the free cholesterol checks and other preventative health initiatives Nero's HR people regularly organize. I've always seen her in scrubs instead of the cocktail dress she's wearing, which is what threw me off, but this is her.

The last time I saw her was during a blood drive a few months back.

Was she collecting blood for vampires, by any chance?

"Take over the driving for a sec," Felix says, bringing me back to the reality of our high-speed pursuit. "I want to get them off our tail."

Even grasping the wheel hurts my stupid ribs, but I ignore the pain and glue my gaze to the road in front of me.

Felix points his gun behind us and curses.

In the rearview mirror, I see the car with three Johnnies behind a minivan.

We slow down, even though I didn't touch the brake.

I guess Felix only gave me the steering.

The Johnnies/Baba Yaga must know what Felix is up to, because they slow down and put a sedan between us.

Felix trains his gun on them, speeds us up, and waits.

The Johnnies slow down again, putting another car between us.

"Fine," Felix says. "We'll just lose them then."

The speedometer threatens to roll over as we leap forward at NASCAR speed.

My road intuition hands in the towel, and I readjust my earlier crash probability estimate to 99.999999%.

CHAPTER THIRTY-EIGHT

FELIX MIRACULOUSLY PASSES every car in front of us without crashing.

I see the light at the end of the tunnel—unless, of course, we've already crashed and that's the *other* kind of light at the end of a tunnel.

We whoosh out of the tunnel in an eyeblink.

Felix signals a right turn and slows down to just five times the speed limit.

We fly through the turn and barrel down a street at the same breakneck pace.

With a rev of engine, the car with three Johnnies appears on our right.

My phone rings again.

Felix shoots his gun at our adversaries, and one of the three falls inside the car—except it's not the driver.

I tell my phone's AI to accept the call without looking.

"Sasha," Nero's voice says from the screen. "What—"

I miss what Nero says next because the Johnnies ram us from the right.

The force of the impact jerks me in my seat, and my ribs crack in a few new places.

Favorite episodes from my life swirl through my adrenaline-soaked brain.

Felix and I must be sharing control of the wheel; that's the only way to explain why we don't steer off the road.

The Johnnies slam into us again.

The passenger-side windows shatter into little pieces.

Nero is yelling unhelpful curses and chilling threats from the speakers.

With rubber burning and pieces of Tesla falling off, we careen onto our street.

The Johnnies follow.

Felix speeds us up.

If Vlad feels murderous about the condition of his poor car, he might not have anyone to take the rage out on.

The revving of the Johnnies' car gets louder.

We're half a block away from our building's entrance when the non-driver Johnny starts to climb out of the back window of their car—the one nearest us.

The wind resistance blows his sunglasses away, but Baba Yaga doesn't care, so his body climbs farther out.

Then the driver pulls on the wheel, and my road

intuition—or common sense—predicts what's about to happen.

He's about to—

The driver-Johnny rams us again, which, as I feared, causes the stunt-double Johnny to fly from his car window into what's left of ours.

He lands in the back seat of our car, and Felix turns to shoot the newcomer.

The Johnny grabs a jagged piece of crumpled metal separating the ruined windows, showing no sign of pain from it cutting his hand to the bone.

"Felix, duck!" I scream, but it's too late.

The Johnny slices through Felix's gun-holding hand with the sharp piece of debris.

Felix drops the gun, and the Johnny slashes his face.

Felix screams in pain, clutching at the bleeding wound.

The Johnny's makeshift blade swipes at my neck next, missing by a hair.

I realize I'd already started screaming a few seconds ago, so I just scream louder.

"Whoever you are, this is Nero Gorin speaking." My former boss's voice booms over our screams. The adrenaline must be playing tricks with my mind because Nero's tone seems more frightening than our situation. "You will cease your aggression against me and mine *right now*."

The Johnny freezes.

His black-filled eyes stare at Nero's image on the

screen intently; then Baba Yaga shouts something through the man's lips in Russian.

Nero barks something back—also in Russian.

I steer the car toward our quickly approaching apartment building and fight the urge to ask someone why and how Nero speaks Russian.

Baba Yaga's speech speeds up; she sounds conciliatory but firm.

Nero's seemingly fluent replies are as scary as the prospect of the crash.

Baba Yaga says something challengingly.

Nero's next reply is shorter, and this time, he tones down the violence in his voice by a small fraction.

"Fine," Baba Yaga says in English as the Johnny faces me. "Looks like you managed to be useful to me, after all."

Before I can reply, she causes the Johnny to slice his own throat with his makeshift weapon.

His colleagues' car's brakes screech, and at the same time, my earbud hisses.

"They all stopped fighting," Vlad says in a confused tone. "Even Koschei. Whatever you did—"

I don't hear the rest of Vlad's great news because I see a ten-year-old boy jaywalking right in front of us in a typical New Yorker manner.

I try to brake and find that I can't.

"Felix, brake!" I shout.

He doesn't.

I spare him a glance. He's passed out from either the blood loss, or the sight of said blood.

I jerk the wheel as far left as my ribs allow—which puts us on a trajectory to collide with the doors of our apartment building.

I pump the brakes.

Nothing.

I scream for Felix to wake up.

Nothing.

Nero calls out blood-chilling threats at Felix if he doesn't brake right now—but even that doesn't work.

The front entrance of my building grows to encompass the whole universe.

With a shower of broken metal, plastic, and glass, we slam into the doors.

My head whips forward from the impact as the airbag punches me in the face and the seatbelt crushes my aching ribs.

The mostly glass door doesn't slow us, however, and our car rockets through the lobby, right into the wall with the elevator door.

The sound of metal and plastic compressing is apocalyptically loud.

"This isn't survivable," I'd say in that last moment if I could still talk.

Instead, I blank out.

CHAPTER THIRTY-NINE

AN ARMY of nails claw at a planet-sized chalkboard.

Am I dreaming, or are these the sounds you hear in the afterlife?

Masculine fingers gently brush my face.

That's not very afterlife-like, but who knows.

A pleasant energy flows through me, and I feel my broken bones begin mending.

Then my cuts and bruises get erased in a familiar sensation.

I felt this kind of warm energy after I battled Beatrice—when some anonymous healer made me look presentable for the Council.

My ear becomes whole again, and my neck bruises and broken ribs are but a distant memory.

The pleasurable relaxation spreads into every repaired muscle, and I exhale a relieved breath.

"That's it," Nero croons nearby. "Isis will take care of you."

ISIS? Like the terrorists? Is Nero saying that my long abstinence has turned me back into a virgin, and that I'm in Heaven to be an ISIS member's reward? Doesn't that make this Heaven a Hell for me? And why would anyone want virgins in Heaven in the first place? If my version of Heaven had to include forty sex objects—which is a big *if*—they would have to be hot dudes with a ton of varied experience, but without STDs and with—

My concussed mind gets clearer. It's as though I've gotten a massage, used a banya (one not owned by Baba Yaga), and then slept for fifty hours, all in a span of seconds.

The fingers on my face add to the slew of pleasant sensations as they send sparks of purely feminine awareness down my body.

I sigh in pleasure.

Someone clears her throat.

I open my eyes as Nero, who's crouching next to me, pulls his hand away.

He was the one stroking my face?

I take it back. It wasn't as pleasant as I thought.

It didn't turn me on. Nope.

I turn my head slightly and see the nurse/doctor from Nero's limo. She has a Mandate aura and is shooting an arc of golden energy at me.

She must be a Cognizant healer, judging by how that energy makes me feel.

The Enforcer from the limo is here too, his reaction hard to read with the sunglasses and the stone-carved face.

Basking in the glow from the healing energy, I glance around.

I'm still sitting in the driver's seat, buckled in, but there's no car around me. Instead, what remains of the Tesla looks like a paper that's been run through a shredder over and over by a spy who wanted to make sure the secret information would never see the light of day.

In fact, I've seen shredded chunks of matter like this before—only it was orc flesh instead of Tesla remnants.

Did Nero do his claw-ripping thing to get to me? Were those the sounds that woke me?

Before I can ask him, my gaze falls on Felix, and the pleasant relaxation evaporates, replaced by an arctic chill in my belly.

Still in his own seat, buckled in like I am, Felix is covered in blood, with his limbs at odd angles.

If he saw himself now, he would definitely faint.

Forgetting Nero and the golden energy still being shot at me, I unbuckle my seatbelt and jump up to check on Felix.

His shallow breathing is slowing with each faint inhale.

My panicked gaze falls on Ariel, who's lying in the rubble behind the seats.

Without a seatbelt to hold her still, she's in an even worse shape than Felix—and her staying intact at all is probably the most impressive feat of her super strength.

"Can I stop?" the woman asks Nero.

"Yes," he says. "She looks much better."

The healing energy stops streaming at me—and even through the stress, I feel its loss.

Urgently, I turn to the woman. "Please do that same healing thing for my friends."

Instead of complying, she glances at Nero.

"One sec, Isis," he says, unruffled. "Sasha and I need to reach an understanding first."

The healer—Isis—nods and runs her delicate hand through her glossy black hair, looking vaguely bored.

"Heal them!" I shout at her, stunned by her indifference. "They're dying."

Isis looks at Nero again, so I pivot to face him.

His expression is unreadable, but the limbal rings in his eyes are extra dark and thick.

"Their fate is in your hands." His voice is low and deep as he steps toward me.

I suppress a torrent of violent urges, allowing myself only a fantasy of slapping his manipulative face.

It's obvious what he wants: his Sasha-shaped golden goose to lord over again. And I don't have a choice but to give in. I'd do anything to get my friends healed, even make a deal with the devil himself.

Then again, no one says I can't do this on my terms.

Angling my body in such a way that Isis and the Enforcer vamp can't see what I'm about to do, I walk toward Nero, staring him down.

He holds my gaze—which is good, because he

doesn't see my hand sneak into my pocket and come out with the FELLATIO device palmed within.

"I'll come back to work," I tell him. "And you can resume being my Mentor—even if that means sending some more orc goons to beat me up."

His mouth tightens, and his eyes narrow dangerously.

Good. I've got his attention.

"Do you need me to swear an oath?" I stop within kissing distance of him and say softly, "Or was there more that you wanted… *boss?*"

Without waiting for a reply, I reach toward his groin area with both hands.

His body tenses like a predator about to leap at prey.

Hoping he's distracted enough, I carefully deliver the palmed device into his pant pocket and continue the motion, brushing my fingers very gently across his crotch.

Eeek. My breath hitches, and heat floods my cheeks.

There's a bulge there I don't recall seeing earlier.

I snatch my hands away, as if from a venomous snake.

A very *big* snake.

A python, maybe? Wait, those aren't venomous.

He catches my wrists before I can pull them away. His fingers are warm and impossibly strong, his grip unbreakable.

He leans in, his hot breath wafting over my neck as he growls, "The status quo is all that's required of you."

I expect him to add a "for now," but he lets go of my wrists and steps out of my reach.

I back away, staring at him as I attempt to catch my breath. My wrists still feel the ghostly imprint of his touch, and my pulse is way too fast.

It was all a charade, so why is a part of me disappointed that he pulled away?

Thankfully, the rest of me wants to smack that part on the head before giving her a sanity check, a timeout, and a cold shower.

"Proceed," Nero says to Isis and the vampire.

Isis points her hand at Felix, and the vampire slices open his wrist with his fangs.

"Wait," I say. "No vampire blood for Ariel."

The two look at Nero, and he nods.

Isis points her energy at Ariel, and the vamp walks toward Felix.

"I'm not sure I want Felix drinking that poison either," I say.

"I'm nearly tapped out," Isis says to Nero. "It will be nine hundred to do both."

"You're going to charge me a premium?" Nero raises an eyebrow. "You don't think it's too steep? You're going to be pretty much tapped out regardless."

"But with two, I'll feel like shit afterward," Isis says. "*That* costs extra."

"Fine," Nero says. "Hurry up before one of them dies."

As they talk, the vampire's wrist closes up.

Isis demonstratively sighs before pointing her right hand at Ariel and left one at Felix.

The golden energy streams at both of my friends.

Almost instantly, their grievous wounds close up and broken limbs straighten.

Isis's healthy olive skin tone pales, and some gray hair pops out of nowhere on her temples.

Felix's throat produces a disturbing moan, and Isis stops his treatment with a knowing smirk.

Felix jolts up and looks around with wild eyes.

"You okay?" I ask him.

"Yeah." He doesn't sound certain. "You?"

"Peachy," I say with as much sarcasm you can cram into the name of a fruit.

He nods, and we both stare at Ariel.

She looks whole again, but she isn't moving or making sounds.

Isis stops the healing energy, shakes her right hand a few times as though to improve blood circulation, and then shoots Ariel again.

Ariel still doesn't come to.

"She was knocked out with this," Felix says, picking his mangled Gomorrah gun out from the rubble. "I'm not sure you can get her out of *that*."

"Let's get her inside their apartment and figure things out from there." Nero looks at what used to be the apartment building entrance.

Following his gaze, I see emergency vehicles gathering.

Did someone call 911?

It's likely. After all—

Powerful arms grab me without any warning.

"Hey," I shout at Nero—who's got me in the same new-bride grip he used when I passed out during my presentation at his conference. "I can walk."

"You're still weak from the treatment," he says, ignoring my ineffectual struggles as he strides toward the staircase.

Felix and Isis trail after us, and the vampire carries Ariel the way Nero is carrying me.

Fine. Whatever. The elevator is probably broken from the collision, and I don't particularly want to schlep up all those stairs. Still, this is not the ideal scenario by any means.

I don't like how good it feels to be held by these strong arms. Don't appreciate how inappropriately yummy Nero smells, or how—

Nope. Must think about something else.

Anything else.

How much is all this going to cost Nero?

Yeah. There's a non-sexy topic.

Given Nero's reaction to Isis's price of "nine hundred," I can presume she didn't mean "dollars." Nero keeps that kind of money in his pocket as spare change. Unless it's some Cognizant currency they were discussing, she must've meant "nine hundred thousand"—as in, nearly a million dollars. Way more expensive than any hospital.

On top of that, Nero owns this apartment building, which means the insane bill for the upcoming renovations is also going to be his problem.

Oh, well. In for a penny, in for a pound—or a million dollars.

"Can you buy Vlad a replacement Tesla?" I ask brazenly as Nero reaches the fourth floor with an Olympic sprinter's speed. "The car I crashed was his, and he was—"

"Anything else?" His eyes gleam at me with dark amusement.

"Sure," I say. "You can get Isis to heal Rose's voice, and you can call Vlad to see if he's all right."

"Spoke to Vlad already," Nero says. "He's on the way—but his car is going to come out of your next bonus."

I almost thank him for being a pain again. Makes it that much easier to ignore the tingling warmth in my body—heat that has nothing to do with Isis's recent treatment and everything to do with my inappropriate proximity to my boss's powerful body.

Maybe I should count sheep, like when trying to fall asleep.

No. That makes me think of sleeping with Nero, and I do *not* need my mind going there.

To my relief, we reach my floor.

The door to my apartment is open, and Rose is standing there, fanning herself with her hand.

She tries to speak, but an unhealthy hiss comes out of her throat instead of words.

How loudly had she been screaming?

"Isis," Nero says over his shoulder. "Rose could use your services."

"Looks like my bill will be a round number," Isis says grumpily and shoots a little arrow of her mojo at Rose.

"She's going to charge you a hundred thousand to fix Rose's voice box?" I whisper.

Nero shrugs, steps over Fluffster, and carries me inside.

"You're back," Fluffster screams in my head. "I was so worried."

"I'm fine," I whisper to Fluffster. "I was healed and everything."

What I want to know but can't ask out loud is: how come Nero wasn't afraid of Fluffster just then? Gaius, Pada, and Vlad were all wary when they first saw the domovoi, but Nero is acting like Fluffster is really the small furry rodent he pretends to be.

On his end, Fluffster looks to have conveniently forgotten his earlier bravado. I distinctly recall his suggestion to invite Nero over so that he could "teach him some manners."

Bending down, Nero carefully deposits me into a lounge chair.

He then leaves and comes back carrying Ariel—and I'm not jealous at all at the gentle way he holds her.

Nope. Not jelly at all.

"I'm so glad you're okay," Rose says as she runs into the room, her voice clearly repaired. "But why is Ariel unconscious?"

Isis strolls in, and Felix comes in behind her, dragging his feet and panting like a dehydrated dog.

Plopping into a chair next to me, he complains, "*I* didn't have anyone to carry me. Though even if Maya were here—"

"Don't finish that sentence," I say. "I don't have the cash to pay Isis to put you back together if—"

Isis clears her throat, and when we stop talking, she walks up to Ariel and gives her a thorough examination.

"Her vitals are fine," she says. "Just let her rest like this, and she'll come to her senses soon enough."

"Sasha should rest also," Nero says to Isis, then looks at Felix. "Him too."

The healer demonstratively sighs and points her hands at us again.

"Wait a sec—" I start, but the healing energy makes me drown in blissful drowsiness, and I blank out.

CHAPTER FORTY

I WAKE up to a bergamot scent and open my eyes.

Rose is handing a cup of what must be Earl Grey to the already-awake Felix.

"Hello." I stretch, noticing how amazing I'm feeling. "How is everyone doing?"

"Felix seems to be good as new," Rose says.

"What about Vlad?" I ask.

As though in reply to my query, Vlad steps into the room.

The only thing wrong with Vlad is his clothes. I never imagined him to be a *Matrix* fan boy, or to wear movie t-shirts for that matter.

"I hope it's okay," Rose says to Felix. "I took some of your clothes to replace his bloody rags." She whitens at the memory.

"No problem. I have ten of those, so you can keep that one," Felix says, studying Vlad with a tinge of jealousy.

If Felix is thinking those clothes have never looked as good on him as they do on Vlad, he's right. The borrowed outfit seems custom made for Vlad's wider shoulders.

I look at the couch.

Ariel is still out.

"Do you want a cup of tea?" Rose asks me.

"Sure," I say. "I'd love some."

Rose grabs Vlad by the elbow and drags him away.

The front door slams shut. She must've gone to make the tea at her own apartment, where she has better options.

That or she and Vlad couldn't keep their hands off each other and went for some hanky-panky at her place.

Fluffster walks into the room and looks us over.

"That was extremely stressful," he says. "Don't ever do that again."

"Sure," Felix says. "*That's* why we will never battle the hordes of hell again—to make sure *you* are not stressing out too much."

"Good," Fluffster says, ignoring or not catching the sarcasm. "Now I think I'm going to go take a nap also. Wake me when Ariel comes around."

"Will do," I say.

The chinchilla leaves, and I look at Felix. "Where is Nero?"

"Wasn't around when I woke up. Why? Do you miss him already?"

He winks at me.

"If you hadn't just gone through the wringer, I would punch your smug face," I reply, only half-jokingly.

"Rose said he and the others left as soon as we passed out." Felix blows on his tea.

I test standing on my feet again.

Totally fine.

Even better than fine. I think I can run a marathon or two.

"Did you know that Nero spoke Russian?" I ask Felix, sitting back down.

"No." He greedily slurps his tea. "But as I've told you before, with the last name of Gorin, it's not that much of a leap."

"What did he and Baba Yaga say to each other?" I glance around, feeling as if Nero might be lurking in the shadows.

"I wasn't in the best condition to listen." Felix cringes at the memory. "I did get the gist of the exchange, though."

"And? Tell me."

"At first, Nero sounded like Liam Neeson in *Taken*," he says animatedly. "He reminded Baba Yaga that, and I paraphrase, he has a very particular set of skills that make him a nightmare for people like her—or anyone really." He chuckles dryly. "Baba Yaga is truly crazy, because she didn't agree right away. Which is when Nero started with the threats." Felix's enthusiasm wanes at this memory. "It was bad. He said he'd go full-on Keyser Söze on her ass—though not in those exact words. He said he'd go after her and the rest of her mob, killing them slowly. That—and again, I don't recall it all verbatim—he'd kill her people's kids, their wives, their parents, and their parents' friends. He'd burn down the Izbushka restaurant and—"

"Dude, I've seen *The Usual Suspects*," I say. "What did Baba Yaga say to all this?"

"She's a tough lady," Felix says. "She said if she's going to die, she'd rather die gloriously and while standing her ground. Oh, and that she doesn't give two shits about what happens to anyone else after she's gone."

"And what did Nero say to that?"

"He asked what she wants. But the way he said it made it sound like if Baba Yaga asked for the wrong thing, the Keyser Söze reaction would still be on the table."

I feel pride swell my chest for whatever reason. I guess I like the visual of Nero putting the old woman in her place—especially since he did it for me, a mere cog in his financial machine.

"Baba Yaga said she wants Nero to leave her alone for a year," Felix says. "To not go after her people or her for any reason, no matter what she does—provided she leaves *you* alone."

"And?" I ask when Felix pauses to take a breath.

"He said if she keeps to her word and otherwise stays out of his business, she has herself a deal. He then said that he knows about her New York Council ambitions and couldn't give a rat's ass one way or another—which seemed to make her happy."

"So I'm safe from her?" I clarify. "I was afraid I'd have to look over my shoulder or stay home for the rest of my days."

"You're safe," Felix says. "As long as you stay away from her and Brighton Beach in general, she stays away from you. There was even a mention of putting together a written contract to that effect, and no one breaks those once they exist."

"Great," I say with a grin. Then my mood darkens as I recall the cost of this arrangement—me going back to being Nero's slave girl.

Or his minion.

Yeah. That has fewer sexual connotations.

Ugh. I need to break my stupid abstinence. How else to explain that a part of me finds the phrase "Nero's slave girl" perversely arousing?

"Earth to Sasha," Felix says, and I thank heavens his superpower is not telepathy. If he'd caught that last thought, I'd have to murder a good friend.

"Sorry," I say. "Back to business… Did you get a chance to finally penetrate Nero?"

"Did I what?" Felix chokes on his tea.

"Oh, maybe I forgot to tell you," I say. "I put the FELLATIO gizmo in his pocket."

"You *what?*" he yelps. "When? How?"

"Before you got healed," I say, ignoring both the how question and the flashbacks to the feel of that "snake."

"Well," Felix says in a much calmer tone. "Even if you had told me, when would I have gotten the chance to do that? Have you seen me touch a computer? Is Nero even back in his office? I need him next to his—"

"No need to get testy," I say. "You can get on it starting now. Since we've learned that Nero speaks Russian, what I saw in my vision—my name written in Cyrillic—could be his password after all."

"You're right." Felix leaps to his feet, spilling half the tea. "Let me get my laptop and—"

Ariel moans from the couch and starts moving with jerky, agitated motions.

CHAPTER FORTY-ONE

I JUMP TO MY FEET, and we stampede toward the couch.

Flailing her arms, Ariel opens her eyes and looks around, her pupils dilated and gaze unfocused.

"How are you feeling?" I ask her soothingly.

"Gaius?" she says, and though she's looking at me, I get the feeling she doesn't recognize me.

"Gaius isn't here," I croon. "Relax."

"Gaius," she says again, her forehead breaking into a sweat. "I need him."

"He's in Russia," I say.

"You're better off without him anyway," Felix mutters, saying what I was being too kind to add.

"No." She begins trembling. "Call him. Bring him here."

"If that vampire dared to come here, Fluffster would make sure it's the last thing he does." Felix's tone is uncharacteristically menacing. Then his gaze softens as he registers the misery on Ariel's face. "I'm sorry, but either way, I don't think he cares enough about you to come to the rescue, especially from Russia."

Ariel starts thrashing erratically, and Felix and I exchange worried glances.

"Ariel." I gently touch her shoulder. "Please st—"

With a spasmodic slap, Ariel swats my hand away, nearly dislocating my shoulder. "I need it," she gasps, tossing her head from side to side. "Don't keep it from me."

I recall something Baba Yaga said on the phone—something that seemed like hyperbole at the time. "Your girl still has major withdrawal symptoms," she said. "She'd be a danger to you and herself right now, but I can keep her clean for the few weeks she needs to get over it."

Ariel leans over the couch and vomits soup onto Felix's shoes.

He and I exchange glances again, our worry upgraded to panic.

Ariel continues to fall apart, moaning and thrashing on the couch.

I reach for my phone to call Nero, to see if he might be able to help. At the very least, he should demand a partial refund from Isis. Her healing abilities are clearly lacking.

A squeak in the hallway announces the opening of our apartment door.

Ariel suddenly looks alert and hopeful. Does she really think Gaius just arrived?

"Vlad and Rose," Felix guesses, a moment before they step into the room.

Ariel sniffs the air like a dog and stares at the newcomers with watering eyes.

"I have your t—" Rose starts to say, but then she lays eyes on Ariel and turns ghost pale.

"Please," Ariel says, extending her shaking arms toward Vlad. "Please…"

Vlad's eyes narrow.

Ariel sits up and swings her feet to the floor.

"Ariel," Felix says. "What are—"

Moving with insane speed, she pushes Felix aside and rushes toward Vlad.

Cup in hand, Felix flies a few feet and slams into another lounge chair, the hot tea spilling all over him as the cup falls and shatters into pieces.

Groaning, he rolls over on the floor, and I wince as I see his palm land on one of the shards. He yelps, raising it to his face, and I fear he'll faint at the trickle of blood.

Ariel freezes mid-stride, the sight of Felix's blood jolting her out of her addiction haze. "Is that… Did I do that?" Some semblance of sanity returns to her eyes, and she starts toward Felix, her hand extended as if to help him up.

Then her shoulder jerks convulsively and she stops.

Her eyes glaze over again, and she turns back to stare at Vlad with zombie-like determination.

"What are you doing?" Rose screams, but Ariel is already leaping at Vlad.

She's not the only one with good reflexes, however. The vampire catches her in mid-air and very ungently throws her back onto the couch.

Something wooden breaks inside the couch with a crack, but Ariel doesn't look like the landing even tickled her.

She slides from the cushions to the floor and starts crawling on all fours in Vlad's direction.

"Please," she moans, her gaze fixed slavishly on him. "Just a sip."

"You have to go to rehab," Vlad says. "You're in the worst stages of withdrawal and—"

"Just a little." Ariel's crawl picks up speed. "I'll do anything you want."

Pink energy dances on Rose's palm, and she angrily points her hand at Ariel.

"Do not take her strength, love," Vlad says to Rose. "She'll need it."

Rose reluctantly lowers her hand, the pink energy dissipating.

Ariel is now next to Vlad, her head precariously close to his crotch.

"Whatever you want," she says, and though I think she meant to say the phrase seductively, it sounds creepy instead. "I need it."

She reaches for Vlad's zipper, mumbling x-rated promises.

Vlad catches her wrist and forcefully pulls her up to her feet.

She looks hopeful for a moment, but then he grabs

her hair in his steely grip and forces her to look at Felix —who's still on the floor, cradling his bleeding palm, his eyes wide from Ariel's abominable performance.

"You're going to hurt everyone you love," Vlad says. "Is that what you want?"

A semblance of comprehension appears on Ariel's face.

She tries to look away, but Vlad doesn't let her.

"I'm sorry," she half sobs, half mumbles. "Please. Please. I need it. I need it so bad." She wipes her runny nose. "I need… I need help." The last line is so faint it's barely audible.

Vlad's eyes become pools of mercury once again, and he jerks Ariel's head back to face him.

"I *will* help you," he says in that hypnotic voice. "You will stay at the Tranquility facility in Gomorrah, until you can make your own choices."

"I will stay at the Tranquility facility in Gomorrah," Ariel parrots in a hollow voice.

Vlad lets her go, and she stands rod straight, awaiting further instructions.

"You used glamour on her?" Felix painfully sits up. "I didn't think it could work this well on our kind."

"The blood addicts are even more susceptible to it than regular humans," Vlad says, his mouth tightening. "Now we better take her to Gomorrah."

"How long will she be under your spell like that?" I ask, extending my hand to help the clearly shaken Felix get to his feet.

"Couple of hours, unless the glamour is reapplied,"

Vlad says. "But they have better methods to keep her comfortable at Tranquility—which is where we're going right now."

"I'm coming with," Felix says, swaying on his feet as I let go of his hand.

"Are you okay?" I grab his arm again.

"Fine." He wipes his bloody palm on his shirt when I release him. "It was more scary than painful."

"Go wash up while I get us a cab to the airport," I tell him.

Felix slinks away, and I pull out my phone to summon a ride.

"The car will be here in five minutes," I say a moment later, doing my best not to meet Vlad's gaze. I feel guilty that he has to ride in a Ford Fusion instead of his shiny Tesla.

"I'll stay here with Fluffster," Rose says, bending to pick up the shards of Felix's cup. "Go help Ariel."

Vlad herds Ariel to the front door, where we join up with Felix, who's now wearing a shirt identical to the one Vlad borrowed and sporting a Band-Aid across his palm.

"The elevator probably doesn't work yet," I say, leading the group toward the staircase.

"When did Baba Yaga nab you?" I ask Ariel, then look at Vlad. "Can she talk in this state?"

He catches Ariel's gaze and commands, "Answer."

"I was on the way home that Saturday," she says in a monotone. "I had just finished escorting Gaius to JFK for his trip to Russia when Koschei attacked me. I thought I killed him at first, but—"

"Did they hurt you?" Felix asks, and it's clear he's afraid of the answer.

"I don't know," Ariel says. "My memory is blank after Baba Yaga used her energy on me."

We walk the rest of the way quietly, and everyone except Ariel looks extra gloomy as we pass by the wreck that used to be the building lobby.

At least someone got rid of the broken bits of Tesla. Vlad already looks pissed enough as it is.

By the time we get into the cab, I feel like the guilt might drown me.

I suspected Gaius wasn't good for Ariel, but I didn't do anything about it.

I should've also realized that Ariel had been kidnapped so many days ago. I didn't even get the hint when Baba Yaga almost admitted to having Ariel in her clutches.

Hell, if we go deeper, I should've ignored Ariel's wishes and pried and pestered her about the PTSD she claims not to have. She's been self-medicating for a while now—using drugs I knew couldn't be that great for her—but I never took decisive-enough action, just gave cautious advice. Now I wonder if her traumatic experiences in the Army are why she was particularly vulnerable to vampire addiction.

Oh, and let's not forget that her first taste of Gaius's blood was after she got hurt helping *me*.

Midway to JFK, I break from beating myself up to

fantasize about obliterating Gaius for what he's done to my friend. It's possible I currently hate him more than I do Baba Yaga.

My gloom continues as we exit the cab and trek through secret corridors to the gate hub.

Felix must pick up on my mood because he leaves me alone, opting to speak to Vlad in Russian in a loud whisper.

I slightly perk up when I see the gate that leads to Gomorrah—then feel guilty for that.

My friend is going to rehab, not on vacation.

When we exit the gate on the Gomorrah side, however, the view of the sky yanks me out of my self-flagellating funk.

Like on my last visit, the time here doesn't match home. We reached JFK around dinner time, but it's late at night here already. On the bright side, the night sky is as spectacular as I remember it, with a majestic fire-and-brimstone-looking nebula instead of a moon.

Also like on my last visit, the size of the city takes my breath away. It's like a Platonic ideal of a megapolis that every huge city tries to futilely reach.

We use the speedy elevators to get down again, and though I've seen it before, I gawk at the building's museum-like lobby.

The pattern of gawking continues as we walk down the street. The last time we merely crossed it to get to Nero's Earth Club, so this longer walk should be a treat.

"It's like every sci-fi and fantasy movie blended into

one," I whisper, staring at the exotically futuristic clothes of different types of Cognizant on the street.

We walk by a green orc man in a skintight shiny outfit, then by a blue-skinned being of indeterminate gender who has both a nice décolletage and a bulge in his/her pink leather pants. When I ogle the four-foot-tall bearded dwarf, she narrows her beady eyes at me and gives me the finger.

Feeling like a dumb tourist, I turn my attention to our inanimate surroundings.

The unusual storefronts all around us beam holographic ads of life-sized supermodels onto the pavement, giving me a small glimpse of local culture. Clearly, the unrealistic expectation of Gomorrah's fashion industry states that a female orc must be around linebacker size, but the elf-women models would make even their most anorexic human counterparts feel obese.

We turn the corner, and I stare at a glass structure that I guess to be a parking lot.

Wow. The drabbest car here—not to mention, out on the street—would make Vlad's deceased high-end Tesla look like one of those vintage clunkers they drive down in Cuba.

Before we enter the lot, the wind picks up, and the most delicious odor I've ever smelled wafts from a little shiny vehicle that looks like a landed flying saucer. It must be this place's version of a food truck.

"I'll get some food for you," Vlad says, noticing my gaze.

"Thanks," Felix says.

Vlad walks up to the contraption and does something I can't make out.

He then comes back holding three packets made out of papery material.

"Eat in the car," he says when Felix snatches a packet out of his hands. "Let's go."

We enter the glass structure, and Vlad swiftly walks up to one of the parked cars, seemingly at random. I don't catch what he says to the car, but it must like it, because it automatically opens its rounded doors.

We all get in the back seat, so the thing must be self-driving. Vlad orders, "Tranquility Center," in plain English, and the car closes the doors and pulls out of the lot.

The streets we pass are teeming with more types of Cognizant dressed in uncanny outfits, and my earlier sense of being in a futuristic fantasy movie intensifies.

And this is at night. Like NYC, this city must never sleep. Even Times Square isn't this crowded at this time of night. People must crawl all over each other during the daytime here.

"Try the food," Felix says, opening his treat.

Vlad hands me and Ariel the remaining packets, and I taste mine as Ariel stuffs hers robotically into her mouth.

Yum. Though the food visibly resembles something like a knish or a pierogi, the concentrated savory flavor reminds of my favorite umami Japanese dishes—all rolled into one.

In fact, the food is so good I momentarily forget about our surroundings—but only momentarily, because we soon enter an area so gorgeous that my gawking recommences.

The closest Earth approximation might be the Gardens by the Bay in Singapore, only this is much bigger and with a slew of plant-covered skyscrapers disappearing into the night sky.

I make a mental note to come back here during daytime; it must be even more majestic then.

We glide into a parking lot next to the greenest of the buildings and exit the car.

As Vlad leads us inside, I'm so distracted by everything that Felix has to drag me by the hand.

"Something will fly into your mouth," he tells me.

I close my wide-open maw, only to have my jaw drop again soon after.

If this is the Tranquility place, maybe I should also develop an addiction.

If a spa had a child with a fancy resort and it grew to the size of a theme park, the result might look like this rehab.

Despite the late hour, the place is teeming with people. I can't tell the patients from the staff; there are all kinds of Cognizant mingling together, creating a Comic Con feel.

"Wait here," Vlad says and leads Ariel away.

"We should've said goodbye," I say to Felix, my guilt raising its ugly head.

"It's okay. She's not herself," Felix says, looking around distractedly.

"True. By the way, how are we going to pay for Ariel's stay here? The place looks expensive."

"There's a universal healthcare system here on Gomorrah," Felix says, still looking around for something. "Everything health-related is free, even for visiting Cognizant like us."

"Cool," I say. "Do they also have healers here, like Isis? I thought you lose powers if you stay."

"I think they entice some to visit," he says, his head swiveling from side to side. "The Cognizant with practical powers, especially healers, are highly sought after here, as they can help with difficult cases that even the most advanced technology cannot yet cure."

"Are you looking for someone?" I ask when I can't take any more of his ADHD.

He looks back at me apologetically and sighs. "I have an old friend who works here. I was hoping to bump into her and ask her to keep an eye on Ariel."

"Isn't there a secretary here somewhere, or some other way you can locate your friend?"

"I'd have to leave you alone," he says.

"I can manage."

"If you're sure—"

"I'm positive."

"Then I'll be right back." He rushes off in the same direction as Vlad and Ariel.

I resume gawking, and do so for a couple of

minutes until a woman approaches me with a huge smile on her face.

I know her, I realize in shock.

This is Councilor Kit—the sneaky shape changer who'd turned into Nero at my Jubilee and tried to seduce me.

"Sasha," she says in her distinct anime-character voice. "This is very exciting. I didn't realize you were also here." She either claps her small palms together or rubs them like a supervillain; I can't tell which. "What is *your* poison?"

"I'm just here escorting a friend," I say when I find my tongue. "What about you?"

My guess is addiction to hotdogs made out of dachshund puppies, but I don't share this out loud.

"Believe it or not, I'm a sex addict," Kit says, looking somber—an expression that seems foreign on her tiny, animated face.

"I would've never guessed," I lie. "You, a sex addict? Get out of town."

Her attempted seduction of me aside, I also caught her trying the same trick on Darian—and that time, she'd turned into me to get what she wanted. So not only can I easily believe she's a sex addict, I also think she has major kinks on top of that—but hey, live and let live.

"And yet, here I am," she says, and I congratulate myself for my lying skills yet again. "I check myself into this place when my condition gets a little out of control."

Wow, okay. If the two episodes I'd witnessed are her normal, I'd hate to see her "out of control."

"So, who is the friend you're escorting?" Kit asks. "Is it Felix?" She makes herself look like him. "Or is it that delectable—"

"Sasha," Vlad says from behind me, causing me to jump. "Where is Felix?"

"He has a friend who works here," I say, turning to face Vlad.

What the hell?

Vlad is looking at Kit like he's ready to rip her head off—something that's now all too easy for me to picture.

I glance back and see why. Kit has made herself look like Rose, only Rose in her mid-twenties—or at least the way I've always pictured Rose at that age.

"Councilor," Kit says in her own voice.

"Kit." Vlad relaxes his fists. "Incorrigible as always."

"Hello," Felix says, looking at Kit's young-Rose guise in confusion as he approaches. "Have we met?"

"We met at the Jubilee." Kit turns back into herself and licks her lips lasciviously. "It's Felix, right?" She looks at Felix and Vlad's identical *Matrix* shirts. "Are you guys playing at being twins? Because it's a game I—"

"I'm sorry, Councilor," Vlad says as she transforms her top into a third copy of Felix's favorite attire. "We're in a rush."

Without letting us say another peep to Kit, Vlad

herds us out of the building and doesn't slow the brisk pace until we get into another futuristic car.

"Do we have time to explore Gomorrah?" I ask as soon as we depart. "This place is amazing."

Felix clears his throat. "Did you forget about that computer project I promised to do for you at home? I thought you needed it done posthaste."

He's right.

Nero might discover the device in his pocket, and not only will we not get a chance to hack him, there might be consequences for Felix.

"Never mind," I say quickly. "Were you able to talk to your friend?"

"Yes," Felix says, looking relieved. "She's promised to look after Ariel. She's a dream walker, so it should really help."

Vlad appears impressed at this, so I ask, "What's a dream walker, and how does she retain her power if she works in this place?"

"Dream walkers can enter other people's dreams and even control what happens—a bit like in *Inception*, only cooler," Felix says. "It's a rare, very practical power, and I think she maintains it with frequent trips off world."

I nod thoughtfully. "You know, that might well help Ariel with those nightmares she never admits to having."

Both Felix and I have heard Ariel scream in her sleep, but she always claims not to remember anything come the next day—and maybe she doesn't, but I doubt it.

"Not just nightmares," Felix says. "My friend has a bunch of therapies she's developed. She's highly sought after. It's lucky we go way back."

"Sounds great," I say. "There's only one thing I'm worried about now—vampires at rehab."

"I took care of that," Vlad says, and both Felix and I look at him, waiting for him to elaborate.

He doesn't.

"Let's just hope Ariel stays away from Kit," I say after an awkward silence.

No one replies to that, so I resume my gawking all the way to the gate building.

On the ride back from JFK, Vlad and Felix talk in Russian again, and I nap.

When we get back home, Rose grabs Vlad, and they run back to her apartment with all the enthusiasm of young lovers after a year apart.

"You left without talking to me. Rose told me some of what's happened," Fluffster says grumpily when we enter the now-spotless living room—likely courtesy of Rose. "You should've woken me up."

"Get on your computer and hack Nero," I tell Felix. To Fluffster I say, "I'll fill you in on everything right now."

The chinchilla looks pacified, so I launch into my tale as Felix leaves and returns with his laptop, then plops on the couch and starts banging away at the keys.

"So the password *is* your name," he exclaims just as I finish my story.

Fluffster and I look at him. As he stares at something on his screen, his eyes grow wider, and the unibrow seesaws back and forth, like a drunk caterpillar.

"What is it?" I ask, sitting down next to him. "What did you learn?"

"It's one of those things you have to see to believe," he says and reverently hands me the laptop.

I stare at the screen.

There are a bunch of documents that look to have been scanned from a paper version. Must be Nero's obsession with the paperless office striking again.

When I actually zoom in on the very first of these documents, however, I gape in disbelief.

What *is* this?

The meat computer that is my brain feels like it's about to crash.

CHAPTER FORTY-TWO

THIS IS my transcript from first grade.

My scores were perfect except for one lonely S in "participation and conduct." S stands for "Satisfactory," or for "my first-grade teacher is 'Such' a bitch for lowering that grade over a few harmless practical jokes."

How does Nero have this and why?

Even my mom, a hoarder of sentimental junk, does not own my transcripts from before middle school.

Puzzled, I close the transcript and pick another file at random.

This is something my mom *does* have. It's a picture from my middle-school graduation, where I pretended to be an innocent angel that I wasn't.

Again—why does Nero have this? This picture might be available to the general public from the school archives or something like that, so it's not as weird for Nero to have as the transcript, but it's plenty weird nevertheless.

Next is an essay I wrote for my tenth-grade English class. I had to pick someone I admired, and it was a difficult choice between Houdini and Criss Angel. I settled on Houdini since he was the more famous of the two and because I didn't want to say things like "I drool when I see him on TV" in my essay.

Where did Nero get a copy of this and for what purpose? I know hedge funds do background checks on potential employees, but this is a level of thoroughness that crosses the line into creepy and leaves it far behind.

Then I look at the next thing on the screen and realize the creepy town is just beginning.

This is a letter from Columbia University addressed to Nero's Upper East penthouse.

The letter thanks Nero Gorin for his generous donation, double-checks that he doesn't want the building named after him, and informs him that Sasha Urban has been accepted as per his request.

What the…?

I lift my eyes and catch Felix's gaze.

He looks as disturbed as I feel.

Nero got me into Columbia?

Why?

How did he even know about me back then?

And… I didn't get in on my own merit? My grades were awesome. I was so proud when they accepted me. Have I been deluded about my abilities all along?

I blink a few times, trying to fathom why Nero would do something like this, but all I come up with is that this is obviously much more than a background check.

It looks more like grooming someone for a specific role ahead of time.

But that's crazy.

Yes, Nero is a control freak, but to personally oversee a future minion's education is not something I've ever heard of—especially without any strings attached.

Terrified at what I might find next, I minimize the donation letter and bring up another picture.

This one doesn't seem to fit with the others.

It's a picture of a man kissing a girl. A very young girl, one in her early teens.

Does Nero think that girl is me?

Because it isn't.

Criss Angel aside, I'd never even thought about kissing an older man at that age, let alone acted on the fantasy.

Then I recognize the man.

It's the cop who busted me at a party I attended my freshman year at Columbia.

He caught me holding the only joint I'd ever smoked during my college career and took me to the station, terrifying me with promises of an arrest on my previously spotless record.

Wait a minute.

That episode never fully made sense to me because

after the cop went to the trouble of bringing me to the station and leaving me there for hours, he mysteriously let me go with a warning.

He did not try to flirt with me or anything else, just mumbled something about not wasting government money on nonissues like me—which made me wonder why he'd bothered dragging me there in the first place.

Had my lucky break been due to this picture?

Had Nero intervened via some kind of blackmail?

He paid good money to get me into Columbia—a fact I'm still wrapping my mind around—so I could see him looking after that initial investment afterward.

But how?

He would've had to have the photo prior to my troubles—that, or acquire it extremely quickly.

He also would've had to know I got into trouble in the first place, which means he'd been watching me at the time—an idea that jibes with all these new revelations but is extremely disturbing.

It is possible that Nero keeps blackmail material on all the cops in the city? Or does he simply know some shadowy person who does?

Come to think of it, does he also keep blackmail material on HR departments all over the US? Is that how he kept me from getting a new job?

But why not glamour the cop? Did Nero not have a vampire handy that night or something? Glamour would've worked just as well, unless the cop is one of the Cognizant.

Well, whatever the case, I do hope that along with

blackmailing him to let me go, Nero told the guy to keep his grabby hands away from anyone younger than eighteen in the future.

I minimize the cop picture and scan a few more documents.

That's my lease—fine. He does own the building we live in.

There's a scan of my DMV records—creepier.

Then I see another file full of text, so I start skimming it.

This is my private conversation with Ariel that someone transcribed into text.

Oh yeah. I'd almost forgotten. Nero was spying on me using the company phone—and this must be one of the million resulting files.

Since I now have fewer documents on the screen, I can spot the underlying folder.

It's called "Sasha," only written in Cyrillic like the password.

I click on a file in this folder at random.

It's a copy of my mom's therapist's notes. On this particular day, Mom had discussed her feelings about dating again, soon after her recent divorce.

My chest tightens. He'd been spying on my *parents*?

Though I'm tempted to read the notes, I close the file. Mom deserves her privacy—a concept that's clearly foreign to Nero.

Why would he want to have this?

What is wrong with him?

Frantically, I scan the folder for something even worse than this.

There's a video file.

I play it.

It's me levitating a dollar in front of Darian's nose on the night we met at the restaurant I'd worked at.

Looks like Nero had been spying on my magic gig, too.

The next video is all foggy at first; then the camera zooms in, and I watch myself kissing Nero in the middle of a deep mist.

My face burns.

This is the recording of me kissing Kit that night at the Jubilee—which means Nero knows I kissed him.

Well, not *him*, but a sex addict who happened to look like him at the time.

Given everything else, I shouldn't feel outraged by this, of all things. We *were* at his fund when this was recorded. But I still feel more violated by this video than by most of the other evidence of his spying.

How could he know about that kiss but act like he doesn't?

Then again, maybe he *has* been acting like he knows. Maybe he always hires orcs to assault women who he thinks want to kiss him.

Fuming, I look at Felix again.

Did he see this?

He stares back at me, his face annoyingly blank.

"Say something," I demand. "Tell me this makes any sense to you."

"It looks like he's watched over you since you were little," Felix says, glancing at Fluffster as though for help. Getting none, he continues. "Also... he speaks Russian."

"He does." I put down the laptop and massage my temples.

"And he's been helping you," Felix says, as though this is supposed to click something for me. It doesn't. "He's been watching over you," he continues. "Protecting you."

"Your grasp of the obvious is superb," I snap. "Tell me something I don't know."

"We know at least one of your parents is Russian." His tone is extremely patient, even as the right side of his unibrow lifts higher than I've ever seen it.

"No." I stop massaging my temples and stare at Felix with my mouth so wide it actually hurts my jaws. "You can't mean what I think you're saying."

"It's possible," Felix says and looks at Fluffster for support—again without any luck.

"No," I say. "It's *not* possible."

"What are you two talking about?" Fluffster mentally demands. "I'm not following this at all."

"Could Nero be Sasha's father?" Felix enunciates.

"My father?" I leap to my feet without knowing why. *"Nero?"*

My legs take me to the door as my heart pounds erratically in my chest.

A set of human and chinchilla feet follow me at a run, but I ignore them.

"Where are you going?" Felix asks worriedly.

"To his office." I jam my feet into my boots.

"Nero's leaving his office," Felix says. "I checked the cameras before destroying the FELLATIO in his pocket."

"Then I'm going to his penthouse," I grit out, and before anyone can reply, I'm out the door.

I rush down the stairs as though another zombie is chasing me, run through the lobby debris, and jump into the first cab I find.

As we drive to the Upper East Side, it takes all my meditative breathing experience to calm down enough to think semi-coherent thoughts.

Could Felix possibly be right?

Could Nero somehow be my father?

A huge part of me is screaming in denial.

Wouldn't I know it? Wouldn't I feel it if he were?

Wouldn't I have sensed something when we first met?

Well, if I'm honest, I did feel something when I first met Nero—but lust is the opposite of what a daughter should feel for her father.

Isn't it?

My head feels like it might explode, so I cradle it between my palms.

If this turns out to be true, does it mean I'll have to blind myself like Oedipus in the Greek myth? Or—

The cab driver clears his throat, and I realize we're already next to Nero's swanky building.

"I'm expected," I lie to the security guard as I rush

in. "My name is Sasha, and I'm here to speak with Nero Gorin."

The overweight man looks through some paper journal on his desk and says, "Sasha Urban?"

I blink in disbelief. "Yes."

"You're on the VIP list," he says. "May I see your ID?"

In a haze, I show the guy my driver's license, and he tells me which elevator bank will take me to the penthouse.

My heartbeat is through the roof and my mind is blank the whole way to Nero's front door.

Channeling my tumultuous emotions, I bang on the door so hard that my palm stings.

No reply.

I punch the doorbell with my finger.

Nada.

Is he not home yet?

Or is he watching me through some hidden camera and refusing to face me?

"I'm not leaving without an explanation," I shout for the sake of the hypothetical camera and pull the lock picks from my tongue.

Nero's fancy lock takes a few seconds longer than usual to defeat, but defeat it I do.

"Looks like breaking and entering can go into your nifty dossier on me," I say to Nero's hypothetical hearing devices. "Ready or not, I'm coming in."

CHAPTER FORTY-THREE

NO ONE GREETS ME INSIDE, so I ogle my surroundings.

There's a sort of Spartan opulence to Nero's grand foyer. Despite the modern art on the walls, eighteen-foot ceilings give the place a cathedral vibe.

I start walking aimlessly.

Each of the pieces of furniture I pass looks like it costs more than a decade of my salary, and was handpicked by the best interior designers.

Following some intuition, I take a left hallway and find myself in an art studio.

"So you do paint," I whisper to the hidden mics as I stare at the various breathtaking oil-on-canvas landscapes.

Then I see it.

Me.

Or rather, a drawing of me—only I don't look this radiant in real life.

I'm standing on a white-sand beach wearing a skimpy bathing suit that I retired soon after college.

"This is from my trip to Grand Cayman," I say. "A trip I took *before* we ever met."

No reply from the secret speakers or microphones.

I examine the painting.

The detail the artist paid to my physique would not be appropriate if said artist was my father. I'm at least a cup size bigger in the picture and my waist-to-hip ratio is much closer to the ideal than my actual proportions.

This is me through the eyes of a flesh-and-blood man with lust goggles on, not a father.

Shaking my head in the hopes of clearing it, I let my intuition lead me farther into the depths of the penthouse, until I reach a smallish office with a heavy-duty safe inside.

Even without my seer powers, it's clear that something important is in this safe, so I examine it closely.

There's no lock that I can pick, and unfortunately, I've never looked into safe-cracking as part of some illusion.

Nor have I read anything about high-tech safes like this.

I touch the LCD screen on the safe door.

It lights up, and a weird alphabet appears.

When I spot a reversed "R" and "N," I realize I'm looking at Cyrillic again.

Interesting.

Nero's digital master password was my name in Russian. Would he use the same here?

Racking my brain for what the spelling actually was, I locate a letter that looks like a 'c,' then 'a,' then a weird letter that reminds me of a flattened 'w,' and finally another 'a.'

The safe doesn't open, but there is a space button on the screen, so the password could still be my full name.

I type the space and focus on the second word. A 'Y'-looking letter, followed by 'p,' then one that looks like a '6,' then the 'a,' and finally the one that looks like an uppercase 'H' written in a small font.

The safe chimes.

I hold my breath and pull on the handle.

The door opens.

There are a bunch of folders inside, but my hands leap for the one that has "Саша Урбан" written on it, as that's my name in Russian.

My hands a little shaky, I open the folder.

There's an intricate yellowing piece of paper inside, all in Russian.

I look at the next paper.

Another old document in Russian.

I flip the page and find yet another ancient Russian document.

What the hell?

What do these have to do with me?

I take out my phone, take pictures of the three papers, email them to Felix, and dial his number.

"Sasha, where are you?" he says, picking up. "Fluffster and I are—"

"Check your email," I say urgently.

Something in my voice must be telling, because I hear him fuss with something before he exhales a shocked breath.

"Felix?"

"I don't believe my eyes." He sounds equal parts awed and scared—a combo that worries me. "This is incredible." He clears his throat. "I don't even know what to say."

"You better find your words and quickly." I grip the phone tighter.

"One is a Russian birth certificate for a girl named Alexandra Rasputina," he rattles out. "The 'a' at the end of the last name makes it the female version of the last name Rasputin. And Alexandra, of course, is the formal version of Sasha. The birth date is Tuesday, October 31st, 1916. Only a father is listed—Grigori Rasputin."

"You think that's my grandma?" I ask, my voice shaking. "Or mother? Was I named after her?"

"No." Felix sounds strongly subdued. "You don't understand. Let me tell you about the rest of the documents."

"Yeah, stop stalling."

"Okay, but this one makes no sense, unless it's a hoax," he says. "It's written in antiquated Russian, so I could be misinterpreting it, but it appears to be a set of prophesies made by Rasputin."

"Oh?" I say, unsure how this will come back to me but trusting Felix to eventually get to it.

"Yeah," he says. "This is also dated 1916, and covers the hundred years since then."

"What?" I glance at my phone, debating if I should video call Felix to see if he looks as crazy as he sounds.

"I know. This predicted it all." He speaks faster. "The Russian revolution a year later. World War II and the Nazis. Pearl Harbor's exact date and time. Sputnik and the first man in space—as well as on the Moon." He noisily inhales. "It goes like that through all the history—every war, the rise and fall of major corporations with specific dates and stock prices, the dot com and the housing bubbles, 9/11 and—"

"This document must be a hoax," I say, my insides growing cold. "Something someone recently put together. I know several methods of how to age a—"

"It could be," Felix says. "But then legends do say that Rasputin was a powerful seer, so in theory, he could've had a vision to cover even this length of time —though judging by your experiences, he must've been out of commission as a seer for a long, long time after, if not forever."

"Fine," I say, fighting dizziness as I imagine living a hundred years in a vision as Rasputin would have to have done. "What does this have to do with me? Am I a pinnacle of some prophecy of his?"

"That's where the third document comes into play," Felix says. "This one is even harder to discern because besides being written in antiquated Russian, it's also a type of legalese."

"What does it say?"

"I'll try to translate it as best as I can," he says. "It's even harder to believe than the previous one."

"I'm going to kill you if you don't stop stalling right this second," I grit though my teeth. "Seriously."

"Fine," Felix says. "Here goes."

CHAPTER FORTY-FOUR

I JAM the phone painfully against my ear, unwilling to miss a single word.

"What follows is a contract between Grigori Rasputin and a man henceforth known as Nero Gorin," Felix starts.

"What?" I stare at the three yellow papers, unsure which one he's currently translating. My mind latches on to a random tidbit. "Did Nero have another name before?"

"You heard Rose and Vlad. Even *they* consider him old. He must've had tons of identities throughout his life," Felix says. "Now let me go on."

"Sorry," I say. "Go ahead."

"The first part is the secrecy clause," Felix says. "The legal jargon is dense here, but I think it states that the parties signing this document aren't allowed to disclose any details of the document to anyone for any reason. There's also a list of topics they agree not to discuss—"

"Let's get back to that," I say. "Go on to the next section—and it better be the meat of the document."

"The two parties exchange services," Felix says with an intonation I'd expect in a courtroom. "Grigori Rasputin will provide Nero Gorin with a hundred-year prophecy that will make Nero Gorin the richest Cognizant to have ever walked the Otherland named Earth." Felix takes a breath. "In exchange, Nero Gorin is to look after Grigori Rasputin's daughter, Alexandra —henceforth known as Sasha—Rasputina, when she appears on the Otherland named Earth at the beginning of the new millennium according to the local timekeeping."

The room around me spins.

Though Felix translated the words into English, their meaning does not want to register in my brain.

"There's more," Felix says softly. "Nero Gorin is to make sure Sasha Rasputina is adopted by the human family named Urban and treated well. He's also to oversee her education and smooth her transition into Earth society—"

"No." I shake my head. "This can't be true. How could I have been born over a century ago? When my parents found me, I was just a child."

"Rasputin could've taken you to an Otherland where time flows very slowly," Felix says. "Then he could've waited and taken you to Earth after decades had passed here. Whatever danger he escaped might've calmed down by then, or maybe he had a vision that told him when and where to take you." Felix sounds annoyingly rational. "It actually kind of makes sense. Your adoptive parents found you in JFK, near the hub. Whatever Rasputin was afraid of on Earth, he only had to stay here for a few minutes—"

I stop listening.

Like a violent storm, a new paradigm is realigning everything I've ever known.

All the facts fit now.

The Russian connection. Fluffster's last owner. Me being abandoned at JFK airport. Nero keeping tabs on me all my life.

When I first learned about Rasputin, I considered that he might be an ancestor of mine, but he's so much more.

He's my *father*.

Could he still be alive? Between Otherland time differentials and the longer Cognizant lifespan, it's entirely possible.

But if so, where is he? Why did he give me up?

"Sasha?" Felix says. "You there?"

"I'm processing," I say. "It sounds like Nero has all the answers. If he knew my father, he might've known my mother. He might be able to tell me where—"

"I'm afraid it's not so simple," Felix says. "If you had let me complete the secrecy clause section, I would've told you. Nero can't talk to you about your heritage at all."

"What?" I barely resist the urge to throw my phone at the wall.

"Breathe, Sasha," Felix says soothingly. "You've learned a lot today. Just think—"

"Let's talk later," I say. "I want to take pictures of the other documents."

"Wait a sec… Where did you get these documents?"

"From the source. Where did you think?"

"You're in Nero's apartment, aren't you?" Felix whispers.

"And that's why I've got to go," I say. "Time might be limited and all that."

"Mr. Gorin, sir, I had nothing to do with this," Felix says loudly. "When Sasha called me, I had no clue. Please don't kill—"

I hang up and look at the next paper.

It looks like some strange hybrid between a map and a Venn diagram. I'll have to figure out what this is and what it has to do with me at some later date.

I look at the next document.

It's an exact duplicate of my high school diploma.

I look through the next ones, and they turn out to be every transcript, diploma, and certificate I've ever gotten. Someone has gone out of his way to keep the evidence that he's upholding his end of the bargain.

I keep flipping through the papers.

Nero's collection is a lot more thorough than my mom's.

The last paper in the folder is the work offer letter I signed when I started working for Nero.

I chuckle mirthlessly.

My stupid job is the culmination of events over a hundred years in the making.

And Nero used it all to get obscenely rich.

Then it dawns on me.

He's still trying to stay rich.

When his hundred-year cheat sheet expired in 2016, he must've decided to use *me*, the daughter of a powerful seer, to keep the money flowing.

The shoe fits Cinderella well.

I snap the folder and stare at my name written in Russian.

Had I spoken this language in my early years? Given that most babies start talking at one year of age, I must've had a small Russian vocabulary that I've now forgotten. Unless my mother spoke English.

I still know nothing about *her*.

Then a sense of déjà vu hits me.

I have stood in this exact spot and stared at this folder before.

Of course.

That super-short vision in which I saw my name in Russian.

That time, there was a noise behind me—

My heart jumping into my throat, I spin around— just as I hear that same noise again.

It was the door banging open so hard it could've flown off its hinges.

His face a mask of fury, Nero strides into the room.

CHAPTER FORTY-FIVE

WE LOCK EYES.

His fury morphs into confusion.

On my end, I realize he's wearing only a towel, and blood rushes treacherously to my face.

This explains why he didn't answer the door.

He was in the shower.

Soaping up. Scrubbing. Rinsing.

I swallow.

Loudly.

There isn't an ounce of fat on his broad, utterly male body. Every muscle looks carved out of a solid block of ice—and I suddenly want to lick an icicle.

On his part, Nero seems just as stunned to see me, his blue-gray eyes traveling over me with disbelief and something else.

Something disturbingly heated.

That is, until his gaze falls on the folder I'm still holding.

He launches into motion.

In a blur, he extricates the folder from my hands, stuffs it into the safe, and locks it.

I back away, deeper into the office, my mouth going Sahara dry.

He lost the towel during that bout of super speed.

Holy crap. Thank heavens we're not related. Though I have to say, even if he'd been my second cousin…

No, stop. This is insanity.

Willing my shaky limbs to move, I eye the exit.

He steps in front of me, blocking my path. "How much did you figure out?" He seems gloriously oblivious to his lack of clothes—and I am definitely not.

I swallow again. *Gulp, actually.* "Everything. I know who I am—and all about your meddling and spying."

His jaw hardens. "Fine. But it doesn't change anything." His voice turns low and hypnotic, his eyes peering into mine as though he's trying to X-Ray my soul. "I hope you realize that."

I dampen my dry lips. "It changes everything."

His gaze is on my mouth, avidly following the movement of my tongue. "We made a deal." His voice is low and deep as he steps impossibly closer. "You are going to work for me, and you will remain my Mentee."

I nod, my breath caught in my throat. I can't debate him right now, because I'm too distracted by the reaction in the region previously covered by the towel.

A very strong, very *big* reaction.

Talk about below-the-belt tactics.

I somehow manage to recall a shred of reason. "I should go. I will... see you at work." I try to step around him, but it's impossible.

He's taking all the space, stealing all the air in the room.

"Yes, you should," he agrees softly, but he doesn't move.

My pulse is throbbing in my temples, and my face feels like it's about to blister as his gaze falls to my mouth again, as if waiting for me to lick my lips one more time.

And I fight the urge to do just that.

Instead, I find myself saying, "You made a deal with my father. You're... supposed to look after me."

His nostrils flare. Dipping his head, he growls, "I know."

His face is now directly over mine, his lips a tiptoe-rise away, and I want to run and scream.

Or close the distance.

Maybe both at the same time, as impossible as that would be.

I feel like I'm torn in two, repulsed by his machinations yet drawn to him... for no good reason at all.

Worst of all, judging by the pulse beating in his neck, he might be suffering from the same madness.

He bends his head another fraction.

My heels leave the floor.

It's as if we have super-strong rare-earth magnets stuck in our mouths, pulling us together.

A muscle ticks in his jaw as his eyes darken, his pupils expanding until they blend with his limbal ring.

Our lips are almost touching. I feel the warm puffs of his breath and smell the minty scent of toothpaste.

I can't.

I shouldn't.

And then my lips press against his, my body rising up on tiptoes all the way as my arms wrap around his neck.

His reaction is as violent as it is instant. His powerful arms close around me, pressing me against his steel-hard body. His mouth turns devouring, deepening the kiss, taking it further, and I breathlessly reciprocate, channeling all my confusion, anger, and frustration into the movements of my tongue.

Something hard presses into my stomach, and I tremble with a growing need to end my cursed abstinence. The rollercoaster of sensations is blinding, and the desire to rip my clothes off is overpowering. The stupid things are between us, and I want all obstacles gone.

A growl rumbles deep within his throat, his hands roaming over my body with intensifying hunger, and a glimmer of sanity awakens somewhere in the back of my lust-soaked mind.

What am I doing?

This is Nero.

With a steel-bending effort of will, I push away—just as Nero lets me go.

I stumble back, panting, and see his chest heave with a similarly rapid rhythm.

"Leave," he snarls, his large hands suddenly resembling claws.

What the hell?

Painful flashbacks of the orcs hitch my breath in a whole new way.

He steps aside, visibly shaking with the effort to restrain himself, and I snap out of my lust-panic paralysis.

Turning on my heel, I flee the room, then the apartment, then the building.

———

THE CAB RIDE home passes in a blur, and I barely recall how I made it up to my apartment. Felix and Fluffster are waiting for me inside, but I ignore their questions as I rush into the bathroom to splash cold water on my burning face.

Nero kissed me.

Actually, I kissed *him*.

Which confirms it.

I'm certifiably insane.

Turning on the shower and setting it to cold, I strip and step under the spray, shivering under the freezing water until the unwelcome heat inside me is but a distant memory.

I may have just gotten a boatload of answers, but none of it really makes sense—especially the enigma that is Nero.

Maybe I'm just too tired to analyze it all?

Yeah, that's it. The shattering kiss has nothing to do with it.

If I get a good night's sleep, I will surely be able to make heads and tails of everything in the morning.

Frozen, I stumble to my bedroom and lock the door before plopping on my bed and wrapping the blanket around myself.

I will sleep now. Dreamlessly, if I'm lucky. And tomorrow, I will somehow find the strength to face Nero.

Between his contract with my father and my own deal with him, we're bound to each other.

For better or for worse.

Thank you for reading! I hope you're enjoying Sasha's story! Her adventures continue in *Sleight of Fantasy (Sasha Urban Series: Book 4)*. To be notified when it comes out, please visit www.dimazales.com and sign up for my mailing list.

Love audiobooks? This series, and all of my other books, are available in audio.

Want to read my other books? You can check out:

- *Mind Dimensions* - the action-packed urban fantasy adventures of Darren, who can stop time and read minds
- *Upgrade* - the thrilling sci-fi tale of Mike Cohen, whose new technology will transform our brains *and* the world
- *The Last Humans* - the futuristic sci-

fi/dystopian story of Theo, who lives in a world where nothing is as it seems
- *The Sorcery Code* - the epic fantasy adventures of sorcerer Blaise and his creation, the beautiful and powerful Gala

I also collaborate with my wife on sci-fi romance, so if you don't mind erotic material, you can check out *Close Liaisons*. Visit ww.annazaires.com for more information and to get your copy.

And now, please turn the page for an exciting excerpt from *Upgrade*.

A successful venture capitalist with billions in the bank, Mike Cohen has it all figured out. That is, until the life-changing new technology he's developing lands him in the middle of a global conspiracy, and the only way to save himself, his loved ones, and his tech is to embed the highly experimental Brainocytes in his own brain.

Brainocytes transform the human experience, making you smarter, faster, and more powerful. With enemies at every turn, Mike must use his newly enhanced capabilities to save his family, his friends, and ultimately, the world.

———

"A cure for dementia and Alzheimer's?" Uncle Abe's

gray eyes pulse with excitement, the way Mom's often do.

"It's not exactly a cure," I say at the same time as Ada says, "It's mostly a treatment for the symptoms."

"How cute," Uncle Abe says in Russian. "Your chick is already finishing your sentences."

As though she understood the Russian words, Ada's face lights up with an impish grin.

"We're not a couple," I tell Uncle Abe in Russian.

"Yet?" He gives me a knowing wink.

"It's not polite to speak in Russian in front of Ada," I say in English.

"I'm okay," Ada says. Only the shadow of a smile lurks in the corners of her eyes now, making her look like a punky version of the Mona Lisa.

"Still, I'm sorry," Uncle Abe tells her, his accent softening the *t* and the second *r*.

As we stroll through the hospital corridor, Ada takes the lead. She's a typical New Yorker, always twitchy and multitasking. I surreptitiously look her up and down, my eyes lingering on one of my favorite assets of hers—that special spot between the soles of her Doc Martens boots and the tips of her spiky hair.

Ada glances over her shoulder, her amber eyes meeting mine for a second. Did she feel me gawking at her just now? Before I can feel embarrassed, she stops in front of a green door and says, "This is the room."

The three of us walk in.

Unlike my dream, this isn't an operating room. It's spacious, with big windows and cheerfully blooming plants on the windowsills. At a glance, it's reminiscent of my stylish Brooklyn loft—if a mad scientist's wet dream was used as inspiration for the interior design.

Staff members from Techno, my portfolio company that designed the treatment, are already in the back. Mom is sitting on an operating chair in a white hospital gown, with a plethora of cables attaching her to a myriad of cutting-edge monitoring tools. Completing her getup is a headset—something straight out of the old *Total Recall* movie. It must be the "latest in portable neural scan technology" that JC, Techno's CEO, mentioned to me. I make a mental note to define *portable* to him.

I hear a "hi" from the farthest corner of the room. The person who spoke must be hidden behind the wall of servers and giant monitors. The other Techno employees keep working silently, though it isn't clear whether they didn't hear me come in, or if they're being antisocial.

Many folks at Techno could stand to improve their social skills. A psychiatrist might even label some of them as borderline Asperger's. Personally, I find those types of labels ridiculous. Psychiatry can sometimes be as scientific and helpful as astrology—which I don't believe in, in case that's not clear. A shrink back in high school tried to attach the Asperger's label to me because I had "too few friends." He could've just as easily concluded I had Tourette's based on where I told him to shove his diagnosis. Then again, maybe I'm still sore about psychiatry and neuropsychology because of how little they've done for Mom. Pretty much the only good thing I can say about psychiatry is that at least they're no longer using lobotomy as a treatment.

I look around the room for JC. He's nowhere to be found, so he must be in a similar room with another participant of the study.

Mom turns her head toward us, apparently able to do so despite the headgear.

My heart clenches in dread, as it always does when Mom and I meet after more than a day apart. Because of the accident that damaged Mom's brain, it's feasible that one day she'll look at me and won't recognize who I am.

Today she clearly does, though, because she gives me that dimpled smile we share. "Hi, little fish," she says in Russian. She then looks at her brother. "Abrashkin, bunny, how are you?"

"Mom just used untranslatable Russian pet names for us," I loudly whisper to Ada and wave hello to the still-uninterested staff in the back.

Mom looks at Ada without recognition, and I inwardly sigh. They've met twice before.

"Who's this boy?" Mom asks me in English. "Is he an intern at Techno or something?"

"She's not a boy, and her name is Ada," I respond, trying my best not to sound like I'm talking to someone with a disability, something my mom deeply resents. "She's not an intern, but one of the people who programmed the nanocytes that'll make you feel better."

"Nice to meet you, Nina Davydovna," Ada says as though they haven't done this before.

Mom's eyebrow rises at either the girlish resonance of Ada's bell-like voice or her proper use of the Russian patronymic. She quickly recovers, though, just like the last time, and also like the last time, she says, "Call me Nina."

"I will. Thank you, Nina," Ada says.

I realize Ada addressed my mom so formally on purpose—to lessen Mom's stress—so I give her a grateful nod. Of course, if Ada wanted to go the extra mile, she could've worn different clothing or changed her hairstyle to eliminate Mom's confusion about Ada's gender. Then again, Mom's confusion might be part of her condition, because to me, despite the leather jacket and black hoodie obscuring much of her body, Ada is the epitome of femininity.

"Is she his girlfriend?" Mom asks Uncle Abe conspiratorially in Russian. "Have I met her before?"

"I'm not sure, sis," Uncle Abe says. "From the way he looks at her, I suspect it's just a matter of time before they hook up."

"Oh yeah?" Mom chuckles. "Do you think she's Jewish?"

Blood rushes to my cheeks, and not just because of this "Jewish or not" business. It's something that became important to Mom only after the accident— unless she's always cared but only started voicing it after the brain damage lowered her inhibitions. My grandparents certainly often spoke about this sort of thing, going as far as blaming the situation with my father on him being non-Jewish—something I consider to be reverse anti-Semitism.

It's unfortunate, but their attitude was forged back in the Soviet Union, where being Jewish was considered an ethnicity and used as an excuse for government-level discrimination. Since one's ethnicity was written in the infamous fifth paragraph of one's passport, discrimination was commonplace and inescapable. My mom was turned away from her first choice of universities because they'd hit "their quota of three Jews." She also had a hard time finding a job in the engineering sciences until my father helped her out, only to later sexually harass her and leave her to raise me on her own. Even I was affected by this negativity before we left. When my seventh-grade classmates learned about my heritage from our school journal, they told me that with my blue eyes and blond hair (which darkened to brown as I got older), I looked nothing like a Jew. Though they used the derogatory Russian term, they'd meant it as a big compliment.

What makes the topic extra weird is that in America, where Judaism is more of a religion than an ethnicity, we're suddenly not all that Jewish. I mean, how can we be if I learned about Hanukkah in my mid-teens and when I had a very non-kosher grilled lobster tail wrapped in bacon last night?

Yeah, I also learned what *kosher* means in my mid-teens.

Either way, I couldn't care less about Ada's

Jewishness—though, for the record, with a last name like Goldblum, she probably is Jewish. I don't know what that term means to her either, since she's just as secular as I am. I think my biggest issue with Mom's question is that I simply loathe labels applied to entire groups of people, especially labels that come with so much baggage.

"It's hard to say," Uncle Abe says after examining Ada's dainty nose and zooming in on her pierced nostril. "With that hair, she's definitely not Russian."

Here we go, another label. To my grandparents, the term *Russian* was interchangeable with *goy* or *gentile*, but I don't think my uncle is using it in that context. Though in Russia we were Jewish, here in the US we're Russian—as in, the same as every Russian speaker from the former Soviet Union. I'm guessing my uncle is saying that Ada doesn't look like she's from the former Soviet Union, since a certain way of dressing and grooming typically accompanies that, at least for recent immigrants.

I decide to stop this thread of conversation, but before I get a chance to put a word in, Mom says, "When I was young, that kind of haircut was called an explosion at the noodle factory."

They both laugh, and even I can't help chuckling. I know the haircut Mom is referring to, and it's an eighties hairdo that may well be a distant ancestor to what's happening on Ada's head. The bleached, pointy tips make her look like an echidna with a Mohawk—an image reinforced by her prickly wit.

The door to the room opens, and a nurse walks in.

Seeing her scrubs raises my blood pressure, though I'm not sure if it's from the standard white coat syndrome or a flashback to my earlier nightmare. Probably the former. There was no anesthesia in Soviet dentistry when I was growing up, so I developed a conditioned response to anything resembling dentist clothing. Anyone in a white coat gives me a reaction akin to what someone suffering from coulrophobia—the irrational fear of clowns—would experience during a John Wayne Gacy documentary or the movie *It*.

The nurse walks over to Mom and reaches for a big syringe lying stealthily by Mom's chair.

The Techno employees in the back collectively hold their breaths.

The nurse doesn't seem to understand the auspiciousness of the occasion. She looks like she wants to finish here and move on to something more interesting, like watching a filibuster on C-SPAN. Her nametag reads "Olga." That, combined with her circa late-eighties haircut and makeup, plus those Slavic cheekbones, activates my Russian radar—or Rudar for short. It's like gaydar, but for detecting Russian speakers.

I bet Mom is insulted by the hospital assigning this nurse to her. It implies she needs help understanding English. Having earned a Bachelor of Science in Electrical Engineering after moving to the States in her mid-thirties, Mom takes deserved pride in her skills with the English language—skills the accident didn't affect.

In the silence, I can hear Mom's shallow breathing; her fear of medical professionals is much worse than mine.

Olga grips the syringe and raises her hand.

———

If you'd like to learn more, please visit www.dimazales.com.